Dorothy M.
Nampa, Id.
466-86

Books authored or coauthored
by Blaine M. Yorgason

To Soar with the Eagle

Secrets

Prayers on the Wind

Namina: Biography of Georganna Bushman Spurlock (private printing)

The Life Story of Roger and Sybil Ferguson (private printing)

Obtaining the Blessings of Heaven

To Mothers and Fathers from the Book of Mormon

Receiving Answers to Prayer

Spiritual Survival in the Last Days

Into the Rainbow

The Warm Spirit

Here Stands a Man

Decision Point

KING — The Biography of Jerome Palmer King (private printing)

Pardners: Three Stories on Friendship

In Search of Steenie Bergman (Soderberg Series #5)

The Greatest Quest

Seven Days for Ruby (Soderberg Series #4)

The Eleven Dollar Surgery

Becoming

Bfpstk and the Smile Song (out of print)

The Shadow Taker

Tales from the Book of Mormon (The Loftier Way)

Brother Brigham's Gold (Soderberg Series #3)

Ride the Laughing Wind

The Miracle

The Thanksgiving Promise

Chester, I Love You (Soderberg Series #2)

Double Exposure

Seeker of the Gentle Heart

The Krystal Promise

A Town Called Charity, and Other Stories about Decisions

The Bishop's Horse Race (Soderberg Series #1)

And Should She Die (The Courage Covenant)

Windwalker (movie version — out of print)

The Windwalker

Others

Charlie's Monument

Tall Timber (out of print)

Miracles and the Latter-day Teenager (out of print)

BLAINE YORGASON

TO SOAR WITH THE EAGLE

Deseret Book Company
Salt Lake City, Utah

For Lindsay, Jessa, and Taylor
with love, from Gampa

I express my sincere appreciation to Gloria B. Benson, chairperson, and to the other members of the Kaibab Paiute Tribe, Pipe Springs, Arizona, for their assistance and cooperation in the writing of this book. Appreciation is also expressed to members of the Hatch family for their encouragement and support.

Prologue

Y‌ou going alone?"

Nineteen year-old Samuel Loper, straining to tighten the cinch strap on his saddle, did not look up. It was October in the year 1855, and despite the lateness of the season, the air on the Santa Clara was hot. Kneeing his horse in the stomach to force out the animal's sucked-in air, Samuel pulled again on the strap. The big bay mare, impatient with what was happening, sidestepped with her hind feet, moving away, and only then did Samuel look up.

"I reckon," he replied simply, giving his friend Thales Haskell a wry grin. "Leastwise if I can get this hoss saddled."

"Jacob know?" Thales pressed.

"He does." Samuel threaded the strap back and forth between the cinch and the saddle, finally feeding it back under itself and tying it down. As leader of the Indian Mission, Jacob Hamblin kept pretty close tabs on what all the missionaries were doing. Samuel knew that Thales understood that. He also knew that Thales, who had become one of his best friends in the time they had been on the Santa Clara, wanted only to help. So Samuel responded, taking no offense at the man's curiosity.

"We talked last night after Tanigoots' runner came." Samuel reached up and pulled the stirrup back across the saddle, dropping it into place. "Seems Jacob wants you boys to visit the tribes down toward Vegas Springs. Right away. There's been a little trouble, so I know you're needed."

"That's no call for you to go off alone, Samuel."

Samuel Loper grinned. "Maybe not, but that's how she cuts out. Besides, Tanigoots is camped this end of the Kaibab, so I won't be gone more'n a week."

"You'll be close to Navajo country."

"Close don't count, Thales, and you know it. Besides, Jacob said he felt by the Spirit that I'd be all right, so I will. Now stop worrying afore I mistake you for my mother and give you a big kiss adios."

Thales Haskell smiled at the young man who had become such a close friend. "Heaven forbid that, Brother Loper. Got any idea what Tanigoots wants?"

"Not much." Samuel shook his head while his mare whisked her tail at a swarm of pesky flies. "I know his wife died not too long ago. Now she's gone, he's thinking of going back to his own people, the Navajo. The runner told me that much. I reckon it has to do with that."

"His wife? She was that Paiute princess gal, wasn't she?"

Samuel stooped and picked up his bedroll and homemade rucksacks, which he carefully secured behind his saddle. "Well," he finally responded, "her grandfather's old Chief Kanosh, if that's what you mean. She seemed like a fine woman, but I'll be dogged if I can remember her name."

Thales was surprised, and his look showed it.

2

"Aw, don't rub it in," Samuel groused. "I remember most of 'em, and you know it."

Thales laughed. "Don't I know it! Tell me about Tanigoots."

"Well," Samuel responded as he rubbed his mare's nose tenderly, "that there's a history, all right. He's the son of a Navajo chief, but when he was just a kid he was captured by one of the old men of the Kaibab-its."

"Was the fellow who captured him Paiute or Pahvant?"

"Paiute. Tanigoots' wife was Pahvant, I think. But them people are kissing cousins, so to speak, and it gets real iffy telling 'em apart."

Thales laughed. "Paiute, Pahvant, and Navajo all in one lodge. Does sound comfy, all right."

"It worked out," Samuel responded, grinning at Thales' sarcasm. "The old man raised Tanigoots as his own son, and he did a good job of it. *Tanigoots* means 'He did tell the truth,' and so far as I know, he's been a square shooter with me."

"He was accepting of your message this last spring, wasn't he?"

Samuel smiled. "You could say that. You surely could." Quickly he pulled himself up into his saddle. "Now Brother Haskell," he said as he reined the mare around, "you figuring on jawing me to death afore the Navajo get to me, or what?"

Thales grinned in return. "Fat chance. I reckon I'll leave that up to the future Mrs. Loper, whoever and wherever she might happen to be."

"Then she'll do it a long way in the future," Samuel stated with a laugh. "You know how I am with women. They scare the bejeebies out of me!"

Thales chuckled. "Maybe so. But that won't stop some enterprising young sister from setting her cap for you. And when that happens, scared silly or not, you'll follow her to the altar thinking all along it was your own grand idea. You wait and see."

"I'll do that," Samuel stated as he wondered at the strange sense of foreboding his friend's words had given him. "I'll just do that. So long, Thales."

"Adios, partner. God go with you."

"I reckon he will. And Thales?"

"Yeah?"

"Tanigoots' wife's name? It just came to me. It was Ungka Poetes."

PART ONE

CHAPTER

1

Beneath her back, blood pooled quickly where the jagged edge of *timpi,* the rock, had broken the skin. Yet the young woman, who was called Iitats, the meadowlark, lay still as death. Too startled to have yet felt the pain, she stared upward, her mind unable to understand. Near her head, *mu-u-pi-chats,* a fly, buzzed, and for a moment it landed on her outstretched hand, lightly tickling the skin. Involuntarily the muscles in her fingers closed, and the insect buzzed away, leaving her as before. Then all was silent again, the only sound a soft whisper of wind in the pinion pines that surrounded the Paiute Indian encampment.

"*Mumpi,*" another woman exclaimed by way of surprise, her voice quiet and distant. For truly this that she and the few others had seen was a bad thing, a thing none of them had ever seen before.

Her mind slowly clearing, Iitats tried to focus on the angry countenance of her older brother, struggling to understand what she was doing on the ground below him. But *tavaputs,* the sun, hid behind his head, and so she could see nothing but darkness against the light. Yet still her brother stood over her, his breath coming in ragged gasps, his anger hot in his belly as he waited to strike his younger sister again.

Realizing finally that she had indeed been struck and knocked to the ground, young Iitats moved a little, and it was then that the pain in her back made itself known.

"Ei-agh," she gasped as she fell back down. "*Imik-a num-pi-cant*! You are crazy, my brother."

With an exclamation of anger, the young man lifted his arm and leaned down to strike again.

"Peokon!"

The voice cut across the stillness like a knife, and the youth stopped as if he himself had been hit. Slowly then he straightened and faced his father.

"My son," the man called Tanigoots questioned, his voice soft as befitted a man of the People, "what is this that you do?"

Drawing a deep breath, Peokon stared at the man who had emerged from the wickiup. A woman across the small clearing coughed, and only then did the youth realize that he was the center of attention of all the others in the encampment, men, women, and children—that all were either regarding him with stupefied, silent amazement or were slowly turning their backs on him.

"It is nothing," he growled in self-defense, doing his best to ignore what the people were doing.

"That is a thing I will decide, my son. Now explain yourself."

Peokon grinned thinly. "This . . . this *mama'uts*, this woman," and his voice rang with sarcastic contempt as he said it, "is *nah-dahm-euahd-ahm*, she is lazy. I told her to do a thing, and she did not do as I told her."

"If it is as you say," Tanigoots pressed, his mind filled with wonder that a son of his could strike the daughter of his beloved wife, "then how does she come to be lying

8

upon the hard breast of *tu-weep*, the earth, instead of doing as you asked?"

The young man's eyes blazed. "I put her there! As I would put a dog in its place, so did I with her."

Amid soft exclamations of surprise and fear from those who surrounded him, for this was a thing that was never done among the People, nor were such harsh words ever spoken in all the broad land, Peokon glared defiantly at his father.

"Ah, my son," Tanigoots said softly, sadly. And then, without another glance at his son, he strode to where young Iitats still sprawled on the warm ground. Kneeling, he tenderly examined the bruised flesh on the side of her face. Then, with soft and gentle words of pity, he helped her to her feet and turned her so he could examine the wound the rock had made in her back.

Wonderingly Iitats allowed her father to do as he was doing. In all the days since she had become a woman, which admittedly had not been many but which were nevertheless some, he had spoken no words of tenderness to her, neither had he held her close as she had been so accustomed to him doing. Yet now—

It was late in the afternoon, and the sun was *tavi-mum-wiski*, sinking rapidly toward the distant horizon. Yet still it was warm on Iitats' bare skin. The air was startlingly clear, and almost directly overhead a puff of *Pah-cun-ab*, the cloud man, hung against the blue, almost as if it had been painted there. Down off the mountain to the west, the grays and pale greens of the Uinkaret Plateau faded into the blues of distance, and Iitats stood still, feeling the blood trickling down her back and the wind moving her hair now that her burden cap had been knocked free.

A few feet away Peokon stood glaring at her, his face still revealing his hatred and defiance, a thing that Iitats did not understand and that filled her with fear. She had

9

always loved her older brother, and yet now, with no provocation that she could think of, he had hit her face with the back of his hand, had hit her angrily and viciously. And no man of the Nung-wa, the People, ever struck another person —

It was strange, she thought, that this had happened to her. Already she was being treated differently from the others. Yet she did not wish it to be so, and a tear that was born more of sadness than of pain flushed from her eye and trickled down her dusty cheek.

"*Nuni pat-sun*," Tanigoots stated over and over as he held her and wiped the blood from her back. "My daughter, my daughter." Then, with a sigh, he pushed Iitats gently away. "This is a bad thing that Peokon has done, a very bad thing, and I will speak to him of it. Perhaps his mind has already left on our journey, I do not know. As the father of Peokon, my daughter, I make for you the sign of sorrow."

Indicating to the watching women that he wished Iitats to be looked after, Tanigoots turned and reentered his small brush lodge. After a moment Peokon followed, and for the next few moments the young girl was subjected to the solicitous clucking and cleaning of the other women of the encampment. But then they were off about their own affairs, and again Iitats stood alone in the late afternoon.

Truly now had her laughter died. So too had the songs of happiness that had always flowed so pleasantly from her lips and that had given rise to her name — the meadowlark. For a moment longer she stood motionless, trying to understand the pain and sadness that filled her heart. Below her, near the spring, some children were playing again, their carefree squeals of laughter rending the air. Wistfully she listened to them, thinking that only a short season before, she had been one of them. But now it was at an end, and that terrified her — not her childhood, for that was to be expected for any girl who reached the age of twelve snows. No, what was at an end was life as she had known it. Life, love, security, joy, happiness — all these were at an end, and soon she would be alone, so very alone!

Involuntarily she lifted her eyes and scanned the horizon. She knew the man would be coming from *qui-am-er tavi-awk-er*, the northwest. Yet she could see no sign, no dust.

Shuddering, and with tears suddenly filling her eyes, young Iitats turned to the low fire she had been working at before . . . before Peokon had struck her, and with tongs made of willow, she picked up a heated cooking rock. Forcing her mind to abandon the empty terror that filled her soul, she carefully placed the hot rock in the watery stew she had prepared in the resin-covered basket her mother had left her. One after another, six heated rocks she dropped into the liquid. To these she added cakes of dried grasshoppers, for that was all she had. And then, lest the hot rocks burn through the cooking basket, Iitats stirred them carefully with her willow tongs while the water boiled.

Wistfully she thought of the fact that there was no meat for her stew. Even a rabbit would have made it better. But for her father and brother, who were too busy preparing for their journey, there had been no hunting. Neither had the three other hunters in the small camp found game. Though it was late in *Cang-am-a-ro-its*, the month of October, for some reason *tu-ee*, the deer, had fled away, and each day the men returned empty-handed.

In the wickiup behind her, the murmur of voices caught Iitats' attention. She did not want to listen, for it was man talk. Yet it concerned her, and so she strained to hear, doing her best to put out of her ears the many sounds of the Paiute encampment.

"My son," her father was saying in a firm but gentle voice, "that which you did to your sister was not seemly. Such behavior does not befit a man of the People."

"I am not of these people!" Peokin stated scornfully. "These Paiutes are dogs who yap at the heels of the Diné, the true people. I would strike them as quickly as I would strike *moowav*, the mosquito."

"Do you suppose a man may live that way among the Diné?" Tanigoots pressed. "My son, since Tobats and Shinob first peopled this world with men and animals, making them all part of one great tribe, it has been the same. In anger, a true man never strikes one who is weaker.

"More than this, a true man honors the life of each brother and each sister in his world, the two-footeds, the four-footeds, and the wings of the air. If life must be taken because of hunger, thanks is given to the brother or sister who is to die, as well as to the great Shinob, for that life. If the life of an enemy must be taken, thanks is also given. In this a true man shows respect for all the creations of Tobats, and the great circle of life remains unbroken."

Peokon sneered. "You speak of the foolish traditions of the Paiutes, my father. I am now of the Diné, and these traditions have become as empty words to me."

Tanigoots shook his head. "What you say is true, my son. These are the teaching of the Paiutes. Yet from what little I remember of the words of my father, the Diné hold to these same *too-veets*, these same truths. The names change, for tongues differ from people to people. Yet a man must always be a man, and no matter his tongue, the way is the same. To change this, as you are now trying to do, is to break the sacred circle of life, and such behavior will lead only to unhappiness."

Slowly Tanigoots leaned back, his eyes suddenly far away. "I would have you understand that it has been good, my life among the Paiutes," he said softly. "Your mother and her people have given me much—"

"I hear your words," Peokon growled as he spat upon the earth, "but they are emptiness to me. I am of the Diné, the only true people. To me, these others are less than nothing!"

"Strong words, my son," the older man observed slowly. "Strong but sad, for you are casting aside much that is worthwhile. If you have indeed cast aside your sister, would you also cast aside your mother's memory?"

Fiercely Peokon glared at his father. "My mother is dead and of the earth," he growled. "Henceforth I speak no more of her. As for my sister, I have none! According to the law of the Diné, which you yourself taught me, if a woman be of mixed blood she is good for nothing but to be a slave. I will be brother to no slave."

Tanigoots looked at his son. "And are you not also of mixed blood?"

"I am of your blood," the youth stated proudly. "You are Diné; I am also Diné! I am Peokon of the People!"

"Yes," Tanigoots said almost sadly, "so you are. Perhaps it is good that such a fire runs in your veins. Perhaps that will help you lead my people in war if that time comes. But for myself, O Peokon, the passing of many seasons has taught me the value of a little tenderness, a little compassion. After all, even a fleeing dog has something to teach us."

"Paugh." Peokon spat angrily at his father's words. Then, realizing that he had again overstepped the bounds of social graces, the young man made the sign of apology.

Tanigoots sighed deeply. "I accept your words, my son. And because your heart has become as *timpi*, the rock, we will speak no more of this now."

Picking up a stick, Tanigoots changed the subject. "You will go with me," he instructed softly as he drew on the

13

ground. "If the white man comes for Iitats, or if he does not come, then in one sun, perhaps two, we leave, and in two suns after that we will cross the river—here."

With a slow arc of his wrist Tanigoots drew the course of a river, and then with a quick thrust he jabbed his stick into the earth at a certain bend he had drawn.

"The Diné will be not far beyond, and each of us will take our rightful place among them—I as a chief, and you, my son—after you have gained more wisdom—as the heir of a chief."

The dark eyes of Peokon gleamed, but other than that, he made no sign that he had heard his father. Slowly he rose to his feet.

"I will see to our horses," he said as he backed from the wickiup, almost backing into Iitats as he did so.

"And when the white man comes," Tanigoots pressed, seeing his daughter cowering beyond the tall form of his son, "will you not bid farewell to your sister?"

The youth did not answer. Instead he turned and, without a glance in Iitats' direction, walked with measured tread toward the tethered horses.

Chee aree, che-che, chick-chick-chee aree." Iitats' voice was soft as she sang one of the happy songs her mother had taught her. It was a nonsense song, imitating the sound of the tiny Brewer sparrows that flitted through the junipers early on summer mornings. Iitats loved the song, for it always brought happiness to her soul. In fact, she loved to sing every song she knew. Thus now, with a sense of impending doom permeating her soul, she did as she had always done—sang the chants of her people as she performed the tasks her father and brother expected of her.

The sun had long before fled below the earth, and in the gathering twilight Iitats quickened her pace, then emptied the cooking pit of the layers of pine cones she had placed there earlier to roast. Now she would take the nuts from them and grind away the shells later on. Then she would form the nut meat into cakes that would be eaten during the time of cold.

The white man still had not come, and Iitats did not know how to feel. Part of her was filled with joy, for

15

perhaps this meant he would not come at all. On the other hand, with the departure of her father and brother she would be left alone, and the custom of the People made her the property of any man who wanted the responsibility of caring for her. If more than one wanted her, they would fight for her in a squaw-pull; if no one wanted her, she would be left behind to starve during the coming winter. Iitats shuddered at both thoughts and wondered again that one so recently a carefree child could be plunged so quickly into such adult misery.

Even now, after two months, she did not enjoy the role of a woman. It had been much simpler being a child playing at womanhood, when she could weep as she chose, laugh as she chose, and run and laugh freely with the other children.

Well she remembered the seasons of laughter shared with her brother Peokon, who had been her best friend for all the time she could remember. But then he had begun to change, and that change had become complete when he had accompanied their father for a few weeks south beyond the great river. He had returned a changed person, full of dark looks and silent contempt for all their mother's people, but especially for her.

Not understanding, Iitats had questioned her mother, who had been as mystified as she. Realizing then that it was a mystery no one could fathom, Iitats had put her brother's anger from her mind and had returned to playing at being a woman with all her friends.

But then abruptly her womanhood had blossomed, and for one month she had been separated from the people, living alone in a wickiup to which her mother had come daily to instruct her. While frightening, those had been wonderful days for Iitats, and she had reveled in the new being she was fast becoming.

But then, on the last morning of her seclusion, her

16

mother had not come as was her custom. Instead, *tahp'poots*, the raven, had landed in a tree across from where Iitats was sitting by the fire. Instantly nervous, the girl had done her best to ignore the sleek, black bird, for she had known that it was a medicine bird who had much knowledge about the future. Yet not only had it stayed, but also after a time the raven had broken the silence, speaking directly to her.

"Ho," it had said in its raucous voice, "why do you ignore me, little sister?"

Staring at the earth, Iitats had tried to calm her trembling soul. "I . . . did not mean to ignore you," she had finally answered, her voice hardly more than a whisper.

"And yet you fear me?"

"The words of my mother, they . . . they tell me that you are a spirit bird, and that you know the future."

"Ho," the raven had cried. "Your mother has been a wise woman."

Something in the way the raven had spoken made Iitats lift her eyes. There had been a meaning to his words that she had not been able to fathom, and yet—

"Your heart is right, little sister," the raven had continued, "and you listen politely. Last night your mother heard the owl call her name, and now she has taken her journey to the land of the sky people. Those beings sent me to tell you this, and to tell you that you must not grieve, for in the end your mother's going will bring you much happiness."

"She is dead?" Iitats had asked, hardly knowing what to believe. "But . . . I have not yet finished the *kono*, the cradleboard I am weaving for the child who is to come."

"The child came in the time of darkness, little sister, and he walks beside your mother on the road to the west. Grieve now until the Cry is held by your people, and no longer. I have spoken."

17

With a cry the raven had gone, and when the women from the village had come a little later, Iitats had been prepared for the sorrow they carried with them. Openly she had grieved until the Cry ceremony a month later, and since then she had done her best not to grieve openly. But abruptly she had become a woman, burdened with caring for her father and an older brother who was more than scornful of her, and with no one to assist her in this heavy task.

For a moment Iitats stared ahead, her thoughts racing. Was she not as much of her father's blood as was her brother? If the two of them were Diné, then why was she not Diné? Why was it that she could not be a woman of the Diné?

But no, she realized as her anger quickly cooled, that was not the way things were. She was of her mother's blood, Paiute and Pahvant, and it could not be helped. She was not Diné, and she never would be. Neither could it be helped that she was now a woman, good for nothing but to be a slave. What difference that instead of being a slave to the Diné, she would now be a slave to a white man?

"O Great Shinob," she prayed fervently, "can you not see that this woman who speaks has no desire to be a slave? Look. She is a good worker. Look at the grasshoppers she has made into cakes. Look at the *tuu*, the pine nuts, that she is working to lay aside for the season of cold. Or see the baskets she has woven. Do not these things bespeak her worth, O Great One? Why is it, then, that she cannot become a woman of the People?"

Pausing for a moment to ease the stiffness in her back, the girl knelt upright, waiting for an answer. But nothing came to her ears but the sound of laughter in another lodge, a lodge where a family of the People huddled in joy and peace.

Aching that such would never be her lot, Iitats sighed deeply and looked off toward the northwest. Of course, it was too dark to see well, but still she looked, wondering if the man was somewhere out there, coming at her father's bidding. Of course, he could not be close, for the ever-watchful dogs would have warned of his approach. But perhaps in the distance —

"*Maik mee-ahf'poots-uny.* Hello, Little One."

With a gasp Iitats spun about and looked up. The dark shape of the man standing beside her spoke her own tongue, but not exactly as she was used to hearing it. Perhaps, she thought instantly, he was from another tribe —

"I seek the man called Tanigoots," the man said softly. "Could you point out for me his lodge?"

Slowly Iitats rose to her feet, trying to place this man, trying to —

And then she knew! It was the white man she had watched for all through the day, the man her father hoped would take her away to live among his own people. But it was not possible that he was here. The dogs had sounded no warning —

"Do you know Tanigoots, Little One?"

"I . . . I know him," Iitats stammered, her mind reeling that he would call her such a name of affection. "He . . . is my father. Come, and I will take you to his lodge."

"Wait here a moment," the man said easily, "and then I will follow."

While Iitats waited, her heart pounding, the man moved away down the hill and into the darkness. He was here! He had come, and if he was agreeable, her life would end and she would become as nothing, a slave to a white man. How would she stand it? How could she possibly endure the grief and the loneliness —

"O, Great Shinob," she prayed silently, "do not let this bad thing happen . . . "

"If you are the daughter of Tanigoots," the man said as he suddenly appeared again, his horse following behind him, "then I bring this as a gift for you." Handing Iitats the rucksack, he smiled as she peered timidly inside.

"*Yungumputs!*" she squealed with delight. And then she reached in and pulled forth a fat young porcupine, skinned and ready for the pot.

Suddenly embarrassed at her joyful outburst, Iitats made the sign for "Thank you." Then she turned as if to go.

"There is more," the white man said gently, still in Iitats' own tongue. Reaching into his shirt pocket, he pulled forth a small packet, which he also thrust toward her. "In your hands, perhaps these will one day become a thing of beauty."

Still speechless, Iitats put down the porcupine and took the proffered packet. Opening it carefully, she gasped with delight. Here were all the choice quills of the porcupine, their sharp barbs already removed, ready to be dyed and made into clothing decorations by a woman of her people.

"I thank you," she said timidly, feeling very nervous. "I shall give these to my mo—" Abruptly Iitats again felt embarrassed, for somehow she had forgotten for the moment that her mother had taken the long journey to the land of the west. Kiyiii, but she was a foolish young woman! What horrible things the white man must think of her! Wanting only to run far off into the trees, she instead picked up the porcupine, placed it back in the rucksack, and without a backward glance turned away toward the lodge of her father. Thus she was spared the slight but knowing smile that played briefly across the face of the young Samuel Loper. He did not know much about girls or women, but what little he did know had convinced him that, red or white, their emotions were pretty much the same.

But it would not be until much later that he would learn how little he really knew.

3

Through the camp Iitats moved, her every sense heightened by the empty fear that filled her. She knew the man
was following, but only because she occasionally glanced
back to make sure. He made no more sound than the
whispering of the wind, and because he was a white man,
she felt true amazement. But she was even more amazed
at his person, of which she could remember every detail.

Not large, but in fact thin and scrawny, this white man
had the longest arms she had ever seen. Or perhaps it was
the strange way he had of walking—silently but with a
stoop-shouldered roll—that made his arms seem so long.
Whichever, in the near darkness Iitats felt certain his
swinging hands were dragging near the earth, and she
suddenly realized it was difficult to keep from *kee-eung-
koo*, from laughing, each time she glanced his way.

Marveling that she could experience such an emotion
at such a horrid time, Iitats came at last to the lodge of her
father. She was about to announce the presence of the
white man, but suddenly her father was standing before

her, looking past at the white man, and so she withdrew silently into the background.

"Ah, my friend Samuel Loper," the Indian said gravely, speaking in Paiute. "You honor my lodge with your visit."

"And you, Tanigoots, honor me with your invitation," Samuel Loper replied in the same tongue. "I did not remember that you had a daughter. She is both lovely and gracious."

"As was her mother. Come, my friend, and you shall eat. Iitats?"

Surprised, for she had been staring again, young Iitats spun away toward the still-warm fire. Building it up and setting her stones to heat, she put water and the meat from the porcupine into the pitch-covered cooking basket. To the mix she also added wild onions, wild potato, and a cake made of grass seeds, which would thicken the water.

Plucking up the heated cooking stones and rinsing them in clear water, Iitats set them into the basket. Then patiently she stirred the contents as the water boiled and the stew cooked. Nor were the girl's eyes still as she worked. She watched as her father and the white man spoke for a moment in front of the wickiup. She watched as the white man staked his horse, removed the saddle and bridle, and rubbed the animal down with handfuls of long grass. She watched as he made his way past her again, carrying his saddle and packs toward the lodge of her father. And with all her watching, she made certain that the white man would see nothing but her busy hands. And as busy as they were, her eyes she kept downturned and hidden.

Finally, as she ladled some of her stew into a woven bowl from which her father and the white man would eat, she continued to marvel. This man her father had called his friend was indeed young. Iitats had seen that right away. But she had also seen that he had foolishly allowed his *mohn-chohng*, his whiskers, to grow. And though they were not many, yet his face looked as fuzzy and soft as the underbelly of *ka-ats*, the packrat. Iitats wondered at that, but she wondered even more at the strange desire she felt to reach out and touch the man's *koh-vahv*, his face.

What strange magic had he performed, she wondered, that enabled him to move so silently, to speak her tongue so well, and to draw her toward him in such a wonderfully painful manner? And it was magic, of that she was certain. Perhaps even evil magic! Thus this man, this white man, was even more to be feared than she had thought.

"O Great Shinob," she pleaded, "protect this woman from the magic of the white man who is called Samuel Loper. If it is so that she is to be his slave, then give her strength—"

"Iitats? Our guest hungers," her father said softly.

And with a gasp of shame that he had been forced to remind her of her duties, Iitats put aside her fears of the white man, took up the small woven bowl of food, and turned back toward the lodge.

CHAPTER

4

It is right for you to know," the Indian said softly into the thick air of the lodge, "that I am no longer called Tanigouts. I am now called Dah-Nish-Uant."

Samuel Loper said nothing, merely digesting the information. As Iitats watched him, she could sense that the smoke from the fire, which curled slowly upward, was making the man's breathing more difficult. Yet he said nothing but merely watched her father.

Iitats thought then of the spring before, when this man and two others had first ridden among the Kaibab-its. She had been a child then, and she had been so astounded by the whiteness of the missionaries' skin that she had spent much time hiding in fear. But now she knew the whiteness was a thing she must get used to.

"Do you return to your people as a chief?" Samuel Loper finally asked.

Dah-Nish-Uant made the sign that it was so.

"Then the Diné will be led by a wise man," he stated softly.

Again silence reigned in the small, brush-covered wick-

25

iup, a silence that did not seem to bother Samuel Loper in the least. Iitats wondered at that, for in the past year others of the white men had visited among the people, and it was the joke that all whites must be children of the magpie people, who were known for their chattering.

Of course, Iitats had no way of knowing that Samuel Loper was long familiar with the ways of the Indian. He had been reared among the Cattaragus Indians of New York, labored briefly among Walker's Utes with Dimmick B. Huntington at the time of Lieutenant Gunnison's massacre, and spent much time with the Paiutes. Thus he had learned that silence was a sign of respect, and now he used it both for that and to carefully study all that was going on around him.

Noting the way his eyes traveled from side to side, seeing everything without seeming to pry into anything, Iitats also examined her father's lodge. It held little, for of a truth the Paiutes were a poor people. Yet there were robes made of rabbit fur and sage bark for the sleeping of three people, and so this white man would know that one of Dah-Nish-Uant's family was missing from the lodge. Because weapons for two hung near the door opening, it could also be determined that the missing one was male. Would the man guess that the missing one was her brother, Iitats wondered? Would he also suppose that the missing one was the cause of the large, swollen bruise on the side of Iitats' cheek? Of course, she could not know, but somehow Iitats felt certain that this man called Samuel Loper would know. Yes, he would know, and he would be troubled by the unseemly anger of Peokon.

For a moment Iitats examined herself, trying to picture in her mind what the white man saw each time he looked at her. For he had looked, many times. Of that she was certain.

So, what had he seen? Though very short, to herself

she seemed very much a woman of the People. She had eyes that were large and dark with the smoke of a thousand generations of campfires; high, wide cheekbones; a body that was only beginning to look womanly; and straight, jet-black hair that was kept covered by her burden cap. Would he find those traits attractive, she wondered? Would he even notice them? Would he notice the careful manner in which she had painted her face, or the way she had put the sacred red pigment into her hair? Among the people she was known for her smile, which lived always on her face. Would he notice that, or the light her mother had told her danced always in her eyes? Would the man notice—

Outside somewhere in the darkened encampment, *sariits*, a dog, barked, once, twice, and then with a frightened yipping was sent scurrying away from whomever it was bothering. Iitats smiled at that and thought about how much better porcupine tasted than dog. Selfishly, that had been one of the reasons she had been happy to see the porcupine brought in by Samuel Loper.

And that was something else about herself that Iitats hoped the white man had noticed. Though only recently become a woman, she had performed all the womanly tasks her father had required of her, and she had performed them well. Surely a man would take note of such a thing, even a hairy-faced white man with the strange name of Samuel Loper.

Iitats almost giggled at that thought, and then, embarrassed, dropped her head. In the small fire the burning branches settled, sending up a shower of sparks. As if that were a signal, her father finally spoke.

"My white friend, soon I go with my son to take my place among the Diné."

Samuel nodded almost imperceptibly.

27

"Because the time of snow hastens, we can delay our journey no longer."

From nearby came the sound of a horse's nicker, a horse that was not Samuel Loper's, and Iitats saw the white man's head lift slightly as he took note. To the Navajo, horses were common, Iitats knew, but among the Paiute such was not the case. Instead the men were runners, fleet of foot and filled with endurance.

Samuel Loper's eyes flicked to the weapons again, and suddenly Iitats understood that the white man had concluded that her brother was with the horses. How she knew that she could not explain, but she did, and she felt strange relief in the knowledge that her brother's whereabouts were known.

"I know little of your people, the Mormonee," Dah-Nish-Uant continued, slipping briefly into Ute jargon, "but I see that your hearts are good toward us, and that pleases me. Do you know the way of the Diné?"

Samuel looked past the fire and into the face of Iitats' father, behind whom she sat. "I know they are a proud people," he responded carefully. "They are fierce in war, and they raise strong sons and daughters."

Dah-Nish-Uant nodded. "Well spoken. What you say is true, my white friend, but there is more. The Diné are an old people, and their legends go back more seasons than a man can count. During those seasons wisdom has piled upon the people like drifting snow filling an arroyo, until even the source of that wisdom has been forgotten. Our chants teach us of this wisdom, and our legends, and our dances, and the power in them is more than a man can withstand."

Samuel Loper nodded, but Iitats did not think that he understood where her father was leading.

"Among the Diné it is a known thing that a man has sons, and a woman has daughters." Dah-Nish-Uant paused and adjusted a stick on the fire, watching as the small flame leaped upward. "Women are heads of each of the clans, and a man may not marry a woman who has been born into the same clan as himself. To the Diné, men and women are equal, and there are no equals beyond themselves. They are the People, and in their eyes there are no others. It is, as you say it, the meaning of the word *Diné*."

Still the white man remained silent.

"When I took a wife from among the Paiute, it was said among the Diné that I had married beneath myself, that I had not married a human being. I understood that, but there was between my woman and myself a feeling that gave me much happiness, and I did not concern myself with the things people said.

"We lived alone here on the Kaibab-its, my woman and me, and there was joy in our lodge. When we needed others, the Paiute were always near, and because I had been taken as son by one who was *ne-ab*, chief of the Paiute, I was considered as one with them.

"In the course of time my woman, who was the daughter of a chief and the granddaughter of a great chief, gave me a son. He grew tall and straight, and in him I felt pride. Soon another son joined him, but that one was not strong, and he took his journey to the land of the sky people. Another young son took the same journey, and then the woman gave me a daughter who also had the strength to live among us.

"More sons and daughters followed, but all were weak, and all soon took the lonely trail to the west, seeking To-bats-kan, the land of the great Tobats. All these things caused sorrow in the heart of my woman. But she was strong and desired to give me one more son."

Again Dah-Nish-Uant paused to adjust the sticks in the fire. Watching him, Iitats was amazed, for she knew

29

she was seeing into her father's heart, a thing she had never before imagined was even possible. These things he was saying were sacred, and she closed her eyes in fear of hearing more of them.

"It was not to be," Dah-Nish-Uant finally concluded. "Now both my woman and the little one who was to have been my youngest son walk together in the land of the sky people, seeking the lodge of Tobats. I am left alone with only my son and my woman's daughter to heal the wound in my soul."

In the silence that followed, Samuel made the sign that he felt sympathy and sorrow for the man who had spoken.

Dah-Nish-Uant gazed without expression toward the white man. "Now it has been determined that I am to go again among the Diné, taking the place of the chief whose son I am. My son Peokon will accompany me, for it is his right as one of the Diné to do so. As for my woman's daughter Iitats, who has now become a woman herself, she is not of the Diné, and my heart is heavy with worry concerning her."

Samuel made the sign that he understood, though in fact Iitats remained certain that he did not.

"Because Iitats is not considered by the Diné a human being, and because she has become a woman, if she accompanies me she will become a slave among my people. It is their way, it is the old way, and one cannot question the wisdom of it.

"If she is left here among the people of her mother, she will either starve or, if chosen, become the squaw of one of the men. Perhaps two or more men will want her. Then she will be placed in a circle between them, her arms outstretched. The two men will take hold of either arm, their friends and family will take hold of them, and a squawpulling will begin. Either one of the men will pull her to his side and so claim her as his squaw, or her arms will be torn free, her weakness therefore shown, and she will be left to perish. To me this is not a good way, but again, it is the way of my woman's people. It is an old way, and who am I to question it?"

Dah-Nish-Uant took a long breath, a deep breath, and the silence in the lodge was intense. Outside the crickets sent out a constant chirping, and the small fire licked hungrily at the remaining wood, throwing out a constantly changing pattern of light and shadow.

"As my woman gave me much happiness," the Navajo finally continued, "so too does her daughter. It is a heart-thing I feel for Iitats, and the pain of what lies in her pathway gnaws like sikuts, the squirrel, at my mind. Long have I pondered the two ways before her, and in neither of them do I feel peace. This has troubled me more than I can say.

"But then Tobats, the great creator, the one whom I remember you called Chee-zoos, put it into my mind that I was to consider you. This I have done, and in the considering I have at last found peace. My white friend, I have asked you to come, for it is in my heart to give to you my daughter."

CHAPTER

5

Young Iitats stared upward into the darkness. Unable to sleep, she let her thoughts wander, trying to make sense of all that was happening to her. Though her head had been bowed as befitted her position during all the times she had been in the white man's presence, she had nevertheless allowed her eyes to steal many glances at him whom her father wished would become her husband.

Now Iitats was beginning to realize that a strange feeling was growing within her, a feeling she could not understand. Part of it, of course, was fear, for she had seen Samuel Loper's expression when her father had explained that Iitats would be his. Strangely, before his coming she had feared going with him. But now she feared that the white man would not want to take her away.

Had it not been such a serious thing, young Iitats might have giggled at the absurdity of it. She recalled the time, many seasons before, when she and Peokon had trapped a small chipmunk. For days it had tried to escape, and all the time they had patiently fed it and cared for it. Then one day, feeling sorry for the little animal, Iitats had finally released it from its woven cage. Though Peokon had been angry, she had watched with wonder as the creature had darted back and forth for a moment or so, then finally made its way back inside the cage, where it remained until they left it behind. The foolishness of the chipmunk had made her giggle then, and she felt the same way about her own foolishness now.

Only there was something about the young white man that Iitats could not get from her mind. Perhaps it was his gentleness, for he was indeed a gentle person. Even her father thought so. When she had asked her father, after he had sent the runner away, why he had chosen to give her to the Mormonee, Dah-Nish-Uant had waited long moments before replying.

"When first Samuel Loper came among this people," he had finally responded, "I saw how he cared for his horse, seeing to its needs before he saw to his own. It is in me to desire that such a man also care for my daughter."

Now Iitats thought of that again and wondered. Off in the trees *mu-u-pits*, the owl, hooted, and then on silent wings it drifted off into the darkness. Iitats listened, wondering with a slight shiver if the owl was now calling her name so that she could follow after her mother into the land of the sky people. But quickly she found herself wondering again about the white man, and so she knew the owl person had not been calling her name.

Earlier, after her father had explained his purpose in calling Samuel Loper to him, the white man had vanished, and Iitats had no idea where he had gone. Had he returned to his people? Had he turned his back on her? Did he consider her unworthy of being his wife? Or his slave? Of course she did not wish to be a slave, but now her thinking was that even as a slave to Samuel Loper there would be great joy. Only he had gone, and surely —

But no, he had left his saddle, packs, and rifle behind,

so he couldn't have gone away. No man could afford to leave behind such wealth. Still, what if he had indeed gone—

The night was very quiet. Only a far-off coyote complaining to the listening *poot-see*, the stars, caused a faint break in the stillness, and its voice seemed only to make the silence more still.

The dull red of the coals left from the fire were a dim light in their small pocket of heat. From time to time tiny flames erupted to seize upon some overlooked bit of dry wood, and then a small blaze would leap up briefly, consuming what had been found.

In the darkness Iitats watched the flames, wondering what was to become of her, and wondering too what had become of the man called Samuel Loper.

"O Great Shinob," she pleaded silently, "this woman does not know her own heart. At one time she does not want to accompany this man at all, and yet at another time she fears that she won't. Perhaps being a slave to him would not be so bad as she has been thinking—"

With a sigh her father rolled over in his sleeping robes, and Iitats thought again of the white man, wondering if she would ever see him again. At the moment she did not care if she never again saw her brother, for he had become something she did not understand. Thus she was now telling herself that he no longer existed. But her father? Suddenly she found herself longing for him, for the strength of his arms as well as his wisdom, but it was as though he had already departed into the land of the Diné. Tears sprang instantly to her eyes, and for long moments she wept bitterly, the ache of loneliness seeming to crush her very soul.

"O Great Shinob," she sobbed quietly, "must this woman die inside at such an early age? The pain within her is as if she has already taken the long road to the west, and she waits only to nourish the earth. Yet the sorrow in her heart does not end, and so she knows that she must continue to breathe. O Great One, if that is so, then give her to someone who feels toward her as her father does—"

Her eyes suddenly wide open, Iitats thought again that thought. As her father considered her to be *mama'uts*, a woman of great worth, so she suddenly understood that to be happy, she must be given to a man who felt the same. Nor would it matter that his ways differed from hers, or even that his people differed. If he could think of her as a person of worth, whether she served as a slave or as a wife, that would be sufficient, and she would be happy.

Outside the lodge, *pan-ah-wich*, the nightbird, made its lonely cry, and a sudden breeze fanned the coals of the fire a brighter red. Another nightbird cried, this time from farther off, and Iitats' eyes opened even wider.

"O Shinob," she prayed again, "forgive this woman from troubling you. But the thought you gave her concerning her father was a clear and happy thought, one she will cherish always. Now *nou-ahd*, the wind, comes, carrying the song of *pan-ah-wich*, which is as the cry of all lonely people. O Great One, now she stands secure. Now she is at peace. The wind has come, and it is the breath of Shinob telling her that in the morning she will walk in the only direction she can, and it will be the path she should walk. Yes, and because the cry of *pan-ah-wich* was answered, surely it is you again, telling this foolish girl that she will not be forever alone, that the man she goes with will be as a husband to her. If that is so, O Great Shinob," and now Iitats smiled shyly as she prayed, "then let the white man called Samuel Loper see her as a person of great worth—"

35

6

These are indeed a happy people." The deep voice of Dah-Nish-Uant sounded emotional, almost reverent, and though Samuel Loper wondered at it, out of respect he did not turn to look.

It was *ich-coot*, the morning of one of the last days of October, and again it was warm and cloudless. The people of the encampment were busy, taking advantage of the unseasonable weather. The three hunters were off again in their quest for venison, Peokon seemed to have disappeared, and Iitats, working with the other women in the harvesting of *tuu*, the pine nut, nevertheless kept herself close to the lodge of her father. At its entrance Dah-Nish-Uant sat with the young white man called Samuel Loper, and though their voices were low, Iitats could hear their words without difficulty.

"Is it so among the whites?" Dah-Nish-Uant asked.

"My people are also a happy people," Samuel affirmed. "Yet there are differences."

Dah-Nish-Uant regarded Samuel questioningly.

"The white people try very hard to be private," Samuel

responded carefully. "Unlike the Paiute, they hide their daily activities from all but their own families."

"How is this done?"

"The lodges of the whites are much larger, and *puow'wan*, the families, live wholly within them, coming out of doors only when necessary."

Wonderingly Dah-Nish-Uant stared ahead. "You speak of the season of cold?" he finally asked.

"Yes, and of all other seasons."

"What a strange thing. I do not—" Abruptly Dah-Nish-Uant paused, and then with a look of understanding he smiled. "If your people do not often see *tavaputs*, the sun, then I see now why you have all become so pale of skin."

Samuel laughed. "Perhaps that is so."

And then there was more silence between them. Although she had been listening intently, Iitats, kneeling nearby, continued to grind piles of nuts between the flat surface of her stone *metate* and the rounded *mano*. Deftly she moved the stone back and forth, back and forth, exerting just enough pressure to crack the shells but not enough to pulp the white nut meat or to grind the shells into it. Once finished, she slid the mass of nuts and shells onto the surface of a large winnowing basket, and then she bent again to her task of grinding more pinion nuts.

"Your daughter is very skilled," Samuel noted with wonder, causing the young girl to flush with embarrassment.

So he had noticed! Perhaps then Shinob would also cause the white man to see her as a woman—

"Yes," Dah-Nish-Uant agreed, interrupting her thoughts. "My woman taught her well. Iitats will make a fine wife, of that you may be certain. Do you understand the harvesting of *tuu*, my friend?"

"It is a thing I have never seen," Samuel responded,

37

while Iitats crushed many pine nuts in her frustration that her father had changed the subject so quickly.

"Then I will explain."

As the man spoke, Samuel watched as a woman using a long pole with a hook on the end pulled the cones from the trees. Two other women, working quickly, gathered the cones in their burden baskets and dumped them into one of three large cooking pits that had been lined with heated rocks.

"Do you see how it is, my friend? The cones must be heated so they will give away their nuts. At the same time, the nuts must be roasted so they will give away their shells. For a day and a night they stay in the fire pits, covered with leaves and earth, and then they are roasted and ready to be ground."

At that moment Iitats rose to her feet with her winnowing basket in her hands. Turning, she was instantly aware that the white man's eyes were upon her. Embarrassed and somewhat confused, she dropped her eyes and began shaking the basket carefully, tossing the nuts and shells into the air and letting the soft wind catch and blow off the pieces of shell. With deft movements she was soon finished, and the self-conscious girl turned away and formed the nut meat into cakes, which she quickly packed in a nearby basket. Then, speaking not at all, she began the process of grinding all over again.

Yet her mind, no more still than her hands, was in a turmoil. Why did her heart race so when she looked at the man? Or when he looked at her, which was even worse? Yes, she had heard the voice of the Great Shinob on the wind, and the cries of the nightbirds had given her to know that she and a man would one day be as man and wife. Yet that did not necessarily mean it was to be this man—

"O Great Shinob," she pleaded silently, "this woman does not understand what is happening to her. Her *sax-*

wayam, her belly, feels empty even when it is not. And *pu-vi,* her eyes, cannot keep themselves from seeking out the man's *koh-vahv,* his face—"

"You look troubled, my friend."

"It is as nothing." Samuel made the sign of deprecation. And then, watching Iitats but not actually seeing her, he continued. "But there is a thing that does tug at my mind."

Though he sensed what was vexing the Mormon missionary, Dah-Nish-Uant remained respectfully silent.

"As the Diné have their ways, and as the Paiute have their ways," Samuel stated slowly, "so, too, do my people have their ways."

"You speak of the whites?"

"Yes," Samuel responded with a nod, "but more than the whites, I speak of the Mormons. Those are truly my people."

"And the Mormonees are not all white?"

Samuel grinned. "It is so that most Mormons are also white. But my friend, that will not always be so. As all men are sons and daughters of the Great God, so will those from all nations who wish it, no matter the color of their skin, become Mormon and worship the Great God as one."

"This God is Chee-Zoos, of whom you spoke before?"

Samuel made the sign that it was so.

"And Chee-Zoos is the peace God, the one you say visited my people?"

Not surprised that the man remembered so much from what he had been taught several months before, Samuel again made the agreement sign.

"It is said among the people in the Great Canyon, the Hava Supai, that a pale God once visited them," Dah-Nish-Uant said softly. "I know of no such tales among the Paiute."

"And the Diné?" Samuel asked.

39

For a long time the man looked out across the vast sage-covered plain to the north and west. "It is so," he finally answered. "Long ago I heard my father speak of it, and even after I was brought among the Paiute, I held on to the memory."

Again the Indian paused, and Samuel, very curious, held his peace.

"To the Diné," Dah-Nish-Uant finally continued, his voice low and deep, "names are very important. They are given for many reasons, but always there is a reason behind a name. It is said that when this pale God of peace came among them, the Diné feared misnaming him. In reverence they asked him the name given in his childhood, far across the great ocean, by his true father. To their questions he gave a name, and even today it is held sacred, so much that only the very old even know of it."

For a long moment there was silence, broken only by the sound of the wind whispering through the pines and the junipers overhead. Samuel heard the far-off laughter of the Paiute children, and then from somewhere nearby a crow called out, once and then again. And during all of that, Dah-Nish-Uant remained still, looking steadfastly at the young Mormon missionary.

"It is said," he finally replied, his voice absolutely solemn, "that the name he gave them was Yeh-ho-vah."

"In the white tongue," Samuel responded just as solemnly, and after an appropriate silence, "this name is also sacred."

"You have this name?" Dah-Nish-Uant asked in surprise.

"We do. But in our tongue it is said this way: Jehovah."

"And this is the God of the Mormonees?"

"It is."

Slowly the Navajo chief shook his head. "It is a thing

to be wondered at," he replied softly. "Surely there is power in this, more than a man can know."

Continuing her labors, Iitats wondered at the things she was hearing. Could it be so that she and the white man spoke to the same great being, the one who was the younger brother of Tobats? It was said among her people that while Tobats thought up the earth, he sent his younger brother Shinob to do the creating. Thus Shinob had great compassion for the things he had created, while Tobats did not. And thus did she always send her prayer-thoughts to Shinob.

Might this God her father and Samuel Loper had spoken of, and of whom she had never heard, be the same great being as the kind and gentle Shinob, who had spoken so mysteriously to her in the last time of darkness? It was truly a thing to be wondered at, and to be considered.

"My brother," Dah-Nish-Uant continued, again interrupting Iitats' thoughts, "you were speaking of the ways of your people the Mormonees."

Iitats was surprised to hear her father refer to the white man as his brother. And as she glanced covertly at Samuel Loper, she was certain the subtle change had not been lost on him. Truly this man, despite his lack of years, was wise in the dealings of men. Truly would it be a good thing if the great Shinob could—

"Among our people," Samuel Loper was suddenly replying, "a man cannot be given to another, nor can one man own another. All men are free, for that is the way the Great God made them."

"And a woman?" Dah-Nish-Uant asked, causing Iitats to catch her breath as she listened.

"It is the same."

Dah-Nish-Uant turned to face Samuel, his own countenance bleak. "This is by way of saying that you will not take my daughter away with you."

It was a statement, not a question, and Iitats paused in her labors to listen. For some reason her heart was pounding in her chest, and even her breathing had grown still. Where only a few hours before she had feared going with the white man, now it seemed to her that she would die if she could not. Surely he could see that! Surely this man called Samuel Loper could understand that she was a worthy person to take away. Why—

Now Samuel Loper made the sign that he had not been understood. "Another way of wisdom among our people," he said then, "is that women do not marry until they are grown."

"Iitats is grown."

"To the Paiute, yes. To the Mormons, a woman is not grown until she is at least sixteen summers, or even more. To my people, Iitats is still as a child."

Shocked, Iitats nearly came upright before her *metate*, a protest in her mouth. But then, realizing that the men did not think of her as one who was listening, she began slowly moving her *mano* back and forth, her ears continuing their work of hearing.

Puzzled by Samuel's statement, Dah-Nish-Uant shook his head. "But she is not a child. I myself have seen that she is a woman. She has spent her first month alone, preparing and purifying herself. And does she not do the work of a woman?"

Samuel nodded. "Surely what you say is so. I speak not of that, but only of the ways of my people."

Now light flooded the Indian's eyes, and he made the sign of understanding, for he well knew that custom was not always based on reasoning or common sense. And slowly he took a deep breath.

"My brother, again I hear you saying that my daughter will not go away with you."

And again, while Iitats listened and watched fearfully, Samuel made the sign that he had not been understood.

"O Dah-Nish-Uant," he finally said, a sound of help-lessness in his voice, "in this thing I do not know my own heart. Perhaps it is right that Iitats accompany me, and perhaps it is not right. If it is right, then I take her neither to be my wife nor to be my slave but to be a young woman who must learn the ways of the whites before she can be anyone's wife."

"And if it is not right?"

Samuel looked back at the man, his countenance show-ing that his heart was heavy with understanding. "Then I will return to my people alone."

There was no hiding the pain in the Navajo chief's eyes. Yet he said nothing, merely making the sign that he understood.

"From where the sun now stands until it awakens on the morrow," Samuel Loper concluded, feeling a sudden flash of inspiration, "I will make a fast that the Great God, Jehovah, will make clear to my heart the path that I am to take with young Iitats."

"Your heart is good, my brother," Dah-Nish-Uant nod-ded with satisfaction, "like the hearts of most of my people. I, too, will make a fast that you will know."

"O Great Shinob," Iitats then pleaded in her mind, still kneeling only a little distance away, "this white man says he does not know his heart, but the woman who kneels before you knows hers. I am certain it is him you spoke of in the time of darkness, him that I would be as a wife to. O Great One, as you have declared, please reach out and bring these two hearts together—"

43

It was still dark, yet day could not be far away. Silently Iitats crept from the lodge of her father, noting in the dim light the rifle and saddle of Samuel Loper, which had not been moved since he had arrived. Standing alone outside the lodge, she breathed deeply of the chill air. For a moment she thrilled to the sweet aroma of pinion pine and *sahng-wahv*, sagebrush, and then crept silently to the trickle of water that ran away from the spring. Dipping her fingers into the clear, cold liquid, she splashed her face with it and then combed her hair with her fingers. After that she rinsed her hand and drank, slowly, for the water was very cold, but deeply, for it was also very sweet.

"*Pa-a tun-kam-ai*," she breathed to herself, "the waters taste good to my mouth. Thank you, O Great Shinob, for allowing Kaibab-its, the mountain lying down, to give his juice to me."

It was still dark, but as Iitats stood again, looking about, the isolated trees and boulders were beginning to stand out. High in the heavens was a faint tinge of pink on a cloud, but that was all. The coolness of the night lay upon the land, and nothing stirred.

Where was he, Iitats wondered? Where was Samuel Loper? Would he have done as the men of her people when they were making a fast? Would he have gone to a high and lonely place? And more important, after the white man had spent the night in such a sacred place, would the great God he called Chee-zoos, who Iitats was now convinced was Shinob, make known to him that he was to take her away with him?

For long moments the girl stood without moving. In her mind was the reality that her father wished her to go with this white man, to be as a wife to him. She also knew that the great Shinob had decreed this thing. Yet Iitats understood well how frail were the thoughts and deeds of humanity—how subject to *un-nu-pit*, the evil one, and his warriors were the hearts of mortal people. Somehow she needed a way to force the issue, a way to guarantee that Samuel Loper would return with the answer from his god that she knew he must receive.

And so she stood in the darkness, pondering. Around her all was still and strangely silent. Even the soft laughter of the water seemed muted. Iitats stood as one transfixed, her thoughts flying in many directions, and when the lone howl of the wolf came to her ears from somewhere across the mountainous plateau, she was not at all surprised.

"*Aru-pax-ai ung-tu-ra'sun-av*," she whispe ed to herself. "The wolf is talking. I must hear his words."

Lifting her head in readiness, she waited, and when a moment later the lonely cry came again, the girl smiled, knowing what it was the wolf was telling her to do.

"Samuel Loper," she declared, her breath hanging on the frosty air, "hear these words, for they are true." And then, raising her hands as her mother had taught her, she spoke again.

Ho.
Hear these words,
you man.
Hear this *um-pug-iva*, this talk of
my mouth.

Ho.
Now I take your heart,
you man.
I take your heart and you see no
other woman.

Ho.
There is no other woman,
you man.
For in *mo'ovi*, my hand, I hold
your heart.

Ho.
Now you must come
to me.

Trembling as much from fear of the strong words of her mother's chant as from the cold, Iitats lowered her arms and returned slowly to the lodge of her father. Sitting on a large stone near the entrance, she pulled her robe more tightly about her shoulders. Then she prepared herself for the return of Samuel Loper. The white man was out there somewhere, she knew that. He had to be! And she was not about to let him creep in upon her again.

Gradually the day brightened, and with the daylight came a heaviness to the eyes of Iitats. She did not wish it to be there. She even willed it to go away so she would see the man coming. Yet for the emotionally exhausted girl, it was not to be, and at last her head drooped in fitful sleep. Nor did she awaken until, with the first warm rays of sunlight, she felt the soft hand of her father upon her shoulder.

"Come, my daughter," he said softly as she lifted her

head and stared upward at the man who was dearer to her than anyone else in all the world. "It is time we made a parting."

Her eyes now open wide, Iitats rose hurriedly to her feet. Only then did she see the rifle in the hand of her father, the rifle that, just the night before, had belonged to the young white man.

And then Iitats knew that her words had been strong enough, and that the white man Samuel Loper had made his decision to take her away with him.

This that you do is not a good thing, my *koo-mahn,* my husband."

Samuel Loper, walking ahead of his horse, looked back in surprise. Iitats, watching him, almost smiled. He looked so awkward the way he moved, and yet *kava,* the horse, had to step quickly to keep up with him.

Iitats had ridden double with him from the camp of her father as they made their way *qui-am-er tavi-awk-er,* northwestward, down the steep slopes of Buckskin Mountain on the northern end of the Kaibab Plateau. Following Jacob's Canyon, they had continued across the foothills at the base, and only when they had come to the relatively flat plain called the Arizona Strip had the white man dismounted to lead his horse.

In all that time, yes, even from the moment her father had awakened her, Iitats had spoken not a word. There had been no farewells for her father, for those had already been done, and Peokon had been nowhere in sight. So truly there had been no one to speak to. She had simply and silently gone about the task of packing what few possessions she would take with her into her new life.

Besides her sleeping robe, Iitats had brought her carrying cap and carrying band. These, with her digging stick, bone needles, and scraping bones, were wrapped in soft bark to prevent breakage. She included her beads and feathers and porcupine quills, decorative items with which she would adorn the clothing she would make for herself and her future family. Those things, along with her oils and body greases and ointments, were all she had to carry away.

When she had finished packing the rucksack in which Samuel had delivered the porcupine only a day before, Iitats had watched as he had saddled and mounted his horse. Removing his left foot from the stirrup, he had motioned for her to give him her hand. Stretching, she had placed her left foot into the stirrup and reached for his hand. Then he easily lifted her onto the back of his saddle. No words had been exchanged. Nor had Iitats looked back once the man had clucked the horse into motion. Dry-eyed, she had simply stared ahead, and not even the curious stares and calls of the children they had passed had affected her.

Now, with hours and miles behind them, her abrupt statement seemed to catch him by surprise.

"What is not a good thing?" he asked, looking back to where Iitats sat in his saddle.

"That a woman rides while her husband is forced to walk," Iitats stated simply and forthrightly.

For a moment Samuel continued to walk, his footfalls raising tiny clouds of dust in the arid soil. Then, with a deep sigh, he stopped the horse, walked back, and lifted the girl from the saddle.

"*Karu kai-ng-o*," he said, pointing to the tiny spot of shade created by the bay mare. "Please sit down."

Iitats did so, and Samuel sat cross-legged in front of her, facing her squarely. Around them *sahng-wahv*, the sagebrush, rose higher than their heads, and so it seemed suddenly that their world had grown very small. To Iitats the position was quite uncomfortable, though she could not begin to understand why.

"Iitats," Samuel finally began, "you are not a wife to me."

"Yes, my husband."

"Oh, for the love of—" Samuel muttered in English, his sounds confusing to the girl. Then, with another sigh he spoke again in Paiute. "Neither am I your husband."

Now Iitats was even more confused, and her embarrassment grew on her face. "Then," she said hesitantly, "I . . . I am to be your . . . your slave?"

Smiling at the foolishness of the idea, Samuel made the sign that she had not understood. Then, as with her father the day before, he sought to explain the difference between the ways of the Paiute and the ways of the Mormons.

Iitats listened carefully, the mare stomped a hoof in impatience, and overhead *kusavi*, the red-tailed hawk, drifted back and forth in lazy circles. Truly was the white man going to great lengths to help her understand his thinking, spending many moments on the explanation. And truly did Iitats hear his words. But just as clearly she could hear in her memory the whisper of Shinob and the strong words of her mother, and so she knew that in time this man would know, just as she did, that their hearts were to come together. Only how could she explain such a soul-thing to him? Perhaps if she took things just one step at a time—

"You seem troubled, Little One," Samuel Loper stated carefully. "Why is that?"

Iitats sighed deeply and dropped her eyes. "I hear your

words, my husband," she said finally, in a voice so low Samuel had to strain to hear. "Yet I saw with my own eyes the rifle with which you purchased me."

"The rifle was a gift from one old friend to another."

"And Iitats was also a gift from one old friend to another."

Instantly Samuel made the sign that it was not so. "You were not a gift."

"But . . . Iitats is now with you . . . "

"Yes," Samuel stated, his voice reflecting a little his frustration, "but only because I agreed to take you to my people, who will teach you of their ways. You are your own person, Little One. No one owns you, and you are not married, least of all to me."

In wonder Iitats stared at the earth, trying desperately to understand Samuel Loper's words. But more than that, she tried to understand the sorrow that now filled her breast. This white man did not want her; not as a wife, not even as a slave did he want her. She was of no value to him, and the thought was so painful that tears started suddenly from her eyes.

"Whoa," Samuel stated in fear, breaking again into English frontier slang as he lunged to his feet, "now don't you start bawling on me, little girl. I ain't never got used to bawling females!"

Not understanding his strange sounds, Iitats continued to sit and weep.

"Aw, for crying out loud—"

Reaching down, the white man took Iitats' hand and pulled her to her feet. "Listen to my words," he said, once again using the more formal tongue of the Paiute. "We will go to my people, and they will make a place for you."

That brought only more tears, and so with a helpless

gesture Samuel took the weeping Iitats under her arms and lifted her back into the saddle. Then, his mind troubled by the sorrow he knew was only beginning for the girl, he resumed his course toward the northwest and the settlement on the Santa Clara.

I . . . would ask a question?"

Samuel did not turn at the sound of the girl's hesitant voice. Instead, he continued his steady progress across the dry plain. It was well into the afternoon, the unseasonable heat continued, and now Iitats walked beside him so the mare might rest.

"*Im-par-vi*, Little One," the white man responded as he swallowed the bite of jerky he had been chewing for some time, "what would you ask?" He had given some of the dried meat to Iitats, but she had eaten little and did not intend to eat much more.

"This . . . Brigham Young?" she questioned. "What is it?"

Samuel chuckled, and Iitats did not understand that he laughed not only because her question was so funny but also because of how she pronounced the prophet's name. Instead, the white man's laughter seemed rude to the Paiute girl. Yet she put his rudeness from her mind and waited for his answer.

"Brigham Young is the name of a man," he answered,

"a great Mormon. He is called by our people a prophet of God."

Iitats digested that, doing her best to understand. "Is he . . . great like you?" she finally asked.

Now Samuel really laughed. "Uung. Yes, only more so—much more so."

"But how can that be?" Iitats questioned, truly puzzled. Never in her life had she known a man like this Mormonee Samuel Loper, and she could not imagine another greater than he.

"Little One, Brigham Young is God's prophet, a man of high soul stature—maybe higher than any other man. I am only a missionary, and a young missionary at that."

"But . . . you are filled with great wisdom, greater than a man with so few seasons upon his shoulders can have."

"Why do you say this?"

"These are the words of *nuni muang,* my father."

Finally slowing to walk beside the confused girl, Samuel spoke earnestly. "Listen, Little One, and hear my words. I am *tang-wats,* a man like all men. That, and no more."

"And a missionary."

Samuel laughed. "And a missionary. That is correct."

Again Iitats paused in thought. "I would ask another question."

"Speak."

"Why is Brigham Young?"

Impressed, Samuel looked at the girl. "Now that's a right good question," he responded in English. Then, in Paiute, he continued. "All men are sons and daughters of God."

"You speak of Shinob?"

"That is right. But the white people call him by another name. We call him Jesus."

"This great being must be known by many names. I heard you and my father speak of one other?"

"Yes, that is so. Among both the Navajo and the whites he is also called something like Jehovah. But that is a very sacred name, and so I call him Jesus when I speak of him."

"And this Chee-zoos is the younger brother of Tobats?"

Samuel scratched the back of his head, thinking. "Among the white people it is said he is the son of the elder God, whom we call the Father."

"And has this Father no name?"

"He does. But it, too, is sacred."

Iitats nodded her understanding.

"And so," she said as she *pahkk-kae-koh*, made a walking around a large ant hill, "we speak of Chee-zoos and his Father, whom you say are Shinob and Tobats. But I do not understand what our words have to do with the man called Brigham Young."

"It is this way," Samuel replied as he circled the ant hill on the other side. "Jesus wants all people to live good lives, to do as he tells them. But there are many people in many places, and it is difficult for him to speak to all of them at one time."

Iitats was silent, listening intently.

"That is why Jesus makes for himself a prophet, one who speaks with God and who then carries God's words to the people."

"This man Brigham Young sees Chee-zoos?"

"Sometimes," the white man replied matter-of-factly. "And he always hears Jesus' word. Then he brings that word to the people, so they will know how Jesus wants them to live."

"Brigham Young is Mormonee?"

"Yes. But Jesus' word is for all people, not only Mormons. That is why I come to the Paiute—to tell them of Jesus' word."

"This man Brigham Young sent you?"

Samuel made the sign that it was so.

"Do you know this great Mormonee?"

Samuel made the sign for a little bit. "That is why I allow you to accompany me to my people," he then added.

Iitats made the sign that she did not understand.

"Jesus spoke to Brigham Young, and his word was that the Mormons are to go among the Paiutes and other Indian peoples and tell them of him. His word is also that the Mormons are to love the people of the Kaibab and other lands, and to help them learn of Jesus' ways."

"Are the ways of my people not Jesus' ways?"

The question, asked innocently, bothered Samuel, and Iitats could see that immediately. "Why are you troubled?" she asked quickly.

Samuel sighed. "I do not know if I have the words to make answer, Little One. There is much about your people—many of their ways—that seem more like the teachings of Jesus than the ways of the whites."

"That is a strange answer."

Samuel made the sign agreeing that it was so. "Yet there is more to Jesus' teachings than just the ways for people to live." Samuel scratched his head again, thinking of how to say what he needed to say to this girl who had dug so deeply into his mind. "There are . . . uh . . . keys of authority that come only through the prophet," he finally stated.

"Keys? I do not know this word."

"Well . . . uh . . . keys are powers, Iitats. Jesus gives the prophet all powers, and then the prophet gives them to others."

"I do not think I understand, my husband."

"Neither do I," Samuel stated, breaking into frustrated English. "I mean, how in tarnation can I explain this to you, little girl? How can I tell you that parts of Indian society are closer to Christ's teachings than my own, white or Mormon, but that we have a fulness of truth and you don't? Even if it's true it doesn't sound true, so how in thunder can I say it?

"Besides, Brother Jacob says over and over that my mission has less to do with that than with bringing you folks back to a knowledge of your Redeemer—or at least to a knowledge of his true identity. After all, you're already an amazingly honest people, mostly moral in your relationships with each other, and willing to give your all to one of your own who is in need. So you do follow his teachings. Yet somehow, in the two thousand years since Christ walked among your ancestors, you folks have lost his identity. You no longer know who it is you worship. That's my calling—to tell you that the one you call Shinob is actually Jesus Christ, and that the account of his walking among your ancestors is contained in the Book of Mormon.

"Now, them's the facts, pure and simple," he said, speaking now to all the empty land. "But how in thunder am I supposed to say them to an innocent little Paiute girl who probably ain't committed a sin in her life, and who has no more idea of white-man thinking than she does of how to go out and turn altogether evil before the sun sets!"

"I . . . do not know your words," Iitats stated carefully, wondering as she spoke why the white man had suddenly started jabbering so loudly in his own tongue.

"The ways of your people are good ways," Samuel finally responded, doing his best to simplify things, if not for the girl then at least for himself. "But they do not include Jesus. He is lonely, and he wants all people to worship him, not just a few."

"The man Brigham Young told you to say this?"

Samuel made the sign that it was so. Then he and the girl continued in silence, scrambling down the side of a deep ravine, walking along in the deep sand of the bottom for a few moments, and finally finding a sloping bank up which they could climb.

"It is good to know of these things," Iitats said over her *tso-av-uvi,* her shoulder, once they were walking single file again.

Once more Samuel made the sign that it was so.

"If Shinob and Chee-zoos are truly the same great being," Iitats continued, "then it is good to do as Chee-zoos says. Now that you have spoken these words, it is in my heart to always do as Chee-zoos says. Will you give my words to the prophet Brigham Young so that he may tell Chee-zoos that which I will do?"

Impressed even more with the girl's innocence and faith, Samuel made the sign that he would do as he had been asked.

"There is one thing more," Iitats said after another few moments of silent walking.

"What is that, Little One?"

"It is that you must promise to tell me all that Chee-zoos tells Brigham Young that I am to do."

And with a warm smile at the young girl who looked back at him, Samuel made the sign that he would do so.

I will return," Samuel said quietly as he slipped from the horse and helped Iitats down. She did not respond, and so without a backward glance Samuel began climbing up through the rocks of the steep ridge above what would one day be called Pipe Springs.

Iitats watched him go. And then, knowing what was expected of her, she turned and immediately began gathering firewood to prepare for their evening meal.

It had been interesting to see how the white man Samuel Loper had come to this place, which she and her people had used for more seasons than one could count. He had been very careful, Iitats had noted, riding in a wide circle as he drew near the springs, his eyes busy seeking tracks or other signs of travel. There had been none that Iitats had seen, but she also knew that war parties of the people called Ute, as well as Navajo and Apache warriors, occasionally used this spring. And often such men intentionally destroyed the signs of their passing, or they circled and came down to the water from above so they would leave no trail. It was this that the white man was concerned with now, and Iitats appreciated his care.

Below the spring and before it disappeared into the thirsty desert, there were many cattails, some *kah-nahv,* or willows, and a few *so'veev,* cottonwood trees. From these Iitats gathered an armful of dead limbs and dry bark. In a low place that had been used by her father and others in seasons past, she kindled the bark and quickly built up a smokeless fire. Then, while the rocks for cooking were heating, she took her digging stick and walked to the stand of cattails.

Quickly she worked, wasting no motion, and she felt good in the knowledge that she was doing well what good women had always done. It would be good for the white man to see more of her skills, she thought as she dug in the black mud. In that manner he could better understand what a fine wife he had purchased—

Moments later, hurrying to a sandy shelf where her people had made a planting, Iitats glanced up at the top of the ridge. The man was there, she knew, even though she could not see him. And he would be studying the agunt, the country through which they now traveled. In her mind Iitats could also see it, for many times she had climbed the hill above the rock spring.

Pe-tan-am-i wintook, south for several miles, and stretching both *tavi-maus wintook,* or east, and *tavi-awk wintook,* or west, as far as he would be able to see, was the sage- and grass-covered plain the two of them had traversed that day. Now in the early twilight, the strip of land would look softer than it was, and smoother. The fading light would also bring the plateaued heights to the south closer than they were, though Iitats knew that Samuel Loper would be used to such illusions and would pay them little mind.

Off in the distance a small herd of *wan-se-tu,* pronghorn antelope, grazed, and Iitats also knew that the man would study their movements. Closer, in the bushes below the springs, some *kahd-ahm*, Gambel quail, clucked and chattered back and forth as they busily prepared themselves for the night. Iitats smiled, for on this evening she was even busier than they, a thing that made her truly happy.

"My heart is *kee-eung-koo*," she sang, breaking into a happy song that she had known from before she could remember.

> My heart is *kee-eung-koo*,
> My heart is laughing,
> My heart is laughing, indeed.
>
> Now *tu-weap* the Earth
> And *tu-omp-pi-av* the Sky
> Have come together as one.
> They will always be one.
>
> My heart is *kee-eung-koo*,
> My heart is laughing,
> My heart is laughing, indeed.

Back at the fire she worked quickly in the stillness of the late afternoon, making all things ready, and as she worked it was so quiet that the sound of a honeybee buzzing past her seemed inordinately loud.

What else might the man be seeing, Iitats wondered. *Qui-ami wintook*, north over the sand hills, the land opened into a small valley where gushed a spring that formed a clear, cold stream of water. It was much bigger than this spring, and near the stream her people always made large plantings of squash, beans, and corn.

Samuel Loper might be looking in that direction, but the sand hills were too high, and he would see nothing of the valley or her people's plantings. Nor was it likely that he would be considering making a *pahkk-kae-koh*, a walking in that direction. The mountains around the valley were too steep and rugged, and it was much easier to simply skirt them to the west, following a wide trail made by generations of her people that would bring them, by dark of another day, to what they called the cane beds, where she supposed their next camp would be.

Thus did the mind of Iitats keep busy even while her fingers performed their womanly tasks. Finally, about when she had expected, but still moving so quietly that he startled her, the man materialized at the edge of their camp, moving toward her.

"The fire awaits your kill, my husband," Iitats said quickly, hiding her surprise at his sudden appearance.

Shaking his head, Samuel stared at the small fire put together by Iitats. He had not seen it even while descending the slope, nor had he smelled the smoke. The girl had known to pick a spot that was practically invisible from more than a few feet away, and her chosen fuel was burning almost smokelessly. These things he appreciated instantly. Her calling him "husband" again, he did not.

While Iitats watched, Samuel strode to one of the two rucksacks and withdrew his venison jerky and dried biscuits. These he handed to her.

For an instant she gazed at the food, saying nothing. But then with a smile she set to work again, ignoring her amused but admittedly impressed traveling companion.

While she worked, Samuel unsaddled and rubbed down the bay mare, his troubled thoughts considering the girl as much as hers were considering him. By the time he was through and the mare was tethered on a nearby patch of lush grass, Iitats was happily singing as she stirred the boiling contents of her pitch-lined cooking basket.

It was almost full dark when Samuel was handed a smaller bowl, from which both he and the girl would eat. Releasing the bowl, Iitats waited expectantly and nodded with approval as Samuel bowed his head and offered a blessing, in English, over whatever it was he was being served.

Finally ready, he took two carved wooden spoons from his rucksack and handed one to Iitats. "Spoon," he said in English, noting her confused expression. "Spoon." Then he dipped the implement into the hot broth and took a tentative bite.

The food, at first taste, was pleasant, though surprisingly tangy. Samuel took another bite, larger, and then smiled at the girl as he ate happily. Iitats smiled in return, rather smugly, and soon she was also eating, though at first the concept of the spoon eluded her. But by the time the cooking basket was emptied, Iitats had mastered the spoon, and both of them were quite full.

"What was it that we ate?" Samuel asked as he stretched back on his saddle.

"The meat and cakes of my master," Iitats said with a smile, "some wild onions, and some cattail shoots, which I was fortunate to find still growing. I looked for camas root but found none. Camas would have made it better. There was also squash from the planting place of my people."

"Your people plant crops here?" Samuel asked in surprise.

"For more snows than a person can count."

"And there was a squash remaining?"

Iitats smiled. "It is the way of my people to leave a little of their planting on the chance that someone might come along in the season of cold, very hungry, and with no way to obtain food. Thus he will not starve."

"It is a good way," Samuel stated thoughtfully. "I did not know that this spring was known to your people."

"This spring, and another which is *qui-ami wintook*, north of here a short walk. This spring we call Yellow Rock

Water, and it has been called such for more generations than one can count. But even my people were not the first to use this *pah,* this water. Over that way lie what is left of the possessions of a people we call the Old Ones, strangers who my father says went away from this land many generations before the Nung-wa, the people called Paiute, were created by Shinob."

"This is a true thing?" Samuel questioned.

Making the sign that it was so, Iitats then led Samuel Loper to the site of the ancient ruins. Kneeling in the last of the light, he examined several large, painted pottery fragments and then traced the remains of the stone walls. Satisfied finally that Iitats' understanding had been correct, Samuel followed the girl back to the glowing fire, where he again settled against his saddle.

"This that you have done," he said as he indicated the camp and the meal, "is a good thing. Very good. *Imik a-pu-ani.* You are a good person."

Iitats smiled shyly. "Thank you, my husband."

Samuel sighed deeply. "Be seated, Little One. There is a thing between us that you still do not understand."

Slowly Iitats knelt before him, her face suddenly a mask. She knew the man was displeased by her words, but truly she did not know what other words to use.

"Did I not say, only this day, that I was not your husband?"

Iitats made the sign that it was so.

"And did I not ask you to no longer call me that?"

Again the sign was made.

"Yet now you call me husband. Why is that?"

Slowly Iitats dropped her eyes. "Because . . . because you purchased me. That makes me *pee-weun,* your wife."

"It does not!" Samuel exploded in English, his frustration getting the best of him. "You ain't my wife, and you ain't gonna be, and that's a certain sure fact! Why,

64

you ain't no more'n a little kid, and I'll be dogged if I'd . . . Aw, what's the use? You ain't got no more notion of what I'm saying than that old bay mare, and maybe a whole lot less."

Iitats, her head bowed, still did not move, and again Samuel sighed, his frustration gone. "Little One," he said, speaking once more in the gentle Paiute tongue, "hear my words one more time. You are not to call me *koo-mahn*, your husband."

Now Iitats looked up, and tears were streaking her face. "Did I not cook well?"

"Huh?"

"And did I not offer to walk so you could ride?"

Stumped, Samuel made the sign that it was so.

"And did I not refuse to take water until you had quenched your thirst?"

Surprised by that, Samuel thought back and realized that it was so. And again he made the sign.

"And did I not spare the food this day so that you would have plenty?"

Again Samuel was surprised, for he had thought she hadn't liked the taste of the jerked meat. "You did all of those things," he finally acknowledged.

"It shames me to ask, then, but I must know where I have failed that you do not desire me. Why is it that you do not find me *nu-tysuza-ri-mu*, a person of worth?"

Dumbfounded by the girl's reasoning, Samuel was suddenly beyond frustration. This was a serious problem, he now realized, and it had better be dealt with quickly or it would only get worse.

Suddenly he remembered Iitats' agreement to obey all the words of Jesus, and he was certain he had a way out.

"Do you still wish to follow all the words of Jesus?" he asked.

Iitats made the sign that it was so.

"Then hear this. Jesus says that I am to be a brother to you — that, and nothing more."

Her eyes wide, Iitats stared at him. "How do you know this thing?" she asked, and her voice was filled with wonder.

And again Samuel was stumped. If he told Iitats Jesus had told him what he had said to her, she would once again start equating him with a great magician or shaman and be more determined than ever to cling to him. If he told her Brigham Young had said the words, she would know that was not so, for Brigham Young did not yet know of her, and she knew that. Nor did he know how to explain to her that it was a general direction given to all the missionaries. That would make no sense to her, for she tended to think only in specifics rather than generalities. So what was he to do? How was he to answer the girl's simple question?

"How do you know this thing?" Iitats repeated, her *e-awk-i,* her crying, now stopped.

Nearby in the darkness a killdeer cried its plaintive *killdee, killdee,* and in the hills behind them a coyote yipped his loneliness to the night. Praying desperately for inspiration about how to help this girl understand, Samuel heard another coyote answer, and suddenly he had an idea.

"Do the Paiute have tales of *shinava,* Coyote Boy?" he asked, changing the subject altogether.

"Both the people of my mother and the people of my father speak of him," Iitats responded. "He is a wicked trickster."

"But wise. Listen, Little One, and I will make an *um-pug-iva,* a talking, about Coyote Boy and *tahp'poots,* Raven Girl."

Iitats shuddered. "*Tahp'poots* the raven is a spirit bird, even as *mu-u-pits* the owl person is a spirit bird. I know."

Samuel nodded. "Perhaps. Now I will make my telling."

"Are you also *narro-gwe-nap?*" Iitats asked in amazement before he could begin. "Are you also a keeper of legends?"

With a slight smile Samuel made the sign that it was so, and he was immediately thankful that she could not know that the legend he was about to tell would be made up as he told it.

"It is said," he began, "that Coyote Boy came one day to the raven clan. He was starving but he was received well, and that night around their council fire he entertained the laughing bird clan with his jokes and tricks, hoping they would feed him.

"All were spellbound, but none more so than lovely young Raven Girl. Never had she seen such things, never had she heard such things, and before long she took her heart out and handed it to Coyote Boy on a stick—a sign that she wished to be his.

"Now Coyote Boy looked upon Raven Girl and saw that she was fair to see. He saw that of all the clan she was most industrious. He saw that she would do many great and wonderful things. And he saw that she had many deep thoughts for him. All these things were good, and for a moment Coyote Boy forgot his hunger and thought instead of taking Raven Girl for his wife. That thought so excited him that Coyote Boy took Raven Girl's heart and very nearly removed his own heart to give to her.

"But then, looking again, he saw that she was a bird of the air and he was not. He saw that when she was upon the earth she hopped upon hard narrow toes while he ran upon soft wide pads. He saw many things, and each thing reminded him that Raven Girl was one thing, he another.

"Feeling sorry for her, Coyote Boy tried hard to say these things to Raven Girl, but she could not understand.

At length the elders of the raven clan told him it was because she was too young, and her eyes were not yet opened wide enough to see clearly. Worse, they told him that if he did not keep her heart and give her his in return, she would be forever miserable.

" 'Well,' said Coyote Boy, who still had not been fed and who was thinking again of his hunger, 'if she will not understand, I can do one of two things. Either I can eat her heart for my supper and stay here in peace, or I can eat her heart for supper and then go away. Either way she will die and her misery will end, and neither of us will try to be something we are not.' "

Samuel grew still, and slowly Iitats looked up, the light from the fire reflecting from her serious countenance. "What . . . did Coyote Boy do?" she whispered.

"He did not know what to do," Samuel responded quietly. "But he knew the thing Raven Girl was asking him to do was not right. So while it made him very sad, he prepared to eat her heart. Then he would decide what to do with himself."

In the stillness another coyote joined the chorus of the first two, and Iitats, her eyes wide with concern, waited for Samuel to continue. Instead he rose and spread her sleeping robe upon the ground. Then he opened his own bedroll and spread it across the fire from the girl's robe. Next he took the small sticks which were still burning in the fire, and pulled them carefully away from each other so the flames would gradually die. Finally, after a quick glance at the mare, he lay down on one side of the make-shift bed.

"You may sleep there," he said, pulling off his boots and pointing to her robe. "We will leave with first light." Then he lay back, pulled the bedroll over him, and adjusted his head on the saddle.

For a long moment Iitats was still. Then, very carefully,

she crawled to where Samuel had designated, pulled her robe over herself, and slowly relaxed.

Staring upward, Samuel gazed at and past the stars, praying for wisdom and strength to help this girl in the way she needed help. And more than that, he prayed that she would understand what was happening to her so she would find happiness rather than sorrow among his people.

"O Great Shinob Chee-zoos," Iitats was praying at the same time, "this woman has heard the white man's telling, and she finds it an empty thing. She does not like what Coyote Boy did to Raven Girl. To this woman, what he did was an evil thing. Perhaps that is because she has heard your whisper in the night, that and the cry of *pan-ah-wich*, the night bird, and the white man has not. Perhaps it is because she heard her brother the wolf talking to her, and he did not. O Great One, please open his ears that he, too, will hear—"

Beyond where Samuel Loper and Iitats lay, the spring gurgled merrily in the darkness, the bay mare munched grass contentedly, and, in the marshes downslope, a chorus of *waxots*, frogs, serenaded each other. It was late in the season for frogs to be out, Iitats knew, but as soon as the weather turned cold they would grow silent.

Even Samuel Loper listened gratefully to the frog chorus, for at least he did not have bad weather to fight as he delivered this girl to his people. Why, if it were snowing—

"That which Coyote Boy did was not a good thing," Iitats suddenly said. "I do not like Coyote Boy's tricks."

Samuel smiled to himself. "What do you mean, Little One?"

"He should not have eaten the heart of Raven Girl!"

"What should he have done?"

For a moment Iitats was still. "Explain the way of things," she finally responded.

69

"What things are those?" Samuel's smile was growing wider.

"That . . . they were not the same."

"She would not have listened," Samuel stated, making himself sound scornful.

"You do not know that."

"I do know it. He explained many times, but she would not hear."

"You are changing the words of your telling."

"It is my telling."

"But . . . it is not a good telling."

Samuel sighed loudly. "Well, I did not yet say that Coyote Boy ate the heart of Raven Girl—only that he had taken it and had decided to eat it. But I myself do not know what Coyote Boy should do, so I do not know how else to make my telling."

"Maybe . . . he can go away and not eat her heart at all."

"What good would that do?" Samuel asked, still grinning in the darkness.

"It would give her time to open her eyes," Iitats stated innocently, "and to see things as he saw them. Then she could add wisdom to her own heart and make it stronger than before."

"Do you think that would help?"

"It would help a great deal. With a stronger heart, perhaps she could make some magic to give Coyote Boy wings like her own."

"Perhaps," Samuel agreed as he shook his head at the girl's foolishness. "Or maybe her magic could open her eyes to see that a pad-toed, furry-backed Coyote Boy was not what she wanted after all."

Again silence reigned, and Samuel wondered where this tale he had been making up would lead. That the Paiute girl was thinking was obvious. Question was, what was she thinking? Of course, he had no way of knowing, and since she had grown still, he rolled to his side and closed his eyes, confident that the child would do the same. Then maybe tomorrow the issue could finally be resolved.

Iitats heard him roll over, but her mind was still racing with thoughts generated by the white man's uncomfortable telling. There was yet another advantage to Coyote Boy's going away, Iitats knew, an advantage she did not feel inclined to say to Samuel Loper. Yet as she thought of it, she knew it was the correct advantage, and suddenly her heart found peace.

"O Great One," she prayed silently, "it is clear to me now that if Coyote Boy goes away from Raven Girl for a time, then surely it will give Coyote Boy time to find that his own eyes have also been closed. Then, once they are open, he can come together again with Raven Girl—"

"If Shinob Chee-zoos wishes that I not call you husband," she said suddenly, surprising Samuel Loper again, "and if he wishes that I not call you master, then how am I to call you?"

"Among my people we call each other brother, or sister. Perhaps I could be your older brother."

"I have no *pah-veets-eeng*, no older brother!" Iitats stated sadly but fiercely. "That one who has been my brother is cruel, and in my heart he has become as dead. I cannot call you my brother."

"Then you know that I am also called Samuel," the white man responded easily, giving the girl plenty of room.

"But . . . it is not seemly for a woman of my people to call a man by his true name—"

"That is so," Samuel Loper agreed, his smile wide. "But two suns from now, Little One, you must give up being a Paiute woman for a time. You will become a white girl who does not yet think of herself as a woman. You will go to school. You will learn things that will seem

71

strange to you but that will be common to the white boys and girls. You will learn more about Jesus. And you will learn the tongue of the whites. As your father wished, for a time that will be your way."

"And then?"

"What is it that you ask?"

"You said I will do those things for a time. What will I do after that?"

Samuel wanted to speak in English, to tell her it beat the bejeebies out of him what she would do. Hang on, maybe. And with a little luck, find a bit of happiness somewhere. Trouble was, he couldn't say that, because he knew that she could never go back to her people, and he was afraid that only in going back would she ever find complete happiness. Instead, in a day or two, or a week, or a year, Iitats would learn the thinking of the whites, and ever after she would be skeptical of the thinking of her own people. She would see how the white men treated their wives, sharing their pleasures and their work, and she would never again be content with a husband who did not do those things. She would learn that to be a Paiute in her own camp was to be free as no white man was ever free, and it was to be as Raven Girl—blind to the rest of the world. That's what she would do. And how could he tell her that he could see no true happiness for her in such a course—

"Do you sleep?"

"Not hardly," Samuel stated in English, and then he translated in Paiute. "I do not know what you will do, Little One. I suppose it will be the same as all others among both of our peoples—you will grow until you discover what everyone must learn in this world."

"And what is that?" Iitats pressed.

"Enough of the meaning of life to be ready to die,"

Samuel said quietly. "Now, *pun-ik-ai-vam ichuk*. I'll see you tomorrow."

Samuel said no more, and Iitats lay still, thinking long thoughts about all she had heard this day from the mouth of the man who was to be as her husband—words that were filled with terrifying wisdom she did not fully understand. But Iitats was also considering her own heart, which, like Raven Girl's, was on a stick, and she knew that she understood it far better than the white man thought she did. One day, she was certain, he would come to know this.

"Sleep well, Samuel Loper," she said softly after his breathing had grown regular and deep. "You are not so much *shinava*, a Coyote Boy, as you may think."

PART TWO

PART TWO

Howdy, ma'am," Samuel stated, removing his hat. "My name is Samuel Loper, and this here little gal is Iitats. She's Paiute."

Samuel and Iitats sat on two horses in front of a small garden in the southern Utah settlement of Harmony, where Rizpah Gibbons was harvesting potatoes with her children. She had paused now, leaning on her shovel, to study the two riders.

Overhead the sky was gray and lowering. As a "V" of wild geese made their way southward, their honking loud in the stillness of the afternoon, Iitats knew that the long-awaited winter would soon be upon them. Now she did her best to still her fears, knowing that what was coming was inevitable but still hoping that somehow it would not happen.

Five journeys of *tavaputs*, the sun, across *tu-omp-pi-av*, the sky, she had spent with the white man, five days during which he had done his best to prepare her to live with the white people and their strange ways. From the Yellow Rock Water they had traveled to the Cane Beds, west across the

Uinkaret Plateau, down the impossibly steep Hurricane Cliffs, and then westward again across what Samuel had called the Forty Mile Desert. They had skirted Sand Mountain to the south, camped at a brackish springs where later Fort Pearce would be built, and then made their way northwestward along Warner Valley to the confluence of the Virgin River, which Iitats' people called Pah-rus, and Santa Clara Creek, which her people called Tonoquint. This they had followed to the small settlement of Santa Clara that Samuel Loper called home.

One darkness she had spent at the settlement, meeting other missionaries, including the one called Jacob Hamblin, who had sad, kind *pu-vi*, eyes, and a funny clump of beard on the end of his chin. It had been he who had suggested that Iitats be taken north to Harmony, where the newly arrived wife and children of a missionary called Andrew Gibbons would take her into their home.

"Land sakes!" the woman called Rizpah Gibbons finally exclaimed while Iitats did her best to pick out words in the conversation that she could understand. "So you're Samuel Loper. Get down off that horse and let me take a good look at you."

Obediently Samuel lifted his leg across the saddle horn and slid to the earth. Tying his horse's reins to the hitching rail, he turned to face the woman.

"Why," she exclaimed, "you're hardly more'n a boy, and a scrawny one at that. Yet Andrew's always telling us tales of the 'great Samuel Loper' that are enough to make a person's hair stand on end. Why, if you and Jacob Hamblin and Thales Haskell and Dudley Leavitt have done half the things with the Indians he claims for you, it's a miracle you're even alive!"

Samuel smiled to hide his embarrassment. "Yes, ma'am, it likely is."

"And this is one of them? One of your Indians?"

Samuel glanced at Iitats, who was looking steadfastly back at him. "Well, Sister Gibbons, she ain't—isn't—hardly mine, at least not exactly. But she is Indian—Kaibab-its Paiute. She's why I'm here in Harmony to see you."

"Do tell."

"Yes, ma'am. Brother Jacob, he told me you had come down with your husband and kids for the Indian Mission, and he reckoned you'd be the right one for the job."

Rizpah Gibbons lifted an eyebrow. "Job?"

"Well, *culling* is maybe a better word. Brother Jacob figures you're the right one to take young Iitats and make her one of your daughters. Your husband, ma'am? He's already agreed, and he thought you'd do a bang-up job of it, too."

For a moment the woman was silent, digesting the news. But then with a bright smile she handed her shovel to a gaping young son. "My goodness, where're my manners? Come inside out of the wind, both of you, and let's see if I can rustle up a bit of grub."

Turning, she entered the rough-hewn cottonwood-log cabin, and after Samuel had helped Iitats from her horse, he and the girl followed the woman inside.

To Iitats the rough-hewn cabins on the Santa Clara had been a wonder that was more than she could comprehend. And so it was with this cabin, which was larger and better built and seemed so much more spacious and yet so much more confining than the simple wickiups of her people. It consisted of one large room that contained a table, benches, a bed along one wall, a fireplace, and a ladder that led to an upstairs loft, which looked to Iitats like a high-up cave. In the cabin itself were the door and one window, and the atmosphere seemed dark, stuffy, and close, making breathing seem more than difficult.

"Goodness but this is a mess," Rizpah said as she bustled about the spotless single room of the cabin, building up the fire and setting out plates. I'd have cleaned better this morning, but with this storm coming on—"

"Sister Gibbons, ma'am, I'm in a bit of a hurry. Maybe I could introduce you to Iitats, and then if you have any questions, I'll do my best to tell you what you want to know."

Again the pioneer woman smiled brightly. "Well, of course!" Then she held out her hand toward Iitats. "I'm Rizpah Knight Gibbons. My husband's name is Andrew, and he's on an Indian Mission same as young Samuel here. The childrens' names are Martha, Andrew, William, and Eliza. Eliza's the baby, you see."

Slowly Iitats reached out and took the proffered hand. "How-do-you-do," she said simply and slowly, doing her best to form the words Samuel had taught her.

Surprised but still smiling, Rizpah Gibbons turned to Samuel. "She . . . doesn't speak English?"

Samuel shook his head. "Not much, ma'am. *How-do-you-do, spoon,* and a couple of other words such as *Jesus* and *Brigham Young.* It sure ain't much of a white man's education, I reckon."

"Well!" The woman's voice was noticeably louder as she turned again to Iitats, almost frightening the girl. "That won't matter. We'll just teach you English, too!"

"Sister Gibbons, ma'am?" Samuel was now grinning. "I said she didn't understand English. That don't mean she's deaf."

For a moment Rizpah didn't know how to respond. Then, abruptly, she sat on the log bench at the table, and her smile was gone. In the fireplace a burning log popped, sending a shower of sparks up the stone chimney. Outside in the corral a mule brayed, and a small dog, standing sentinel near the plank door of the cabin, gave a soft bark in response.

"That was foolish of me, wasn't it?" she asked of no

one in particular. Then she looked at Samuel. "Brother Loper, you might as well know that I've never actually talked to an Indian before."

"Yes, ma'am."

"I . . . I don't know what they're like."

"Well, ma'am, mostly they're just like you and me."

"I . . . I mean, is she dirty? Will she steal? Can she do anything useful?"

Sitting down on another bench, Samuel motioned for the silent Iitats to do the same. Then he turned to Rizpah Gibbons and her children, who were crowding inside the door, staring.

For her part, Iitats kept her head downturned as was the custom of a woman of the people. Yet as always her eyes were busy, and though she was doing her best to listen to the conversation between this white woman and Samuel Loper, she was also watching the children, studying their eyes and very forward mannerisms. They seemed like happy children, she finally concluded, and it was suddenly in her mind that perhaps they could be like younger brothers and sisters —

"As far as being dirty, Sister Gibbons, she's about like you and me. She bathes when she can and does her best when she can't. Twice coming back from her encampment we were near good water. Once she bathed, and the other time she washed her hair with yucca soap — got a real lather up. Then she combed it real good with her porcupine-tail comb. So she ain't dirty, and with that yucca lather I don't reckon she has lice.

"As for stealing, these people don't feel the same about owning things as us white folks do. Where we're mostly selfish, they ain't, and they expect all folks to feel the way they do. If she sees something here she likes, she may just take it, knowing she would willingly give you anything or everything she ever had, and expecting you to feel the same."

"Goodness! What an unusual way to live."

"Yes, ma'am. According to the Book of Mormon it was Jesus' way, too. Now, you asked if there was anything she could do. As far as white ways, not much, though I did learn her to use a spoon. That's why she's here—to learn the rest of it.

"But the rope don't just pull one way, ma'am. I know she's only twelve, but among her people she's already a woman, with all the skills a woman needs to raise a family. It'd seem right smart if you and the youngsters here took a little learning from her."

Rizpah was startled at the idea. "What . . . could she possibly teach us?"

"Plenty," Samuel grinned. "She's already handled births and deaths—fact is, her mother died in childbirth, as did the baby, and Iitats had to take care of both of 'em afterward. She told me that herself. So you see, already she's a regular midwife. She's a cook, too, ma'am, a dandy cook. Any woman who lives on the frontier ought to learn her methods. And she can scrape together a meal where you'd think there was nothing but sand and rock and a few dead weeds."

"But . . . but out of what?"

"Most anything, I reckon. Besides pinion nut and grass seed cakes, which they use to thicken stews, she can make a fine stew out of roasted grasshoppers and crickets, ground to powder and used as flour. From a hundred yards off she can spot wild potatoes, wild onions, and wild rhubarb, not to mention sego lilies, and she can do any number of things with the yucca besides eating the fruit. Not only do the roots make soap, but the fibers are good for sewing and wrapping arrow tips.

"Why, she could probably write books about how to

use serviceberries, chokecherries, squawberries, currants, gooseberries, raspberries, elderberries, sour buffalo berries, buckthorn berries, wild strawberries, and wild roses, all of which she could put up for the winter without ever seeing a tin can.

"The only sweets you likely have is molasses, but this little gal can get sweet sap from willows or quakin' aspens just by sticking a hollow deer bone into a slash she's made with a stone knife. And believe me, that sap is mighty fine eating.

"Then, of course, there's the common variety of food — snakes, gophers, rabbits, deer, porcupine, and whatever else her folks can lay hand to. Not only can she cook those things seven ways from Sunday, but she also knows how to prepare 'em so they'll taste good either right now or last the winter just like the seeds and berries.

"She knows how to tan hides so the hair stays on and the leather is soft and warm, or how to tan them without the hair so they're even softer. She knows how to cut and sew leather into clothing and shoes, and more than that, she knows how to make 'em pretty, using quills and feathers and other such foofaraw as she might have handy.

"Iitats knows a good bit about doctoring, too, ma'am. She told me she cooks down a particular sunflower plant, and what's left does wonders for boils. A person can also bathe in the water that plant's been soaked in, and the water will relieve the pain of skeeter and no-see-um bites. Show her a creosote or greasewood bush, and besides using it for fire-starting, she'll boil the leaves to make a poultice for open sores. And the sap, dried on the branches, makes a dandy glue for cementing arrowheads, something she'd know how to do for her husband right off, happen she had one. And that wild rhubarb I mentioned? Besides cooking the leaves for food, the roots work wonders for colds and sore throats, and you can bet she knows how to use it.

"No, Sister Gibbons, Iitats may not know our ways or our language, but don't ever make the mistake of thinking she ain't educated."

"My goodness," Rizpah exclaimed. "How did she ever learn so much in such a short time?"

"By going to school, ma'am—the school of life, I reckon you'd call it. You see Indian children at play, and you also see them at school. Each is learning, day by day and season by season, to become the most productive adult they can become. They laugh and run, or they laugh and sit, for they are a happy people, and each grows daily older and wiser. Every boyish activity is designed to develop physical strength and stamina, keen wits, or skill needed to hunt various sorts of game that will feed their future families. There are also some fighting skills the boys develop, but the Paiute are by and large a peaceful people, so I ain't certain how much of that there is.

"As for the girls, they begin their training in womanly skills just as soon as they can walk. They start with carrying wood and building and tending fires, and they soon learn to recognize and gather herbs and wild roots for medicines. They're also taught to gather foods such as grass seeds, fruits, and berries, and soon most girls can make bread, biscuits, and those dried seed cakes I mentioned. They're also taught to weave baskets, and to do every other sort of womanly thing. All this stuff is play to 'em, and they sing and laugh and giggle and have a grand time, all while they're learning."

Rizpah was stunned. "I . . . I had no idea—"

"No, ma'am, I knew you didn't. That's why I said the rope ought to be pulled both ways."

"Well, I should smile it should!" Thoughtfully Rizpah regarded Iitats, who sat with her eyes down but carefully observing all that was going on. "Knowing what you just said, Brother Loper, it seems a sorry shame to make this wonderful child over into a white girl."

"I reckon you're right," Samuel responded. "I've done a sight of studying on that the past few days, and if it were me, I wouldn't do it!"

"Why, what do you mean?"

"Just what I said, ma'am. Why try and make her over when she's got such a leg up on most folks anyway. Instead, why not do for her what her people have been doing for me? Leave her be who she is and teach her all the good things you can about being white. She'll fit into her life what she feels good about, and by the time the cows come home for the last time, the rest sure won't matter."

Thoughtfully Rizpah Gibbons nodded. "I do believe you're right, Brother Loper. And I'll do what you say. By the way, you said her mother died. What happened to her father?"

"Well, Dah-Nish-Uant—that's his name now—returned to his people, the Navajo. From what I understand, their custom is that mixed-blood women—of which Iilats is one, being half Navajo and half Paiute—become slaves. Dah-Nish-Uant is a fine man, and I reckon he wanted something better for his little girl here. I looked likely to him, so he give her to me."

"He gave her?"

"Well, come down to it, I actually traded him my rifle."

"Lawsy," Rizpah exclaimed, "of all the barbaric customs—"

"With one thing or another being different, white folks do about the same," Samuel declared softly. "Only we call it dowries and so forth. Besides, it got her here, didn't it?"

The woman looked at him and suddenly broke into a delighted laugh. "It most certainly did," she declared.

"Uh . . . I have one or two questions more. Is she . . . well, has she been baptized?"

"I don't reckon so, ma'am. But she wants to follow Jesus and Brigham Young, so you teach her the gospel same as your other children, and I reckon her day'll come. Now, you had another question before I get on my way?"

"I did. I . . . I don't want to stop her from being an Indian, but I think she would do better here if she had a different name—a Christian name, I mean. Do you suppose—"

"Let's ask her," Samuel said soberly. Then, turning to young Iitats, he spoke in Paiute. "Little One, it is settled. This woman, Sister Gibbons, will be as your white *pe-ats*, your mother. Her husband, Andrew, will be as your father, and her children will be as your family. But there is a thing she desires of you."

"What is that?" Iitats asked softly.

"She desires to know if you would like to take the name of a white woman."

"I . . . I do not know. Will this white person take away *ni-yaani*, my true name?"

Samuel laughed. "No, Little One. You will have nothing taken from you."

"Then . . . I would hear the sound of this white name that may be mine. Then I will decide."

Nodding, Samuel turned to Rizpah. "She's willing, ma'am, providing she doesn't have to give up her Indian name, and providing too that she likes the sound of the name you give her."

Rizpah Gibbons smiled. "Good! I have always loved the name of Rachel. If it meets with her approval, we shall call her Rachel Iita . . . Iita . . . "

"Iitats, ma'am."

"Yes, that's it. Rachel Iitats . . . What did you say was the name of her father?"

"Dah-Nish-Uant."

"Da . . . Dyah . . . " For a moment the woman struggled with the name, which had rolled so easily off Samuel's tongue. Then, with a shrug, she smiled. "Dawson. That's about as close as I'll ever get and still remember it."

Samuel nodded with satisfaction. "Little One," he stated in Paiute, "listen carefully, for if you choose, this is how you will be known among my people. Rachel Iitats Dawson. Can you say that?"

"Rachel . . . Iitats . . . Dawson," the Paiute girl repeated softly.

"Does the name feel good in your mouth?"

Slowly the girl repeated the name several more times. Finally she made the sign that she was satisfied.

"It is well," Samuel said, breathing a silent sigh of relief.

Suddenly Iitats' eyes lifted, and she gazed earnestly at the young missionary. "Samuel Loper," she questioned then, "does this name make me *nu-tysuza-ri-mu*, a person of worth, to these whites?"

Surprised, Samuel thought quickly. "You are a person of worth to them even now," he finally replied. "I told them a little of your womanly skills, and it is in their hearts to learn of your ways even as you learn of theirs. But yes, this name they have given you will be a help to you."

Iitats made the sign that she understood. Then, while Samuel concluded his business with Rizpah Gibbons, Iitats dropped her eyes but continued watching. Though she was frightened and ill at ease, and though she was determined to make her heart strong in this place no matter how much pain she encountered, there was still a deep emptiness in her soul that she could not understand.

Moments later, as Samuel handed her his rucksack filled with all her earthly possessions, the emptiness grew worse. And when the scrawny Mormon missionary climbed back on his bay mare and turned to ride away toward the Santa Clara, the emptiness became almost unbearable.

Perhaps it was the strangeness of the place she had been left in, or the strangeness of the people who surrounded her, or the strangeness of the language that she could not understand at all. And perhaps it was only that another portion of her life, if only the brief portion of traveling with Samuel Loper, had come to an end. Truly she did not know.

But whatever it was, as the new Rachel Iitats Dawson stood watching the white man Samuel Loper ride away toward the south and whatever he would be doing next, she did not feel like *nu-tysuza-ri-mu*, a person of worth. And it was with great difficulty that she withheld the tears that battled each other to leap from her eyes.

Rachel, do you know where Eliza is?"

Quickly Rachel Iitats straightened and looked around. The little child had been at the edge of the garden plot only moments before. But now she had vanished, and Rachel knew her nature was to go directly toward the fresh-running stream that chuckled along behind the cabin.

"I get Eliza," she stated in her rapidly improving English, and then, dropping her shovel, she hurried away.

It was spring, Rachel's favorite season, and the bright green of new-growing things lay upon the land. In the trees birds sang their brightest songs, insects trilled in the bushes around her, nearby a newborn colt frolicked beside his mother, and ahead of her in the sagebrush a Gambel quail cock and hen led to safety a bevy of chicks so tiny it seemed impossible they could fly. Yet Rachel knew they could, and would, if threatened too closely.

Taking a deep breath, and smiling with the joy of the moment, Rachel reached the stream and found little Eliza, who was swirling the shallow water with a small stick.

"Eliza like water?" Rachel asked as she knelt beside the child.

Her eyes wide, Eliza made no reply.

"Rachel like water too. See? Water good for drink, water good for wash, water good for cook. Water not so good for play."

"Not play," Eliza repeated.

"That right," Rachel smiled. "Not play."

Taking the baby up in her arms, Rachel stood and looked off toward the south and the west. Before her rolled the red and salmon-pink land of her people, the wide, shimmering reality of the desert, broken only by the tabletop backs of upthrust mesas and the dark bulk that was Pine Mountain. This was a wild and lonely land, born as the bed of an ancient sea, cracked and tempered with endless heat and cold, and inhabited by drifting dustdevils and the endless, empty sky. To her it had always been home, but now she thought of it differently, almost like an enemy, for it hid from her the man who would not leave her thoughts.

With a sigh, Rachel tried to think of other things. Six months. She had now lived with Andrew and Rizpah Gibbons and their family for six months. In that time she had learned many of the ways of the whites, and much of their language. There was a great deal about the white settlers that she had come to appreciate, such as their knowledge of the world and the God who made it. But some of their customs she had finally accepted without being certain of their value, such as the need to cover her entire body with clothing. Rachel laughed now, thinking of how Mother Gibbons had labored to get her to cover herself on the days when *tavaputs* was hot and clothing seemed a hindrance. At first she had resisted, not understanding. But then young Martha, who had become for Rachel her *phhch-eets-ahn*, her sister, had found a humorous way to explain the strange white custom, and Rachel had laughingly accepted it.

There had been many such incidents, with much disagreeing and much learning on the part of both Rachel and her host family, and so the six months had gone by rapidly, leaving Rachel a vastly changed person.

Of course, she had not accepted everything about a white woman's clothing, the bonnet being a case in point. Good perhaps for shading the eyes, it was of no further value, and Rachel had discarded it almost instantly in favor of the burden caps she made for herself, sturdy woven caps that protected her head from the chafing straps of the burden basket she carried so frequently. Now Martha also wore a burden cap when she worked, and even Mother Gibbons used one occasionally.

Rachel stood still, her head high as she gazed off into the red, yellow, and purple-hued distance, wondering. Yes, six months had passed, a long season of cold, and all had learned much. And in all that time she had seen nothing of Samuel Loper.

Oh, Andrew Gibbons spoke much of him when he was home, of the lengthy mission he was on to the Mojaves, and of the difficulties he was surely encountering. But Samuel Loper had not returned to the little cabin in Harmony, and Rachel was having greater and greater difficulty keeping his image fresh in her memory. She wanted to, and to that end she thought often of him. Yet somehow his features had grown blurred until she was now able to see clearly only his eyes—that and his long, dragging arms.

With a sigh that was more from resignation than loneliness, the Paiute girl turned her gaze back to the child in her arms.

"We go home now?" she asked.

"Water play?" Eliza asked in response, pointing back at the creek.

"No, no. Water not for play. Unless swim. Then water for—"

Suddenly Rachel paused, remembering a long-ago time when her mother had taught her to swim. And abruptly she began to smile.

"Rachel maybeso teach Eliza swim," she stated happily. "Like Rachel learn swim. Then water good for play."

Hurrying along the bank she dragged the tiny girl to a place where the waters of the creek had run head-on into the roots of a long-dead cottonwood. There the water had swirled and churned and finally changed direction, in the process digging out a hole that varied from three to four feet deep, a wide pond that would suit her purposes perfectly.

Quickly stripping the clothing from herself and the child, Rachel stepped into the eddying hole, caught her breath at the chill of the spring runoff, and then made her way to the center of the mostly still water where she slowly sat down, submerging both herself and the shivering child up to their necks in the water.

"Now," she said, "you learn swim Paiute way." And so saying, she held little Eliza out from her and let go.

Instantly the child's head disappeared beneath the surface of the water, and Rachel crouched with hands ready to grab her if necessary. Seconds later Eliza bobbed to the surface, her eyes wide with surprise and her mouth gasping.

"Swim," Rachel shouted, showing Eliza how to pull the water with her hands. "You swim now."

Back down Eliza went, but seconds later she bobbed up again, and this time she was clawing at the water almost as Rachel had shown her.

"Good," Rachel said as she clapped excitedly. Then, reaching out, she caught the little child and gave her a hug. "Okay. Now you swim again."

Over and over Rachel placed Eliza alone in the water, and now she hardly even dipped beneath the surface. Instantly she was pulling at the water, her feet were kicking wildly, and time after time she made her way across the hole to wherever Rachel was waiting.

Soon it was a game, with Rachel scuttling along on the bottom and Eliza laughing and swimming in slow circles as she tried to make her way through the water to her Indian sister. Suddenly, happily, Rachel broke into a Paiute happy song that her mother had taught her such a long time before.

> Ho, little *ahng-ah-peech*.
> Ho, little baby.
> Now we move with this earth.
>
> Ho, little *ahng-ah-peech*.
> Ho, the water.
> Now it is moving along.
>
> Ho, little *ahng-ah-peech*.
> Ho, we are moving.
> Ho, the grass and the trees are moving.
> Ho, the water is moving.
> Now we all move with this earth.

Finally, her teeth starting to chatter from the cold water, Rachel arose and gave the child a final hug. "That enough today," she said, speaking English again as she began backing through the shallow water toward the bank. "Now water good for play, too. Maybeso tomorrow—"

"Rachel Iitats Dawson, what on earth are you doing?"

Rizpah Gibbons' voice was both loud and filled with anger, and Rachel spun in surprise.

"And look at you! Why, you . . . you're naked as a jaybird!"

"Clothes not wet," Rachel stated with a smile, knowing that dry clothing was a high priority for the white woman.

"Well, I should hope not! Land o' Goshen, girl! Here you are right out in the open where any lallygagger who wants can stand and gawk at you. Mercy sakes! Have you no shame?"

"Shame?" Rachel asked, confused. "What is shame?"

"Well, it's . . . it's . . . why, I mean . . . "

And Rachel, seeing the confusion of the woman, suddenly broke into a wide smile, doing her best to help.

"Shame all the same modesty?" she asked hopefully.

And poor Rizpah Gibbons did not know how to reply. "Yes! I mean, no! Shame isn't the same as modesty. Modest girls keep their bodies covered, and they ought to feel shame when they don't."

"Shame allthesame bad thing?"

"Yes! I mean, no! I mean, well, parading around naked is bad—"

"Why naked bad? Jesus make baby and baby come naked, allthesame everybody naked all time, only cover up. Why cover up when no need? Why make bad what Jesus make good?"

"Why? Because going naked isn't decent!"

"Not know decent," Rachel stated simply. "Not understand all time cover up, either. Is hot, cover up. Is cold, cover up. Is warm, cover up. Is cool, cover up. Not Indian way. Indian way better. Is hot, no cover up. Is warm, cover up little. Is cool, cover up little more. Is cold, then all cover up."

Shaking her head in exasperation, Rizpah shifted the focus of her wrath from nudity to concern for her little daughter.

"And what, may I ask, are you doing taking my baby into that frigid water?"

"No need fear Eliza in water anymore," Rachel replied proudly as Eliza, her face somber, twirled a chubby finger in her hair. "Eliza learn swim now."

"What?" Rizpah was practically screaming.

"Rachel think Eliza need throw in water," Rachel declared then, trying to keep her own voice calm. "Make wet, make understand. Eliza no more play water maybe so drown."

Rizpah studied the girl. "Throw a baby in the water?" she asked incredulously. "What kind of a fool notion is that?"

Rachel smiled. "Good fool notion. Throw deep water, make swim. Child no fear, child respect. And child learn."

"But . . . she's a baby!"

"No," Rachel shook her head. "Eliza no baby. Eliza child. Child learn, allthesame learn cook and sew, maybeso learn swim. Now Eliza no fear water; Mother no fear water."

"Land o' Goshen," Rizpah exclaimed in complete exasperation. "How can I make you understand—"

But before she could say more, Rachel leaned over and placed a smiling Eliza back in the water. Then, backing away from her, she smiled widely as the tiny child paddled furiously after her.

"See?" she said proudly. "Eliza swim. Now Mother no need fear water; allthesame let Eliza play."

For a moment Rizpah thought of what Rachel was saying, thinking of the great good sense it made. After all, the girl was two, and William had been swimming at that age, though who had taught him Rizpah did not know. And there was no doubt that Eliza was swimming. But still—

"Rider coming, Ma! From the west!"

Looking up at the sound of Andrew's distant call, Rizpah Gibbons shaded her eyes and studied the distant rider, who was coming up the rutted road leading a low cloud of dust.

"Merciful heavens," she shouted at young Rachel

Iitats, "there's a man coming, girl! And your brothers are coming, too! Quick! Get out of that creek and get your clothes on, before they get here."

Obediently Rachel picked up the still-swimming Eliza, stepped onto the grassy bank, and handed the girl to her mother. Then, carefully, lest she tear the fabric, she pulled on her underclothing, then stepped into her almost new calico dress. Only after that, while slowly doing up the nearly endless row of buttons, did she turn to look at the approaching rider.

At that distance it was not possible for her to see who it was, and yet she could see that the man rode stoop-shouldered, like someone tired, or like someone who has fallen asleep in the saddle. His hat was pulled low, obscuring his face in shadow, and in every way he seemed nondescript. Even the horse he rode seemed ordinary, and its gait was a plodding shamble more than a walk or a trot. Yet it came on steadily, the man unmoving in the saddle, and suddenly Rachel had the distinct feeling that she was watching Samuel Loper ride toward them.

Hastily she did up the remainder of her buttons. Then, white-woman-like, she lifted her hands unconsciously and smoothed her dress, after which her hands went of their own accord to her hair.

Closer he came, and closer, and by the minute Rachel grew more nervous. Of course she still could not tell his identity. But her heart was pounding, her breath was short as if she had run a great distance, and despite the chill of her body, the palms of her hands were suddenly wet with sweat. It was him! She knew it had to be—

"Can you tell who it is, Andrew?" Rizpah was speaking to her son, who had just arrived with his brother and older sister.

"Naw," the boy said as the rider dipped into the wash

that cut south around the community. "He's too far off, but I don't think he rides like Pa."

"It isn't Pa," Martha stated matter-of-factly. "It's Samuel Loper, I reckon, and it looks like he's come a far piece."

As it turned out, both Martha and Rachel Iitats were right. The man was Samuel Loper, and he was a sorry sight to behold. Sweat streaked his dust-caked wool shirt, spots of red flushed beneath his squinted eyes, and the gray of desert dust clung to the stubble of his unshaven jaws.

Finally reaching the women and pulling rein, he did his best to grin, and Rachel's active nose detected the stale odor of a body having gone long without a bath. It was a strange smell, mingled as it was with the smell of damp earth, smoke from fires long gone dead, and the new green grass under their feet. Yet it was Samuel Loper's smell, and of a sudden she remembered it with fondness from the long ride six months before.

"Appears like I'm a mite late," he said slowly as he looked from Rizpah past the staring children to the still-dripping Rachel. "For the bath, I mean." Then he grinned. "The way your eyes are watering, I must be more'n ripe enough to need a good one." And then he slid slowly from the horse.

13

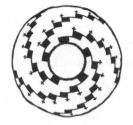

Well, Miss Rachel, in that fancied-up blue gingham dress, you're a sight to behold!"

It was dusk of a warm evening, that wondrous time of day when the sky turns bloodred and bathes the hills in soft crimson and pink, waiting quietly for night to creep out and throw her shadow blanket over the land and tell the stars to light their lamps. But at the moment only two or three bright stars were visible, so night was still hidden away, and the shadows were still asleep. Out in the hills a coyote called, a nighthawk swooped and dived in the air just overhead, and the bats were coming out.

Samuel Loper was leaning against the hitching rail in front of the Gibbons cabin. Rizpah was holding Eliza on her lap as she rocked in her chair before the door, her other children at her feet. And Rachel was standing quietly with her back to the cabin, savoring her own joy at having this man back with her.

Of course, his visit would be brief, and Rachel knew that. Yet it felt so good to see him again, and to hear his funny way of speaking—

"And you speak English real good, too," Samuel stated, his compliment sincere. "Yes, ma'am, Miss Rachel, Sister Gibbons sure has turned you into a regular white girl."

"Not white girl," Rachel stated emphatically. "Rachel Paiute girl, allthesame maybeso Lamanite." At that she pulled a funny face. "Rachel learn white ways," she then continued, "but she no different than Iitats. Why your clothes full holes?"

Looking down at himself, Samuel chuckled. "They're plumb wore out, I reckon. Besides, I ain't got no woman to stitch 'em up or to make new duds for me, either one."

"Rachel make new clothes for Samuel Loper, allthesame buckskin. You see."

Samuel laughed at that, not making fun but trying to cover his embarrassment.

"She'll do it, too," Rizpah Gibbons declared. "This girl's a marvel with buckskin. She made Andrew a shirt that's a pure wonder."

"I seen it," Samuel stated quietly. "Right nice work. A man'd be proud to wear such a shirt. Where's Andrew now?"

"He's on a mission to the Indians over to Kannaraville."

"The Tave-at-sooks, huh? Good folk, from what I hear. And good country, too. Real pretty."

"Where have you been, Brother Loper?" young Andrew asked suddenly.

Samuel lifted his arm and swung it in a wide circle. "Over most of creation, it seems like. Just now I've been on a scout out west, through Mountain Meadows and beyond, getting back a bunch of horses that the Uint-kar-its Indians stole from the Tono-quints. Jacob saw the place where they was camped in a dream and sent me out there. And sure enough, there they were with the horses. So in the dark I called out that I'd come to take back the horses they stole, and they just up and give them to me. No fuss or nothing."

"Merciful heavens," Rizpah Gibbons exclaimed in wonder.

"Yes, ma'am, they have been. Merciful, I mean. Makes a body wonder to even think about it, the way a man perambulates around this country without getting hisself killed. There's no doubt the Lord's protecting us."

"And where before that?" Andrew pressed.

"Andrew, don't be so nosey."

"Aw, I was just wanting to know, Ma."

Samuel Loper smiled. "It's all right, ma'am. You can't learn much if you're afraid of asking questions. Let's see. Since I was last here, young feller, I've been down to the Las Vegas with William Bringhurst and the other brethren who set up the fort there last year, exploring the Colorado. And besides that, Dudley Leavitt and me took a mission to the Mojave, which wasn't no picnic either. Now I'm here to meet Jacob and head to Cedar City for supplies."

For a moment there was silence, and the darkness drew its veil ever more tightly around them. Rachel stood silently, watching Samuel Loper and thinking of so many questions but fearing to ask them, fearing . . . well, fearing she would be so transparent he would see right through her. So she remained silent, and finally Rizpah Gibbons spoke again.

"I keep wondering," she said slowly, "what it's really like out there. Can you tell me that, Samuel Loper? Can you tell me the things my Andrew sees, and maybe even a little of what he feels when he's away from me and on his missions?"

Samuel shifted his feet uncomfortably. "Tell you of what he sees, ma'am? Or feels? I . . . I don't hardly know where to begin or how to describe the things I've seen, let alone the things he's seen."

"Well, at least try and tell me."

Samuel smiled. "All right, ma'am, I'll try. But I don't reckon there are even words to tell of the swift-running streams, chuckling and roaring over rocks, or the mountains that reach to heaven and the clouds that gorge the valleys among the high peaks. What words are there to describe things like that?

"It's a wide, wide country out there, Sister Gibbons, wondrous far and wide. There are canyons where no white man has walked, canyons in the high-up mountains or in the way-down desert, canyons born of volcanic heat or wind-whipped sand now frozen into stone. And here and there, where a little water has seeped to the surface, you'll find pockets of country in those canyons so beautiful it hurts your heart just looking at 'em. Trees reaching like fingers toward the sky, grass and flowers thicker'n a parlor room carpet, and the air so thick with the sweet smell of life it makes your head reel with the breathing of it.

"Then there's campfires, ma'am, where you sit alone over a wisp of a fire watching the sparks rise up and blend with the millions of stars in the sky above you, and you realize how insignificant you are, and how wondrous great God must surely be to have created and numbered all you can see. Abraham saw such things, ma'am, most likely sitting over a lonely fire himself, and I reckon it was on such a night as that when he was shown all the things the Lord had made — people and worlds alike. Out there alone you think of Abraham and other people of the wilderness a lot, and when you're crouched over your fire with the coyotes howling at the moon, and your horse — when you're lucky enough to have one — comes close to the fire for company and looks out into the darkness with pricked-up ears, then you feel comforted, ma'am, you surely do.

"And animals, ma'am? You've never seen such a sight as a herd of desert bighorn come soft-stepping it through the rocks of an early morning to a tiny spring you'd think only birds could reach. Or listened in the darkness to the angry whistling and bugling of two bull elk who have their hearts set on the same trouble-raising cow.

"And the storms, ma'am? You just ain't never in your life seen storms like the Lord sends into that wilderness, with lightning flashing like living fire from the peaks and thunder rumbling and growling down the long valleys, bouncing from side to side like a ninepin ball coming right at you. And the rain? I've seen so much water coming down, all to one place, it seemed like, with washes and arroyos running full and more and pushing along ahead of them trees and boulders that are bigger'n this cabin, that I figured Noah's storm was a piker compared to them.

"And there's nothing prettier than standing alone in a high-up mountain valley with the snow falling soft and thick, and the only sound besides your breathing the soft rustling as the snow settles into place for the winter.

"But it's a hard land, too, Sister Gibbons, and a land that passes judgment on the unwary and deals out its own swift and permanent justice. I recollect the time me and Dimmick Huntington were on a scout way out west of here, in a parched land of no water and alkali soil drawn so tight it was all cracked with the strain, where no one with any sense should ever have gone. It was flat country with no edge but the sky until we rode into a serrated upthrust of mountain, and there in a narrow canyon we found bones, bleached by wind and sun, that had to have been a man, a woman, and a small child. And about them, a weather-beaten, gone-to-pieces wagon.

" 'Some sorry fool,' Dimmick said to me, speaking real quiet, 'met his Maker here whilst he was hard on his way to somewhere else.'

" 'Yeah, and was probably some surprised when the

102

Indians hit,' I added as I gazed at the skeletons at the feet of my horse.

"And so he must have been. Rusted iron tires, a solid oak hub with spokes and a couple of still-attached fellies, bits of burnt wood here and there, and what was left of a burned-out wagon box—wood so powder-dry it fell to pieces at the touch. And not a sign at all of the horses or oxen that had drawn the wagon there, which is how we knew it was Indians. It truly wasn't much for a man to leave behind, but it was all that man had left, and it set me to thinking, it surely did.

"And speaking of Indians, ma'am, they had thousands of years of history and traditions in this land before Columbus was even born. They're part of the country, too, and the reason why your husband and I are on our missions. Like Rachel here, they know what's up as far as living with the land is concerned, and white folks who call them savages and dismiss them as ignorant just ain't got much sense. I've said all this before, but it's a thing I feel, ma'am. It surely is.

"And another thing. There ain't no such thing as a typical Indian, no more'n there's a typical white man. Mostly they're about like us—tall, short, thin, heavy, gentle, cruel, smart, foolish, and about every other way you can think of to describe the human critter. Most of 'em love their children, but where some tribes make women real important, letting them govern and all, in other tribes women are about like cattle, and they ain't treated hardly any different. That's what I mean by saying there ain't no typical Indian.

"Then there's the Indian religion, which some folks call simple but which is anything but. It's about as practical as breathing, something a good many of our white religions would do well to look at. And Indian folks don't all believe in the same things, neither. Some of 'em have real elaborate

103

ceremonies and beliefs, and others keep things plain and simple. But all in all, Indian folks everywhere worship the Creator, they truly respect all living things, and they cherish and care for the earth on which they live. And it ain't a Sunday kind of religion, neither. Day after day she's the genuine article, and if you ever hear of an Indian feller doing something contrary to the way he's been taught— well, I ain't never heard of such a thing, not like what happens most all the time with us more 'civilized' folks.

"Fact is, despite their problems, almost without exception Indian folks seem to sense there's a higher way of living, a way they seek after. For instance, among the Cattaragus Indians of New York, the old women appoint their chief. The man they pick has to have a skin 'seven times thick,' meaning he can't react to criticism, he has to control his negative thoughts and feelings, and before he acts he has to consider the effects of his decisions down to the seventh generation after him. Sure beats American politics, don't it?"

Rizpah Gibbons laughed with appreciation, and Samuel quickly continued.

"Boiled down, the thing I like best about the Indians is that they're always seeking after the soul. While many of our people scoff, the best of their people never stop asking God, whatever they might call him, to show them the way. And once it is shown, by dream or vision or even a sign from nature, they never vary from the direction they've been given. It'd be a wondrous world if all of us were like that.

"Anyway, that's the country your husband sees when he rides out of here, ma'am, and the people he rides to see. But describe it? I don't reckon I can. There just ain't words to do a thing like that."

In the silence that followed, Rachel glanced at Rizpah Gibbons and for the first time saw the faraway look in the woman's eyes, the lonely, empty look that sometimes haunts a woman's face in the dark if her man is gone and she thinks no one is looking. And from that moment, Rachel no longer looked upon the Mormon woman as a mother figure but as a kindred spirit, someone who could understand the far-off, aching feelings she herself dealt with.

Rachel also thought of Samuel Loper, made even more wondrous to her by the words he had spoken so eloquently, and as she gazed secretly at his figure silhouetted against the night sky, she knew he was the only man she would ever want.

Now if she could only get him to see the same thing—

14

Ho, you long-life makers.
Ho, you powerful ones.
I have come to easily
take you.

Ho, you long-life makers.
Ho, you powerful ones.
For this the Creator
sent you.

Ho, you long-life makers.
Ho, you powerful ones.
I thank you for coming to
satisfy me.

Singing quietly but happily to the medicinal plants she
was gathering to carry home to the Gibbons cabin, Rachel
kept in the back of her mind the wondrous fact that she
was alone again with Samuel Loper. Even now he sat near
the fire watching her, and Rachel, very aware of his eyes,
made certain she gave no hint of her knowledge. Yet she

was happy, happier than she could ever remember being, and she knew it was because she was with her man again.

"These are fine duds," Samuel said as Rachel returned to the fire, her basket filled with the herbs. "Yes siree, they fit better, practically, than my own skin."

It had been a year since Samuel Loper's last visit to the Gibbons cabin, a very long year, and now he was back "to see to business," as he put it. Rachel didn't know what that meant, but when he had asked her to saddle up the Gibbons' old mare and take a ride with him, she had been more than excited.

She had also been excited to hand him the buckskin shirt and trousers she had made for him during the long winter months while he had been away. It had taken much work to create them, yes, and much love also, for both items were carefully decorated with the quills of *yungumputs*, the porcupine, dyed red and yellow and then sewn into elaborate designs.

Now the couple sat on the brow of a knoll covered with *wah-ahp*, or cedar trees, while *tab-oots*, a cottontail rabbit Samuel had killed with a thrown stick, roasted slowly over the fire. Below them to the south the ground dropped away into the vast desert country where the Santa Clara ran, and that had once been home to her. But that had been long ago, and to Rachel it seemed almost as if it had been in another life. Now it was a warm afternoon, but pleasant, and because Samuel Loper had returned, Rachel was truly happy again.

Abruptly she laughed, and as he always did, Samuel Loper marveled at her soft and musical voice. He never tired of hearing it, nor did he tire of the lilting, singsong way she had of forming the words of her adopted language. Never would he learn to speak exactly as she did; never would he cease hearing the lovely sound of it in his ears and mind.

107

"You seem happy, Little One."

"I am happy."

"That is good. I was truly worried about you the day I left you with Sister Gibbons. Fact is, riding away was maybe one of the hardest things I ever did."

"You were worried?" Rachel questioned in her vastly improved English. "I did not know of this."

"That don't mean I wasn't. Maybe more than worried, what I was feeling was a great sadness."

"But why?"

"Well, let's see if I can put this right. As a Paiute woman, you had been one with your people—happy, contented, and a great blessing to those around you. When I left you, I knew you would be lost and alone, and you might never develop the skills necessary to be a woman among the whites. Even the thought of such failure scared the beejeebies out of me, for I had seen others fail, and I knew how terrible it could be."

"I did not know you had these feelings," Rachel declared softly.

"Well, I did. Fact is, if I could have kept you with me, I'd of done it in a minute. But being alone and single, I had no way to care for a child such as you."

"I thought of myself as a woman."

"I know that, and I knew it then. But it changed nothing at all. You were a child, and I had nowhere to put you, no way to care for you."

"It seems strange to me, then, that you took me away from my people at all."

Samuel nodded. "Well, it was a tough decision, all right. Yet every time I prayed about it, I felt good inside. Besides, all us missionaries had been counseled, in light of the fact that so many of the Paiute children were being sold into slavery to the Utes, to save all of them that we could, and to raise them as our own children.

"That made sense in a humanitarian sort of way, but it didn't stop me from suffering when I watched children like you feel terrible pain as you tried to be something you weren't. I've thought about it since then, time and time again, and I can't figure out why so many of my people insist that the Indians we take in become white. Why can't they just learn the ways of the whites but be encouraged to remain Indian? After all, Indians are a fine people, with much about them that can be admired and even emulated. Seems to me it would make a whole lot more sense to do as was being done for me— leave me white but teach me the ways of the Indian.

"I figured all that out for the first time while I was bringing you back to the Santa Clara, and I determined that, no matter who took you in, I was going to see that you kept the best parts of being who you really were. I reckon that's why I feel good seeing you happy."

"Mother Gibbons and the children have been very kind to me," Rachel stated quietly. "They taught me much, and they always made me feel a part of them."

"Well, you may be happy," Samuel said as he glanced at the fire, "but you sure have changed! Why, I recollect the first time I saw you after I had left you with the Gibbons family, and it made me feel both good and bad—good that I could see you again, and bad because you were no longer my little Paiute sister. Gone was the shy and eager girl in the deerskin shawl and leggings, with her body oiled and painted and her hair as wild as the wind. As I recall, you wore a blue calico dress, your hair was properly done in a bun, your skin was adorned with neither paint nor body oils, and on your face was the discipline that marked the size of your battle. Truly have you become a white girl."

Rachel sighed. "In some ways, Samuel Loper, it is so. When I rode away with you from my people, it was like taking a knife and cutting a piece out of me. But to fail in becoming what my father wanted for me — that would have been like taking a knife and cutting through my father's flesh and bone."

"Do you miss him?"

Soberly Rachel made the sign that it was so.

"What did he say before you left him? I did not hear him speak, but I have felt certain that he gave you wise counsel."

Rachel nodded. "Yes, he did. He told me to walk straight on with my life. He said, 'Do not look back, my daughter. Do not turn your head, for I have found your way for you.' I said, 'Yes, my father.' He said, 'You will be white now, and that is good. But never forget that you are also Nung-wa, of the People. Walk in two worlds, and in a day to come, you will discover that they have been one world all along.' I said, 'Yes, my father.' And that was the end of his saying."

"And has he been right?"

"Of course," Rachel replied with a smile. "At least, I think so."

"But you are not certain?"

"Who can be certain of such a thing? I am happy, and yet I see also that in ways my life is more difficult than I can say. At the first I could not sleep. I could not eat. I missed my people. I missed my pinion cakes and my cricket cakes and my rabbit stews. And most of all I missed my father. At night when I slept, I dreamed of his bark wick-iup, of the soothing sound of his voice, and of the comforting smells of my camp. But more often at night, I would lay awake, smelling the sagebrush, longing for the feel of the cool night wind off the Kaibab-its or for the sight of the Vermilion Cliffs shouldering against the skyline, for the sunlit flanks of the Paria Plateau or for the purple loom of the great canyon that separated us from the world to the south.

"Truly it seemed as though the white world had swallowed me up, and for a time I did not think I could live outside the world of my people. That was when I began praying to Jesus that he tell you to come and take me home to my people."

Slowly the girl lifted a strand of hair from her face, tucking it behind her ear. "But by the time I saw you again, I knew that even if you took me back, I could never go home again. I had changed too much, and it wasn't my clothing or my hair or my oils and paints. It was my mind that had changed. Do you remember that I told you all of this the night of your first visit?"

Samuel smiled. "Not exactly."

"Well, I did tell you. And then you said some words to me that hung like a lantern in my mind, words I have never forgotten. Do you remember this?"

Slowly the man shook his head.

"You said two things, and though the words are different, they were the same words my father had spoken. The first was that I needed to remember that God's world was in both places, not just one. Secondly, you said, 'Someday, Little One, you will be able to live in both these worlds. You will represent your people among the whites, and your people will be proud of you. And you will find, even though you cannot return, that the kind of woman you are, all that is deepest and best in you, will be there because you are a daughter of Dah-Nish-Uant and Ungka Poetes. And then you will be happy.' "

Samuel smiled. "And was I right, Little One?"

Tenderly Rachel smiled. "I . . . think you are right, just as I think my father was right. I know this, that I have never felt such happiness as I feel today."

"Well," Samuel said as he turned the slowly roasting rabbit, "that's grand, just grand."

For a moment there was an awkward silence, and then

Samuel spoke again. "Uh . . . if you don't mind, I have another question for you."

"And what is that?" Rachel responded, still smiling.

"A year back you pulled a face when you admitted that you was a Lamanite. Why was that?"

"I do not like Lamanites," Rachel replied forcefully. "Lamanites were bad people, not like Nung-wa, Rachel's people. Mother Gibbons says I am a Lamanite, but I do not think I came from bad people!"

Samuel chuckled. "I thought that was it."

"You think I am a Lamanite too?" the girl asked, surprised.

"That ain't exactly what I meant," Samuel replied. "What I meant was, I thought it might bother you, finding out there was a few ring-tailed wonders back along your family tree."

For a long moment Rachel looked at him, completely perplexed. "You talk nonsense," she finally said, using one of Rizpah Gibbon's phrases, and Samuel simply nodded in agreement.

"Sister Gibbons learn you to read yet?" Samuel then asked, momentarily changing the subject.

"*Mia'puts*," Rachel answered in Paiute. "A little. I have been trying to read from Mc . . . Mc . . . "

"*McGuffy's Reader*," Samuel finished for her. He was smiling as he turned the rabbit, and Rachel found that she didn't mind.

"*Uung.* Yes. But I do not read very much. I do not understand words when I see them, not so well, at least, as when I hear them."

"It'll come, Little One," Samuel stated, and Rachel thrilled to the sound of the name this man had given her so many seasons before.

"But I brought you a gift, something you can learn reading from that'll maybe make more sense to you than

McGuffy's Reader. Maybe in some way it'll make up for this fine outfit you've given me."

Reaching into his saddlebags, Samuel drew forth a book, which he handed to the surprised girl. "It's a copy of the Book of Mormon. Thinking on it, it come to me that if you had your own copy, you could read it about when you wanted to."

"This is mine?" Rachel asked, her voice small with wonder.

"As ever was. You make your way through that, and not only will your understanding of English grow by piles and piles, but you'll also find out you ain't got a single solitary thing to be ashamed of concerning your family tree. Was I you, Little One, I'd feel right proud being who I was.

"Now, happen you're hungry as I am, this here rabbit looks about right."

Rachel nodded, and while Samuel took the roast meat from the spit and split it between them, she continued to feel the texture of the leather-bound book. "This smells like buckskin," she suddenly exclaimed as she held it to her nose. "It is a good smell, and a fine gift. Thank you, Samuel Loper."

"You're welcome. Now you'd best eat, or I'll finish my share and yours too."

Agreeably Rachel put the book down and began to eat, and not until they were finished did Samuel speak again.

"Has Sister Gibbons told you much about the Book of Mormon?"

Rachel nodded vigorously. "She tells much, very much, but I don't remember so much as she tells." Suddenly she swatted at some tiny insects that were hovering about her face. "*Ang-iv-its ung nax-wosik-ai ung,*" she laughed. "The gnats are bothering me."

"Me, too," Samuel agreed as he stood and cut some

green cedar boughs which he heaped on the fire. "Seems like a bad year for 'em. Maybe this'll smoke 'em off."

"It is a strange custom," Rachel declared then, slipping into Paiute, "that a woman should be *narro-gwe-nap,* the keeper of legends."

"Among the whites," Samuel responded in the same tongue, "anyone who has the scriptures is the keeper of legends for himself or herself. That is the way God desires it. That way, we can learn all we need to learn, and we can each learn all the time."

"I see that this is good."

"*Poon-eek-ah,*" Samuel said then. "Look at the book, Little One, and I will tell you a little about it.

"Long ago, more seasons than a man can count, one family was led by God into the wilderness of a faraway land, another family joined them, and they were led across the great water to this land. As near as I can figure out, the Nung-wa, the people of the Paiute, are the children of their children's children."

"This was the man called Lehi?"

"That is so. Lehi was a great man, a man who *um-pug-iva Shinob,* who talked of God. He is what we call a prophet."

"Like Brigham Young."

Samuel made the sign that it was so. "Near as I can tell, Little One, in one way or another, most all Indian folks are the children of this man and his wife."

"It is good to have this man Lehi as a father," Rachel said thoughtfully.

"Yes," Samuel agreed, "it is good to be of the children of Lehi."

"Then . . . why does Mother Gibbons call my people Lamanites?"

Samuel sighed. "That is a long story, one I may not be able to tell the way I should. But I will try. Laman was a son of Lehi, and he turned against the ways of his father and did many evil things. His one brother and some others followed his ways, and over many seasons they came to be called Lamanites."

"They are a bad people."

"Well, they did bad things. But that doesn't end my telling. Lehi had good sons, and one of them, called Nephi, was very good, *um-pug-iva Shinob*, like his father. Over the seasons many people followed Nephi, and in time they came to be called Nephites."

"Mother Gibbons spoke of this. Are white people the children of Nephi?"

"No," Samuel replied with a smile, "they are not. It is the Nung-wa, the people of the Paiute, who are the children of Nephi."

"But . . . " Rachel paused, shocked into speaking English, "how can this be so? Mother Gibbons says my people and I are Lamanite—"

"This thing I will explain," Samuel stated, speaking still in Paiute. "After many seasons, Lehi died and took the road to the west. Then Nephi died and Laman died, and more seasons passed than a man can count. Two nations then lived, two great tribes called Nephites and Lamanites. They fought each other often. Many died, and many were left to mourn.

"Soon the people of both nations grew wicked. God was angry at their evil, so he sent a great destruction, and many, many people died and took the long road to the west.

"On a bright, clear day, those who were left to live, both Nephites and Lamanites, gathered together in a *so-par-o-van*, a great council, to discuss what had happened to them. These were good people of both tribes, very good, and they were not at war with anyone.

"As they met in council, a great thing occurred. God

115

spoke to them, and all in the *so-par-o-van* heard his voice. This was truly a great thing, and all the people cast their eyes upward. There they saw the one the Nung-wa call Shinob, the younger God, who was standing in *tu-omp-pi-av*, the sky. In a sacred and solemn manner he came down out of the sky until his feet finally rested upon the earth.

"In silence now all the people, both the children of Laman and the children of Nephi, fell to their knees to worship this great being. He bid them stand again, and then he told them his name, which according to this record is Jesus Christ. Then he told them that he was the son of God the Father, the one your people remember as Tobats. He also told them that he had been killed by wicked men in another land but brought back to life by his Father, this that all men might live after they die, just as he was doing.

"Then, to help the people believe, he called them forth, one after another, until all had come to him and felt the wounds in his body that had taken away his life."

"This is a wondrous thing," Rachel stated, her voice a whisper. "This is what you were speaking of to my father the day before you took me away with you."

"That is right," Samuel replied, pleased with the girl's memory. "Many tribes have not forgotten the visit of this great Being, and though all remember different names that he used, for in the days that followed, as he traveled about the land he did use many, yet all remember him and his promises to them."

"To the Diné he was called Yeh-ho-vah?" Rachel questioned.

"Those are the words of your father," Samuel agreed.

"And to the whites it is the same?"

"One of the names we learn from the scriptures," Samuel responded, breaking into English, "is Jehovah. It is the same."

"Why is it that my people do not remember the name of Jesus Christ?" Rachel was speaking still in Paiute.

"I do not know this, Little One. Perhaps it was considered a sacred name and so was not often spoken. It would be good if that were so among the white people today, for many speak it evilly and bring upon themselves much suffering."

"This I have heard," Rachel stated. "But I would ask again, why is it that the name of Jesus Christ is not remembered even by the *narro-gew-nap*, the keeper of legends?"

"Perhaps here and there it is," Samuel answered, leaning back against the trunk of a tree, "but is not spoken. Perhaps, though, it has been forgotten. After Jesus had traveled among the people, he went away, leaving his promise to return in the distant future. After many seasons, Un-nu-pit, the evil one, came among them again with his *ruan*, his spirit warriors. Soon most of the people, both the children of Nephi and the children of Laman, were once more following his evil ways. All of these evil people formed themselves into a tribe which they called Lamanites. Soon they took themselves to war against the few remaining followers of Jesus Christ, who were calling themselves Nephites, and over time the Nephites were all killed.

"For the people who remained, who were a mixture of the children of Nephi and the children of Laman, it was a strange thing to have no one to war against. Soon they were warring against each other and telling themselves that it was good to war, for they themselves were the only true people on the earth. Of course this was not the teaching of Jesus, who had declared that all were brothers and sisters, children of God the Father, just as he was a son of God. But this was not the only teaching of Jesus that the people ignored or forgot. There were many, and many

117

of them are kept even now in the book I have given you, which you may learn as you read it for yourself."

Rachel nodded. "This is good. But tell me of this book, Samuel Loper. How did it come to be?"

Samuel yawned and then smiled. "I must be tired, Little One," he said in English. "It's been a long, long year."

"Perhaps you should rest."

"Naw, not yet. First I'll answer your question." Shifting again into Paiute, Samuel continued. "The Book of Mormon was written by many people as the seasons passed in ancient times, by wise and holy men who *um-pug-iva Shinob*, talked about God, just as Brigham Young does today. Each of them made their record on gold metal that had been hammered flat and thin. The first of these who recorded his sacred thoughts was the man Nephi, and the last of them was a man called Moroni. It was Moroni's father, Mormon, who wrote so much that the book was given his name. That is why we call it the Book of Mormon.

"When Moroni was about to take the long road to the west, he dug a pit and carefully buried the gold records within it, sealing his pit so the waters of the seasons could not harm the record."

"I myself have learned how to seal pits against *pah*, the waters of the seasons," Rachel stated simply. "It is how we keep our food."

"I know this. And perhaps the method is the same. After the pit was closed, seasons passed, more than one can count. All memory of the record passed away, and all memory of almost everything concerning the children of Lehi also passed away. All that was remembered was that a pale God of high soul stature had once walked the broad land and had promised to return one day from the east, walking through the sky on the morning rays of the Dawn

118

Star. Such is the memory your father spoke of that lives among the Diné and the Hava Supai."

"How did the Mormons come to know of this great book?" Rachel asked then.

"Jesus made known to another prophet where the gold plates were hidden up in the earth," Samuel responded. "He was a wise and holy man called Joseph Smith. You have heard of him, perhaps?"

Rachel made the sign that it was so.

Samuel nodded. "After many days Joseph Smith was given power from God to translate the records of the children of Lehi into the tongue of the white people and to make a book of those sacred things. This is the book I have given you."

Samuel yawned again and then closed his eyes, and for a few moments Rachel was silent, thinking. In a nearby juniper, a cicada sang its day-song, but already the shadows were long enough that an early cricket had started its shrill chirping. Rachel listened to that and found herself wondering if these were the same sounds the ancient fathers of her people had listened to. And were their sights the same as hers, of a wild and lonely land cut deep by canyons, ribbed with red rock walls and dotted with crumbling mesas that were black-topped with lava from ancient volcanos? Among the red walls and the crumbling lava blocks were the greens of pinion, pine, and juniper, and here and there was good water, which her people always knew of and used well. Had the ancient ones also used those same waters, those same rich benches where crops grew so well?

Behind her, Samuel Loper's horse, a gray with dapples splashed across its hips, a horse that loved wild country and quickened its pace with the crossing of each new ridge, switched its tail at a bothersome *mu-u-pi-chats*, a fly. Her own tired old mare stomped a hoof impatiently, and Rachel knew it was time to be going. Yet Samuel Loper was sleeping soundly now, and she hated to disturb him. Besides, she felt so comfortable with this man she had come to think of as hers, so absolutely good—

"Jesus," she silently prayed, "will you not tell this man what he is to do? The seasons pass, and it is hard for me to be alone. Will you not tell him what you told me so long ago?"

The cicada continued to sing in the brush, and the air was hot and still. High above, *pah'see quan-ants*, the bald eagle, swung in lazy circles against the evening sky. Sighing, Rachel thought of how life would be so simple for such a creature, circling effortlessly through the day as it did. From all earthly troubles it was aloof, untouched by argument and quarrel, unfazed by the politics and social posturing of puny humanity. This great bird had only to drift along where the sky trailed its cloudy herds, and for it life was good.

But that could not be her way. No, nor could it be the way of Samuel Loper. To them the great God Jesus had given a higher way, a way of learning, a way of caring, a way of loving, a way of becoming one with him that was sacred. But it took effort, great effort, and she would not give up until she had accomplished it. Only her man could not see that such a way lay with her at his side. And so, like the eagle, she must continue to circle through her life, waiting.

Until such a time as that happened, however, she would learn all the words of the book. Within her breast was a burning desire to know and follow the teachings of Jesus, for she loved him fiercely, and in her mind she could see him coming through the sky, his arms open to her even as hers would be to him. Her ancient fathers had written that it would be so, and within her heart there was no doubt.

But for now she would be happy, her heart at peace because the man of her life was sleeping near her—

"Samuel Loper," she said later as a second cricket joined in chorus with the first, "it is time to wake up."

His eyes flashing open, Samuel stared at her. And then, as comprehension came, he smiled. "Must have dozed off, I reckon."

"You were tired. Samuel Loper, I thank you for your words, and for the great gift you have given me."

"You're welcome," the man stated with a grin as he rose to his feet and tightened the cinch straps on the two saddles. "I sure wish the day was longer. It's been a wonder. But I reckon it's time we headed on back.

"Oh, did I tell you? Jacob says we'll be building a fort down on the Santa Clara. You be sure and tell Sister Gibbons that she and the family will be moving on down just as soon as it's done. Next spring, most likely. I reckon that'll also include you."

And Rachel, clutching her precious new book, could not hide the sudden smile that swept across her not-so-innocent young face.

Brother Loper," Rizpah Gibbons suddenly asked, "what's it like on the Santa Clara?"

Leaning back in the comfortable hide chair, Samuel smiled. "Why, I don't know as I can describe it, ma'am. Now your husband here, he's a grand one with words. I reckon you had ought to ask him instead of me."

Andrew Gibbons laughed. "You ornery polecat, she has been asking me. And all along I've been telling her to wait and ask you. You're the one around here with the gift of gab. So fess up and tell the woman what she wants to know."

Samuel chuckled, and Rachel, who was sitting on the floor with the Gibbons children, marveled at the maturity that had grown on the face of this man she loved. No longer were his whiskers soft and delicate, and the laugh wrinkles that spread out from his eyes had grown deeper and more pronounced. His voice was also deeper, or at least its tone quality had changed so that now when he spoke it was with the quiet voice of a man such as she remembered her father being.

And had she changed as much, she wondered? It was now nearly three years since Samuel Loper had brought her away with him from the Kaibab-its, three years in which she had hardly seen him at all. But now the fort on the Santa Clara was finished, and in one day, or perhaps two, they would load the wagons and move the entire family south. Then perhaps she and Samuel would see more of each other—

In her mind Rachel examined herself, trying to see the changes. Of course she had rounded out now, was perhaps a little taller, and her form was truly the form of a woman. But the real changes had come inside, where her thoughts and feelings lived and grew. And with these she was both saddened and pleased, just as Samuel Loper had told her he was feeling only a year or so before—pleased because she was becoming more and more like him, the man she would soon spend the remainder of her life with, and saddened because more and more she was realizing the significance of the fact that she could never simply pack up and go back to her people.

Oh, they would be the same, and they would accept her readily. But it was she who had changed. In many ways, perhaps even most ways, she now thought as a white woman thought and valued the things a white woman valued. She had not meant for this to happen and had not intended that it should. But in the days and weeks and months of her association with Rizpah Gibbons and the other women of the settlements, it had happened so quietly that she had not even been aware of it.

Of course she still knew the ways of the Paiute, the good ways, and at times it was a great thing for her to consider them and distance herself from the pettiness and meanness she occasionally encountered among the whites.

But there were also the other ways of the Paiute—

She remembered the fall before, when she had accompanied Andrew and Rizpah Gibbons on a trip northward for supplies. They had come upon an encampment of her people—several wickiups that had only recently been abandoned. As she had stood among them, she had known abruptly that she would never again be comfortable in such a home. But more, and this frightened her, she had somehow known that such homes themselves were nearing an end, and that in a coming day all the Paiute would be as she, as much white as Indian, and trying desperately to find the way to walk between two worlds.

Very soon, her impression continued, only the old would be left in their wickiups, and when they died, the young would leave the wickiups forever. They would trade their simplicity for the intricate machinery of the complex white world, and they would lose their contentedness when they were not so accepted as they were accepting.

In a letter, she had written these feelings to Samuel Loper, and he had written back, a letter she had received only a few weeks earlier. It was the only letter she had ever received from him, and she had been surprised not only by the formal and proper way he wrote but also by the things he said.

Many times she had read the letter, so many that she now had it memorized and could read it at will simply by thinking of it. She did so now, thinking of the portion that pertained to her people:

> You are right, Little One. In the end, it seems to me that all the Paiutes will leave their wickiups. That is because they are losing themselves. I have studied this out in my mind, and to me the problem seems one of dominion, the whites exercising dominion over the Indians. Where the white folks are by tradition settlers, taking up water and land and planting deep roots, the Paiutes by tradition follow the circle of life. They go from the deserts to the mountains, and from water source to

water source, according to the seasons and the bounties of the land, which they use fully. And this they do year after year.

This is good for the Paiutes, but to the whites it seems that the Indians are not users but passersby, nomads. Thus the whites cannot conceive that, by taking up the water and the land they think is empty and building homes and farms and ranches, they are actually forcing the Paiutes from their homes, and in the end, I fear, from their way of life.

Already the Paiutes have lost much of their water, and as whites continue to come into this country, and you can be certain they will, the Paiutes will also lose their land. Without land and water the Paiutes cannot live as they have, and so they will be forced to become as the whites. Yet by then all the best water and land will be taken, and so they will become the poorest of the whites, and the most despised. This saddens me, but I fear that it is all as you have foreseen.

But you have forgotten something. They have at least one splendid friend who understands them and will stand by them, one person who can think and walk in both worlds. They have you, Little One, and because you know the way of God, who understands both the Paiutes and the whites, you will be able to teach them to see themselves as people of worth, no matter what becomes of them.

Now Rachel thought of that, and the words of Samuel Loper, stiff and formal and as surprisingly proper grammatically as they were, felt good within her. Truly had she come to know the teachings of Jesus, and as his teachings had grown like a good seed within her, blossoming into a lovely tree of faith and understanding, she had come to the realization that she knew him, and could feel his Spirit working within her.

And other than being in the presence of Samuel Loper, it was this that made her most happy. It was this, she felt, that would finally attract Samuel Loper to her as she had been promised so many seasons before.

"Well," Samuel stated with a grin, bringing Rachel's mind back again, "so far as I can tell, there just ain't no way to describe it."

"Try, Samuel. Please?"

Samuel grinned. "All right, ma'am, I'll take a stab at it. But when you see it, don't you be getting after me. You hear?"

Rizpah smiled. "I hear."

"Tell the truth," Samuel paused, taking a deep breath, "it's a lot like here, only then again it ain't. I mean, the Pine Mountains are to the north of us instead of southwest like here, and they rise high and steep and are blue with distance. Up in 'em the grass is belly deep to a tall horse, and pine trees stand so straight they're using 'em to make the pipes for the organ up to Salt Lake City. It's there that the Santa Clara Creek heads out, with water fresh and clear and cold as you'd ever want it, and absolutely delicious.

"By the time it gets down to us, that water has dropped all the way into the desert and turned muddy on the journey. And that's where we built our fort, under some big old desert cottonwoods and sycamores by that water, smack in the middle of the desert. Our soil there is mighty sandy, but we plow it regular and plant it in crops, and every year we lay aside a good supply of corn, beans, potatoes, and squash. Of course the Santa Clara's a hard creek to tame, I'll tell you. She floods out near every time there's a rain upstream, and I reckon we've built back our dam most of a dozen times."

Rizpah Gibbons smiled, a distant look on her face. "It sounds wonderful! Tell me about the fort."

"Well, as forts go it's a good'un. It's a hundred feet long to a side, and the walls are twelve feet high and two feet thick. Inside are fourteen cabins, seven to a side, and each with its own fireplace. There are regular gun ports on all four sides, and though there are doors at both ends, the thick double doors we mostly use are on the south facing the road."

"Will we live in the fort?"

Samuel grinned. "I reckon you will, since we've reserved a cabin for you. Could be you'll share a cabin, but that ain't so bad, neither. I've been sharing a cabin for a coon's age with Brother Jacob and his two wives, and there's plenty of room. Why, each cabin is more'n a dozen feet wide by twenty feet deep, and some of 'em even have a loft. So you can see there'd be plenty of room for sharing."

"That'd be just fine," Rizpah Gibbons declared. "All I want is to have me and the children close to Andrew and to feel safe there."

And then Rizpah Gibbons asked the question that finally, for Rachel, put it all into perspective. Abruptly she knew not only who she was but also who she would always be.

"Brother Samuel, would you tell us about the Indians? I don't mean the fact that they're fine people, generous to a fault and easy to laugh, which is what you've said before, and which I believe. What we want to hear about are the hard things that have happened to you, the adventurous things, the dangerous things."

And in the silence that followed, Rachel found herself as eagerly attentive as any of the others, anxious to hear what trials those people had put her man through. And that was when she absolutely knew that she could never go back.

"Now, Sister Gibbons," Samuel finally responded, "you don't want to hear such truck, and you know it. Hearing such things only upsets folks, and I don't much like to speak of 'em my ownself."

"I . . . I'm sorry about that, but we truly would like to hear."

"But why? It don't matter much, and besides, I'm always protected by the Lord. All us missionaries are. That was promised us when we was set apart, and it ain't been revoked yet, at least not that I know of. Why, there ain't been no permanent harm come to any of us—"

"Brother Samuel, you avoid this, and so does Andrew. But you've both avoided it long enough. Since Andrew won't talk, you must. What sorts of awful things have happened to you that you don't like to talk about?"

"Andrew," Samuel asked, turning to his friend, "what am I to do?"

"Tell her, I reckon," the man replied. "If you don't do it now, Rizpah'll keep pestering you until you do."

Sighing deeply, Samuel settled back. The nights had now grown uncomfortably warm down on the Santa Clara, and he had been looking forward to a good night's sleep here where the air was cooler. But Rizpah Gibbons' questions—

"Brother Loper?"

"Lawsy, ma'am. You do push a man."

"I want to know!"

"Well," Samuel said with resignation, "there really ain't too much to tell. Mostly being a missionary's just long rides across hundreds of miles of desolate wilderness without enough water. And usually you can add not enough food to that, too.

"Now and then you spend a little time with a tribe of Indians here or there, and sometimes they're happy about that, and sometimes they ain't. When they're happy, it makes it all seem worthwhile. When they ain't, well, that's probably worthwhile, too."

"Is it always so hard?"

"Mostly. I recollect Dudley Leavitt and me were sent

TO SOAR WITH THE EAGLE

on a mission to the Mojaves in '57, and it turned out to
be a hard one. We rode to Las Vegas Springs, where I
found a Paiute who was willing to take us to the Iyats, as
they called themselves, some eighty miles to the west of
there, and be our interpreter. We made the trip in six days
and found the whole tribe angry because the U.S. Army
in California had used 'em up pretty bad. So they were
spoiling to get even.

"They took our horses from us right off, killed one and
roasted it, and invited us to eat it with 'em as our last meal.
So we ate, and afterward when they were ready to kill us,
I asked the chief if I could kneel in prayer before I died—
sort of make my last medicine with the Great Spirit. Chief
Chah-ne-wauts, his name was, agreed, so I asked our
Paiute friend to interpret my prayer as I was going to pray
in Paiute. I then began to pray, pausing regular so each
of my words could be interpreted. I asked God to soften
the chief's heart as we meant him no harm but only wanted
to teach him about the one true God.

"I must have said, 'soften his heart' most of a dozen
times in that prayer. And by the time I was through, it
had worked. That chief's heart was softened enough that
he protected us from his people all through the night,
whilst we gave him much instruction in the ways of God.
Come daylight, finally, and we were allowed to leave. Of
course they kept our horses and all our supplies, and so
it was eighty miles on foot with very little water to be
found anywhere."

"Goodness! What did you ever do?"

"Suffered, and learned how to survive on the desert.
Our Paiute friend showed us how to grind mesquite beans
into a flour that, along with lizards and snakes and mice,
kept us alive, and we got our moisture from cactus— not
good, but wet enough to keep us going. We traveled at
night and shaded up by day, and ten days later we were

back at Las Vegas Springs, where we rested some before tackling the trail back to the Santa Clara. Altogether I reckon we walked about a hundred and sixty miles, all of it mighty hot and rough. But we made it, and though bedraggled, neither of us was much the worse for wear."

For a moment Rizpah was silent, thinking. "But why did the Indians pick on you?" she finally asked. "It was the army they should have been mad at."

Samuel smiled. "That's white thinking, Ma'am. To an Indian, especially a mad one, killing one white's as good as killing another. They live pretty much an eye for an eye, only they don't seem to care much whose eye it is they put out, just so long as it's done real soon.

"I recollect a Muddy Indian killed a Tono-quint, a Santa Clara Indian, somewhere near our fort. Before we hardly knew what was up, the Santa Clara Indians had gone up the creek, tied a Moapats or Muddy Indian woman to a tree, and burned her to death. They said it was according to their customs or traditions and a necessary duty."

"How awful!"

"I reckon. At least to us. To them it made good sense. But mostly they're a real gentle people, especially the Paiutes. But even the Paiutes sometimes have a mean streak. Early in '58, whilst the Utah War was shaping up to end, I was sent alone to help travelers along the immigrant trail from California. I set up housekeeping on the Muddy in a broken-down wagon bed that had been abandoned, and was to receive supplies from travelers as they passed. I had no horse, as that would have proved too much a temptation to the Indians, and I had to hide up my food all day long so it wouldn't get stolen. So I cooked and ate only at night. Still, some Indians found my food, and I was left with little but grasshoppers to stave off starvation."

"Oh, you poor, dear man! What did you ever do?"

"The desert's a great teacher, Ma'am— beautiful, wild, harsh, uncompromising. When a man's alone with nothing but his gun, knife, and blanket, and the only food and water is what he can scrape up from what's around him, he starts to appreciate the simple things. The last swallow of water in his canteen is truly savored, as is the last bite of a rabbit that has happened to wander across his path. Then he starts to notice even the smallest things that might sustain life, and they all teach lessons that can never be forgotten.

"That's how it was with me. To make shade I turned the wagon box upside down and propped it up with willow poles. Then I stacked brush along the sides and had me a tolerable good wickiup. It wasn't long before I came to appreciate that wickiup more than any comfortable home I've ever lived in."

"What in the world did you ever do there?"

"Well," Samuel said as he scratched at the back of his head, "during the day I climbed a small hill to watch for teams crossing the desert. If I saw any, I'd go and do my best to help 'em get safely past the Indians."

"There were Indians there too?"

"Lawsy yes, and some of 'em didn't take too kindly to my meddling in what had been a good business for 'em— robbing and plundering and begging and all. After a bit, some of them got in the habit of shooting arrows at me whilst I was on that hill, seeing if they could make me jump. They also shouted at me, telling me all the awful things they were going to do to me as soon as they were ready. One man in particular, a fellow I called 'Sneak,' tried to cause me real trouble."

"Sneak?"

"Yeah. I called him that on account of he was the sneakiest fellow a body ever did see. He was the kind of man you just couldn't turn your back on. Never!

"One day I caught him going through my things, and when I shouted at him, he ignored me. I ran toward him, and an arrow from another Indian came a little too close and made me mad."

"But . . . but you were only one against so many—"

"Well, I was mad, and besides, I was in the right, and all of them knew it. Like my Pa used to say, it's mighty hard stopping a man who is in the right. So I pulled out my handgun and pointed it at Sneak and the others, and then I told them in their own tongue, which they hadn't known I could speak, that I could kill six of them while their arrows would only go into me a little way. That stopped their nonsense for good."

"Were . . . were you there a long time?"

"Five, maybe six months, though the last couple of months Thales was there with me. That's Thales Haskell. I reckon him and John Young are my two best friends, though Jacob's a close friend, too. But that was a long six months. I was away from folks so long I got mighty indifferent about my grammar, and I still ain't got it back worth a hoot. When Colonel Thomas L. Kane came by on his peace-keeping mission between the Mormons and the U.S. Government, I could hardly understand a word he said. So whilst I acted as interpreter between him and the Indians in the area, Amasa M. Lyman had to be the interpreter between Colonel Kane and me."

"You know Colonel Kane?" Rizpah asked in wonder.

Samuel grinned and held two fingers together. "We were just like that, only closer."

"Brother Loper, you stop funning us!"

"Then stop sounding so worshipful," Samuel teased on. "After all, Colonel Kane's a fine man, but he puts his pants on pretty much the same as me— when I have any, that is."

"With Rachel making you new buckskins every year now, you had ought to have plenty."

"Yes, Ma'am," Samuel replied, looking at Rachel and smiling, "I do."

"With all the awful things those Indians did to you," Rizpah pressed, serious again, "I can't imagine why you didn't just shoot a few of them and be done with it!"

"Now Sister Rizpah," Samuel said wryly, "we was sent to convert 'em, not kill 'em. Besides, Jacob's always preaching kindness, and it sort of gets into a man so's he don't have much disposition to kill. It pays, too, being kind, I mean. One time this past spring me and Thales took a mission to the Muddy and Las Vegas Springs to try again to stop the Indians from killing immigrants. Whilst we was on the Muddy, Jacob passed on his way further south, so we rode with him toward Las Vegas Springs, which was sixty-five miles with no known water anywhere. We'd filled our canteens with water and I'd found a small wooden keg which was also full, so I figured we had just about enough to reach the Springs. Then, about halfway there, we came across an old Indian who'd been left by his people to die."

"What?"

"It's their custom, Ma'am. Not too kind, maybe, but remarkably practical. So far as I can find out, that's why they do it. But this old feller pleaded for water, so Jacob give him some from his canteen. Both Thales and I cautioned him against it, as we knew it'd cause us to run short, but Jacob just smiled and give the old man all he wanted.

" 'Remember what the Savior said,' Jacob told us whilst we was protesting. 'If ye have done it unto one of the least of these my brethren, ye have done it unto me.' Then he hauled that old man up on his horse behind him, and on we went.

"Well, sure enough, the next day we ran plumb out of water, and we still had fifteen, maybe twenty miles of scorcher to go. Our tongues were sticking to the roofs of our mouths, the horses was about to drop, and things was looking desperate. So that old Indian, of a sudden, climbed to the top of a small mound and looked all around. Then he came down and led us to a damp spot on the ground. 'Indian Secret,' he said, speaking for the first time as he pointed down. So we dug, and in about two feet we found good, clear water, all we could want. I reckon that was a good lesson for both Thales and me to learn."

Rizpah smiled. "Brother Jacob is a wonderful man. Any more awful things you have to tell us?"

Samuel shook his head. "Not hardly. I reckon I've done enough storytelling for one night."

"Only if you've told us every awful thing that's happened to you."

Samuel laughed. "Now that'd take a month of Sundays, especially if I was to count all the bad water holes, the dusty rides, the miserable walks, the strange meals, and the angry Indians.

"But all in all, Ma'am, I'd say it's worth it. Wouldn't you say so, Andrew?"

Andrew Gibbons chuckled. "I would, Samuel. I surely would!"

"You mean because of the help you're giving people?"

"Well, yes," Samuel agreed as he scratched again at the back of his head. "That, of course. But there's more, lots more, and I reckon it's all a mite selfish. For me, at least, it's brought me to a greater appreciation of all that is about me, the vast breadth of the sky, the warmth of the sun, the drifting clouds, the gracefulness of a moving horse.

"I'm telling you, Ma'am, the trickle of sweat down my back, the odor of sage on a hot, still day, the smell of the earth after a summer shower, the twittering of birds, the crunch of sand under my boots, the cold, wonderful feeling of water in my throat after a long thirst, the flight of an eagle or even a buzzard against the sky, and the storm clouds on a summer day— these are things I remember and feel, things that I never appreciated until I come to live down on the Santa Clara.

"You see, Ma'am, it's come to me, watching the Paiutes, that happiness can't never be found in accumulating material things, or in struggling to build up your own name. To the Paiute, and I reckon to me, too, life is only worth living when you're widening and deepening your understanding of the living things around you, and being sensitive to them.

"So now maybe I'm finally learning to listen, really listen. Out there on the Muddy those six months, disturbed by no people, I became aware of the smallest sounds you can imagine. The falling of a rock from a steep bank, the rustling of a pack rat, the whisper of wind in the grass or across the sand, the creak of timbers expanding under a hot sun—these I learned and remembered, and hear even today when they occur.

"More importantly, in all that solitude I grew a little closer to the Lord, and learned how to feel his Spirit. Day after day and night after night, he was my only companion, and after a spell it came to me that I wasn't the only one doing the talking. Through the Holy Ghost he was speaking to me, blessing me, teaching me, encouraging me, and in general doing his best to make a silk purse out of a sow's ear.

"Course there's still a heap of work for him to do. But now I see that living with such awareness has enriched my life, and maybe it has prepared me for whatever else I may be called on to endure. I hope so, Ma'am, I surely

135

do. But whether it has or not, I wouldn't trade it for all the tea in China!"

Much later, after all were sleeping soundly, Rachel made her way outside to stand on the cabin porch. The last light had long before faded, the last twinge of sunlight had been swept from the sky. The dark shadows that hid through the day in the deepest canyons had now rushed forth with a vengeance, enveloping the earth and gathering close around her with cooling breath and cooling arms.

Of this sweet coolness Rachel breathed deeply, and then she smiled, for she was truly at peace. Now she knew who she was, and more importantly, now she knew whom she would always be.

"Samuel Loper," she declared, remembering her words from long before, "hear these words, for they are true." And then, raising her hands as her mother had taught her to do before she had become a white woman, Rachel Iitats spoke again.

> Ho.
> Hear these words,
> you man.
> Hear this *um-pug-iva*, this talk of
> my mouth.
>
> Ho.
> Now I take your heart,
> you man.
> I take your heart and you see no
> other woman.
>
> Ho.
> There is no other woman,
> you man.
> For in *mo'ovi*, my hand, I hold
> your heart.

Ho.
Now you must come
to me.

PART THREE

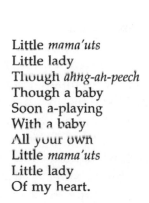

Little *mama'uts*
Little lady
Though *ahng-ah-peech*
Though a baby
Soon a-playing
With a baby
All your own
Little *mama'uts*
Little lady
Of my heart.

Rachel's voice grew still, and with affection she watched five-year-old Eliza playing on the ground with the cornhusk doll Rachel had made for her.

"Lawsy, woman," Martha Gibbons declared from nearby, "you are the singingest soul I ever did see. What was that one about?"

"It was about Eliza growing up," Rachel replied as she worked.

Martha grinned mischievously. "You certain-sure it wasn't about ol' Brother Samuel?"

Unaccountably embarrassed, Rachel remained silent.

"Well, since you won't talk about that, when do you think he's coming back?"

Now Rachel looked up from the deer hide she was stretching. The head end of the hide was tied to the trunk of one of the large sycamores that grew among the cottonwoods along Santa Clara Creek, and she and Martha and little Eliza sat in its shade, as they often did, working together.

It was a lovely fall morning, peacefully silent, drowsy with warmth and the song of the cicadas. Against the deseret horizon, the far miles stood out clearly, the mesas, cones, and cliffs standing boldly outlined. And over all, the shadows of drifting clouds offered welcome respite from the sun.

Breathing deeply of the potpourri of delicious fall fragrances that hung upon the nearly still air, Rachel smiled. Never had she felt so happy, never so at peace. She felt as if all her worlds were finally coming together.

"Maybe soon?" she finally answered her younger sister, her smile of anticipation shy and lovely.

With her teeth Martha Gibbons was splitting into three pieces a long willow that she had peeled only moments before. "Well, I should smile," she said when she was finished. "He's been gone most of the summer. Look at all these yellow leaves. Fall's here, and old Samuel'd better be here soon too. Say, do I have enough split willows here to do my basket?"

Rachel nodded. "Yes, Martha, I think you have plenty."

"Good. How much more do you have to tighten that fool hide?"

"A little." Rachel looked at the hide, trying to gauge what yet needed to be done. It was given to her by John Lytle almost two weeks before, after he had killed the

142

animal for community venison. She had staked it to the ground and scraped it clean of flesh and hair. Then she had washed, soaked, rinsed, and wrung it out, and then thoroughly rubbed boiled animal brains into it. After days of drying it in the sun, she had again soaked and rinsed the hide and then wrung it out by twisting it with a stick. Now she was in the midst of the long, tedious process of stretching the hide for the final time, holding it with her feet and pulling it toward her, inch by agonizing inch. Once it was stretched, she would smoke it for maybe thirty minutes, and then it would be ready for rubbing with white clay and then sewing. Now all she needed was to decide which color she wanted it smoked. Greasewood would smoke it yellow, willow would smoke it brown, and pine would smoke it a very light yellow. Maybe light yellow, she decided. That would be pretty, and it would sew into a nice shirt for Samuel Loper. Very early in the morning she would build a pine fire —

"What do you think he's been doing all this time?"

"Who?"

Martha looked up. "You know very well who. Samuel Loper, silly."

"He has been visiting his family. That is why he went northward."

Rachel's English had become fluent, though she still spoke with a lilting, singsong way of forming her words that Martha loved to hear. She had also learned everything else about the whites that there was to learn — at least that's what young William said about once or twice a day, especially when he was assigned by his mother to show the Indian girl something else.

But true to her word, Rizpah Gibbons had treated Rachel as one of her own daughters, teaching her to sew and cook as she and other pioneer women did it, and teaching her to read well and write her own name and somewhat more besides. Rizpah had also learned much from the Paiute girl and had instructed her children to do the same. Thus Martha was quite adept at weaving baskets that the family used for storage, and even the boys could do it in a pinch. Both Rizpah and Martha could cook in a willow basket using heated rocks, and pinion nut cakes had become a staple of the family diet. Rachel also taught them to find honey by using a little pitch to fasten a blade of grass to a honey bee while it was still inside the flower. Eventually, the marked bee led them to its hive, and sweet honey was the reward.

But most important, Rizpah had loved Rachel the way any woman loves her daughter, and Rachel had reciprocated in kind. After four years, she now thought of the Gibbons family as her own. She and Martha spent many a night in the loft giggling over girl things; Andrew and William, the two boys, teased her every bit as much as they did Martha; and little Eliza came to Rachel with her hurts before she went to anyone else in the family. Though Rachel remained in many ways a woman of the Paiutes, she was also a woman of the white race, and as Samuel had foretold, she was now quite comfortable with the idea of living in both worlds.

"Do you think he found a girl?"

Again Rachel looked up, but this time she laughed. "Pu-am-ey?" she questioned, using Samuel's recently bestowed Indian name, "I do not think so. He is too shy to speak to girls."

"He sure ain't . . . isn't shy around you."

Rachel concentrated on the hide she was stretching. "That is because Pu-am-ey does not see me as a girl. To him I am a little sister; that, and nothing more."

"Oh, fiddlesticks! That ain't . . . isn't true, and you know it. How come the Moquis called Brother Loper *Pu-am-ey?*"

"Because it fits him," Rachel answered without looking up. "It means Eagle-Who-Walks-on-the-Ground."

"I don't understand."

Rachel laughed delightedly. "That is only because you have never seen an eagle walking on the ground. If you had, you would know that the name fits Samuel perfectly. Him with his long arms and fingers, his stooped shoulders, and the rolling way he walks—truly does he look like an eagle who drags his wings as he walks about on the earth."

"Not very complimentary," Martha laughed.

"Very complimentary," Rachel disagreed. "Samuel Loper has always seemed like an eagle to me. But once the Moqui gave him that name, it brought him to the ground where I was, giving me even greater hope that I . . . uh . . . I . . . "

Noting Rachel's awkward stammering, Martha looked up and smiled. "So, when are you going to tell him?"

Again Rachel looked at her younger sister, but now she was suddenly more frightened than embarrassed. "I . . . I do not understand your question."

"Of course you do," Martha stated easily. "But I'll make it plain. When are you going to tell old Eagle-man that he ought to make you more than a sister?"

"Martha!" Rachel cried, sounding shocked. Then immediately she broke into a giggle. "You call him Eagle-man?"

"Yeah," Martha giggled in return. "Sure beats the stuffing out of 'Eagle-Walks-on-the-Ground,' or whatever it was. That's too long a handle in any language."

"You should not talk that way."

"Why? Ma can't hear me, and the boys sure get away with it all the time. Fact is, I think they try a-purpose to butcher the language just like Samuel Loper does. Now stop dodging my question."

"I do not remember what you asked."

145

"You do so. When you going to tell Brother Samuel that you're in love with him?"

Shyly Rachel dropped her eyes. "I . . . did not know you knew this thing."

"Mercy, woman. Only bats and old Eagle-man are blind enough to miss it. You've been carrying a torch for him long as I can remember."

"You . . . see this in me?"

Martha laughed. "I should smile I see it. So does Ma and likely everybody else in the fort. 'Cept him, I mean. Every time he shows up here, you get all flubbergusted. And about every other sentence you've spoken the whole past four years has been about him. I don't know why, neither. Besides being scrawny and homely as a dead bug, he's so thick between the ears he don't know the sun's up. And he sure as heaven's in the sky don't know you love him!"

Rachel knelt in silence, her heart pounding. "Was it true? Did she really love the man called Samuel Loper? She had never thought of it like that—had not allowed herself to think of it, if the truth were known. It was true that she could see no other man, not because there were none but because none of them interested her. It was also true that her heart beat faster whenever Pu-am-ey was near, and her words came more clumsily to her mouth when she was speaking to him. Then there was his voice, a quiet sound more soothing to her than wind in the trees or water tumbling happily down a rocky stream bed. How she loved the times when he was there to teach her about the Mormon religion or to discuss the Book of Mormon, which she had now read from cover to cover almost three times. Of course she enjoyed learning those things, but learning to the sound of his voice made it all that much more wonderful.

So, was she in love with the man? All things consid-

146

ered, including the fact that she could think of no one else as her man, Rachel suddenly realized that she was.

"Do you think I should say this thing to him—about my love?" she asked fearfully.

Martha grinned as she stood to go back to the fort. "I should smile you should! How else is old Eagle-man ever going to figure it out?"

And to Rachel Iitats Dawson, whose heart was suddenly pounding crazily, the answer was as logical as the question.

Now Rachel, I've told you that word before. Sound it out, and you'll know it just fine."

Adjusting her book to catch the remaining light from the one window in the cabin, Rachel did as she had been instructed. "Gad . . . Gadi—"

"Rachel, that 'i' has an 'ee' sound."

"Thank you, Mother. Gad . . . ee . . . an . . . Oh, Gadeeanton! Now I remember. Gadianton. These are the evil men who did not believe in Jesus but who delighted in murder and stealing."

"That's very good. Now read on—"

"Mother?"

Rizpah, flour up to her elbows from the bread dough she was kneading, turned to look at her daughter. She was aware of a subtle change in the girl's voice, and she felt immediate concern. "Yes, Rachel? Is something wrong?"

"I . . . no, I . . . I wanted to ask a question. How is it that a white woman tells when she has love for a man?"

"Mercy sakes alive!" Rizpah said with a smile as she held her hands away from her apron. "Has it come to that already?"

Silently Rachel nodded.

"And who is the lucky young man?"

"It is Samuel Loper. Martha told me everyone knew."

Still smiling, but with her mind racing ahead, Rizpah turned back to her dough. "And how does Brother Loper feel about this?" she asked softly, tenderly.

"This is a thing I do not know. Martha says I should make my heart known to him so that he will marry me, but the thoughts of doing so frighten me."

"How long have you had these feelings for him?"

Rachel shook her head. "I . . . I do not know. Perhaps they have been in my heart since the moment I saw him, and since the moment he paid his rifle to my father so he could take me away with him."

"Four years," Rizpah Gibbons said as she shook her head. "Land o' Goshen. Who'd have thought it?"

"You did not know this thing?" Rachel asked in surprise.

"I didn't mean that, honey child. I . . . uh . . . has Brother Loper ever indicated that he has similar feelings for you?"

Bashfully Rachel shook her head. "Oh, no. In fact, one time he made me a telling that, like *shinava* the Coyote boy, he would take my heart and eat it if I ever handed it to him. But I did not mind that telling, for on the night before I was taken away by him, Jesus told me that one day I would be his wife."

"You heard this?" Rizpah asked, turning again to look at the Paiute girl. "Jesus said it to you?"

"N . . . not as you and I speak," Rachel declared, seeking desperately for a way to explain this spiritual experience that had meant so much to her. "But the breath of

Jesus blew upon the coals of the fire as I prayed, and then *pan-ah-wich* the night bird called from near the wickiup and was immediately answered by its mate. It was then I knew I would marry Samuel Loper."

Nodding soberly, Rizpah turned back to her bread. "Mercy," she breathed to herself as Rachel watched from behind, "what a crazy notion! The breath of Jesus. But she believes it, so how am I ever going to tell the poor child that Samuel Loper isn't interested, and never in a hundred years will be—"

"Ma! Ma!" Young William burst through the door, his whole being animated with excitement. "Brother Samuel's back! And you'll never guess! There's a girl with him! Whadaya bet he went and got hisself a wife!"

Spinning, William was gone again, and with a little squeal Martha scrambled from the loft and ran to the window. "Lawsy! Willy's sure enough right! And just look at her! Oh, glory! She's beautiful as a picture!"

In another moment Martha was also gone, and a stunned Rachel sat with Samuel's copy of the Book of Mormon forgotten on her lap. For some reason she had stopped breathing, and she felt as though a crushing weight had been dropped onto her chest, making it impossible to start breathing again. Neither could she speak, and there was no way at all she could rise to go see the sight that was bringing all the fort out in surprised celebration.

Samuel had brought a woman back with him from Salt Lake City.

Pu-am-ey, Rachel's Eagle-man, had gone away to get married!

Motionless she sat, trying to absorb the news, and Rizpah Gibbons stood helplessly by, not knowing whether to run out and offer congratulations to one of her favorite men in all the world, or to go to her dear Rachel and hold

150

her close while she absorbed the pain the announcement had so obviously brought her.

But finally, knowing where she was needed most, Rizpah took her young Indian daughter and held her tenderly in her arms.

I can't hardly imagine he did it!"

Again Martha and Rachel were seated beneath the huge cottonwoods on the Santa Clara, fifty or more yards west of the fort. There was a brisk breeze, and the cottonwood leaves, bright yellow from a series of frosts, were falling steadily into the water. Here and there splashes of yellow reflected leaves that had settled to the bottom near the bank, though the water was too murky for much color to show through.

Martha, weaving her willow basket, ignored both the water and the falling color. And Rachel, furiously rubbing white clay into the nearly tanned buckskin, was ignoring her adopted sister.

"To the people of my father," Rachel stated to no one in particular, "the wind is known as *niltshi*. To my people it is called *noo'i*—"

"Amanda Richins Loper, her name is," Martha declared, paying no attention to the Paiute girl. "Well, she may be purty, but she sure don't shape up like much to me."

Rachel rubbed on, her mind too numb to focus on Martha's words.

"So old Eagle-man brings her here, and everybody practically falls all over theirselves making her out as something special. Lawsy, they even got their very own cabin for just the two of them, and poor Brother Jacob and his two wives and their kids and his adopted children Eliza and Albert and who knows who all else have all been crowded into one cabin ever since the fort got built! I tell you, Rachel, it's a sorry shame is what it is."

With a final touch Rachel rubbed clay into the last area of the tanned hide. Finished, she straightened her back and eased her straining muscles, all the while her mind trying to grope for some sort of understanding.

Two days had passed since Samuel's return, and in that time he hadn't been to see her even once. Of course he had no reason to come, not unless he considered her a friend to whom he wanted to introduce his new wife. But not even that had brought him, and Rachel was more hurt than she could imagine.

For the entire night after Samuel's arrival, Rachel had sat up on the bluff, trying to understand the terrible pain in her heart. She had prayed for hours, had wept copious tears, but no understanding had come.

"Heavenly Father," she had sobbed again and again, "if you told me he was to be my husband, why didn't you also tell him? Or better yet, why didn't you tell your prophet, Brother Brigham? Samuel always does what Brigham Young tells him to do. So do I. That's why I can't understand why all this is happening—"

After the night on the bluff, the next day had been nothing but a blur of sorrow and pain, and so had the night that followed. But now the sorrow had finally been replaced by numbness, and so Rachel felt that maybe her prayers were being answered.

"You can ignore me all you want, Rachel Iitats, but that won't make me stop talking. Old Eagle-man Loper's got my dander up, and I'm mad."

Was she angry, Rachel wondered as she listened to young Martha spouting off? Perhaps, but it was certainly not directed at Samuel. After all, he had every right in the world to marry anyone he wanted to marry. And he had every right to bring his wife here to the Santa Clara. No, if Rachel was angry, it was directed at herself, Rachel Iitats Dawson. She was the one at fault, for she had been the one filled with foolish dreams. After all, Samuel had warned her plain enough on their first day together that he and she were different, and that if she didn't stop holding her heart out to him on a stick, like Coyote boy he would eat it and put her out of her misery. Well, now he had done just that, and like Mother Gibbons was wont to say when one of the little ones got hurt, it served her fair-to-middling right.

Rachel knew all this and truly felt it in her heart of hearts. But there was another thing she could not reconcile, a thing that now made no sense at all. What had been the meaning of her sacred experience down on the Kaibab-its? Obviously it hadn't meant what she had thought. But then, what had it meant? Was it possible that it had meant nothing at all? She knew that Rizpah Gibbons felt that way, for though the woman had said nothing as Rachel had spoken of it, Rachel was perceptive enough to discern the white woman's thoughts. So was she right? Was she—

For four years Rachel had clung to that memory. Even when she had doubted it she had clung to it, for in all her adversity it had given her peace. Yet now, with the simple arrival of Samuel Loper and his new wife, Amanda, she was being forced to abandon her experience as meaningless. It had meant nothing!

"Go ahead and play Indian on me by not talking,"

Martha was saying matter-of-factly. "I know you're mad as hops, 'cause I seen the look on your face. And I don't blame you a bit. That was a low-down, skunk-mean thing for old Eagle-man to do, and I think you had ought to tell him so."

"Martha," Rachel replied without fervor, finally breaking her long silence, "what Pu-am-ey did was not mean. He had every right to take a wife, and I am happy that she is pleasing to him."

"Pleasing to him! Lawsy, Rachel, what about you? Right now, asleep, you know more about being a good wife than she'll ever know in her whole life! And stop that lying about being happy. Merciful heavens, woman, I know how you feel."

"It doesn't matter," Rachel said quietly, inspecting the hide she had been tanning. "No matter how I feel, he does not find me a person of worth. When he looks at me at all, he looks at me the way William or Andrew look at you—as a sister. I accept that."

"Well, I sure as blue blazes wouldn't!"

The Indian girl smiled sadly. "But you are not me, Martha. You are not Paiute, living in a village of white people, knowing that as hard as you try, you can never be like any of them."

"Say, nobody thinks of you as Paiute!"

Rachel smiled. "Perhaps not. But I do, *neu-nee phhch-eets-ahn*, my sister, for I know it is so. Nor will it ever change."

Abruptly she rose to her feet, pulling the tanned buckskin up with her. "Now, if I can beat the clay off this hide— "

"Rachel!" A man's voice suddenly called, "Rachel,

155

Martha, I been looking all over creation for you two! I want you to meet my new wife!"

And, frozen in place, the two girls waited motionless while a beaming Samuel Loper dragged his new bride across the sandy earth toward them.

CHAPTER

19

It was dark as pitch in the cabin loft. Though Rachel had
lain there for what seemed hours, she could not sleep.
Instead her mind was far away, both in time and in distance, and she was a small child again, standing beside
her father at a stream the whites would one day call Mam-
mouth Creek, which chuckled along quietly at their feet.
As she watched, the rays of the late afternoon sun splashed
off the water and turned golden the rounded rocks of its
bed. On the other side of the creek and beyond the nearest
beaver dam was a vast meadow dotted with many hundred
pah-re-ah, elk, which her father and the other men would
shortly hunt down for a great feasting.

With a quiet sigh, Rachel remembered looking out over
the shadowing acres of green. In her mind she could hear
the wind in the pines and smell the freshness of the high,
cold air. Something stirred deep within her, something
almost forgotten, and for a moment she smiled happily,
as a child would smile.

In the few brief years when she had been a child of
the Paiutes, she had been blessed to follow the lonely,

silent, yet living trails of her people. For days on end they had traveled without much speaking, their campfires surrounded by a vast and empty stillness, their thoughts spreading out wide as eternity.

She remembered the pungent smell of cedar, the smokiness of damp wood, the crisp crackle of pine, the deep red glow of dying fires, the sound of the night wind whispering through the rocks and trees around her. How many fires had she fed, she wondered then; how many meals had she helped prepare, how many bellies had she made content with the bounty so freely given by Giver-of-Life, her Lord Jesus Christ?

For twelve years she had traveled beyond the edge of what was known among the whites as civilization, moving like a whiff of smoke across lands known only to her people and to the Lord. And she had been happy, perhaps more happy than anyone had a right to be.

But now —

There was silence then, silence broken only when she broke into a soft, chant-song.

> Here around me all is still.
> My breath is still.
> My heart is still.
> My thoughts are still.
>
> Here around me my soul is still,
> for I have come to a place where I have not
> stepped before.
>
> Yet the wind blows my steps away in
> the dust, just as the steps of all
> who will yet walk here will
> go with the wind and walk in
> the sky.
>
> Here around me all is still.

Outside in the night a storm was coming, and thunder

was rumbling. A spattering of rain started, grew into a quick flurry, and then raced over the fort and away. In flashes of lightning that made their way through the small rifle porthole that was the loft's only window, she could see the fringe of dark trees along the Santa Clara's edge, and they were bending and swaying in the gusting wind.

Restlessly Rachel turned in her bed, more drops of rain hit the roof over her head, and the wind prowled searchingly around the eaves. It was a fit night for misery, Rachel thought as she stared upward, and she was truly miserable.

What was to become of her, she asked herself for the thousandth time? Now that her dream had been shattered, now that she had been shown for the fool she really was, what was to become of her? She could not go back to the Paiutes, for she had changed too much and there was nothing for her to go back to. Nor could she go forward, for when she thought of her future, she could see nothing but a wall of darkness, an empty nothingness that held only loneliness for her. And all this because her dream had been dashed to pieces on *timpi,* the rocks of reality.

Rachel turned again. The heavy patchwork quilts whispered against her body, and she could not sleep. Outside, the leaves rustled as more wind came, and she got up, lighting her lamp and slipping her feet into her moccasins, a pair that matched almost exactly in their quillwork a pair she had made for Samuel Loper. She felt cold, but she did not want to go down to the stove and rekindle the fire, for that would lead to conversation with Rizpah and Andrew, and right now she wanted conversation with no one.

Samuel Loper had now been back for nearly two weeks, so he had been married nearly a month. And other than the brief moment when he had introduced her to his new wife, Rachel had not spoken to him at all.

So why had he done it? Why had the man she loved,

who was now somewhere out there in the darkness and the storm with his new bride, gone away to get married? And more than that, why had Jesus allowed Rachel to deceive herself for so long? Why? Why? Why?

In the light from the lantern, Rachel stared ahead. The Spirit had given her an intense awareness that heightened every impression of the senses. Now as she sat on the edge of her pole-and-rawhide cot, she looked around at the gray boards, at the cracks, the slivers, the places where her little brothers had whittled with a knife. There was even a heart there, carved on the log lifted over young Martha's bed, a heart with an arrow through it that contained the initials RID and SL.

Seeing hers and Samuel's initials, Rachel almost smiled, and then she was aware of the coolness in the room, of the sound of water dripping from the eaves, and of the strange way the shadows from the oil lamp played on the rafters. Lightning flashed and thunder boomed again, long and loud and very close, and Rachel made a little jump.

"Ur pa-at-wan-an un-vai," she breathed as she looked out the porthole in wonder. "That was a long thunder. Now *u'way-ng wan-xkay-tu*, the rain is coming for certain.

"Dear Heavenly Father," she whispered then as she held her arms tightly about herself, "please help this foolish girl who sits before you to understand why she has been so terribly misled these many years. And if that is not possible, help her to understand what she is to do now. How should she live? Among her people a small voice? In the white world silent? In her world there was never a horizon, but in the white world there is no longer even a sun.

"O Great Father, what is there for this woman now that Samuel Loper is gone? She plants in the white man's way, and what is left then? She hoes in his fields, and what is left for her when she is finished? She harvests, and what is there for her when the harvest is over? Perhaps better crops. That is all, and it is not enough.

"Because she had no choice, she came to learn how the white man lived and to see if he was free. He was not. She came to learn the white man's ways and found them a stranger to her. Yet she learned them all, the wise ways and even the foolish ways, and in the learning she gave up her own freedom, all so that she could be a good wife to the white man Samuel Loper.

"Now he has been snatched away by another, and this woman does not know what to do, or where to turn. Worse, now she no longer even has a dream. Please, O Great One, tell this foolish young woman what she is to do next. In the name of Jesus Christ she asks this— "

Blowing out the lamp, Rachel slipped back into bed. There was a moment's hush, and then the rains came and thunder muttered in the distance, grumbling over the hills and in the deep canyons to the west. Somewhere in the midst of it all, Rachel drifted into a fitful sleep, and in her dreams she was following Samuel Loper from place to place, almost but never quite catching up to him. Yet occasionally he would turn back and ask her when she was going to become his wife—

Rachel? Rachel, wake up."

Groggily the young woman stirred. It seemed only moments since she had been awake, yet perhaps it had been hours. Only it was still dark, the rain was now beating a steady tattoo on the roof, and the lamp in Mother Gibbons' hand was casting eerie shadows about the loft.

"Y-yes, Mother," she murmured groggily, "what . . . is it?"

"Samuel Loper, Rachel. He wants to know if you'll marry him."

With a groan Rachel rolled over and buried her face in her straw-filled pallet. Would this nightmare never go away, she wondered? Now she was dreaming that Samuel wanted to marry her, and she knew he was already married to the girl called Amanda—"

"Rachel, wake up!"

Abruptly Rachel sat up, her eyes wide and staring. "Mother Gibbons," she whispered, her voice hoarse, "what is it?"

"I told you. Samuel Loper is downstairs, and he wants to know if you'll marry him."

Numbly Rachel shook her head. "Is . . . is this true?"

"It most certainly is. Elder Rich is here with him, the apostle who spoke in our conference yesterday, and he says President Brigham Young asked you and Samuel to marry each other."

With a gasp Rachel stared straight ahead. "President Young? Brigham Young asked this thing?"

"That's what they said," Rizpah Gibbons replied.

For a long moment Rachel sat silently, her mind whirling. Was this how God intended to answer her prayers? She had certainly asked him why he hadn't had Brigham Young tell Samuel to marry her. There had been no answer to her prayer, not then at least. But now, not more than two weeks later, the very thing she had wept about not happening had come to pass. To Rachel's mind the conclusion was inescapable. God had done exactly as she had asked him, and now she must do her part.

Nor did it matter that she was not *nu-tysuza-ri-mu*, a person of worth, to Samuel Loper. It was now a principle of obedience, not worth, and she had sworn many years before to always obey God and his prophet.

"Tell them yes," Rachel said with a heavy sigh as she lay back down. "I will marry Samuel Loper in the morning."

Lying in the darkness, Rachel listened as Rizpah descended the ladder from the loft. There was the murmuring of voices from below, and Rachel did her best to make out what they were saying. She couldn't tell, however, and—

"I wouldn't do it, I'll tell you that!"

"Martha, you should be asleep."

"Well, I ain't! And I wouldn't marry him, neither, not if ten prophets asked me."

Rachel giggled. "And what would you do, little warrior?"

Now Martha giggled. "Little warrior? Am I a warrior?"

"Well, you certainly seem ready for a fight."

Martha giggled again. "Yeah, that's right. And I'd fight 'em, too. It'd serve old Eagle-man right if you told him to go take a big jump into a little cactus."

Both girls giggled softly, and then quickly Rachel told Martha about her sacred experience in the camp of her father, as well as her more recent prayers on the bluff and elsewhere.

"Serious? You told Heavenly Father that exact thing? That you wanted Brother Brigham to tell old Eagle-man to marry you?" Martha could not hide the wonder from her voice.

"I did."

"Whoa! That's spooky enough to make the kettle boil all night long, if you know what I mean."

Again Rachel giggled. "You shouldn't talk like that. Mother Gibbons hears you, and—"

"Yeah, yeah, I know! Uh . . . Rachel, maybe you hadn't ought to fight. I mean, knowing all that scary spiritual stuff—"

"Rachel?"

"Yes?" Rachel asked as she sat up again. Rizpah Gibbons was back on the ladder, and in the lantern light Rachel could see that she looked quite upset.

"Brother Rich is leaving for Salt Lake City before daylight. He says since you're willing, he'd like to marry you and Samuel right now. Would you mind very much doing that?"

"May I clothe myself first?"

"Well, I should smile! Of all things, dragging a girl out of bed in the middle of the night! What's this world coming to? Rachel, darling, you take your sweet time, and I'll tell them you'll be down when you're good and ready, and not before."

Both Rachel and Martha giggled again, this time at Rizpah's defiant anger. Then Rachel pulled back the quilts and began sliding her heavy sleeping robe over her head.

"Oh," Rizpah stated, lifting her head back up over the loft floor, "I forgot to tell you. Once the ceremony is performed, Samuel says you can just come on back up to bed. Then he and Amanda will be by sometime in the morning to move you to their cabin."

"Yes, Mother," Rachel replied meekly. And then, her bosom filled with the strangest and most conflicting emotions she had ever experienced, Rachel Iitats Dawson began dressing for the marriage she had been contemplating and longing after for so many lonely years.

Elder Rich, this is Rachel Iitats Dawson."

Shyly the Paiute girl took the proffered hand of the apostle, Charles C. Rich.

"How do you do, Sister Dawson."

"I'm pleased to meet you," Rachel replied quietly.

"Why, you speak delightful English!" Elder Rich beamed. "How long have you lived among the whites?"

"Since Brother Loper brought me here a little more than four years ago."

Elder Rich nodded. "You've done well, Sister Dawson. Very well, especially for such a short time. Tell me, what do you think of the Mormons? I assume you've been baptized into the church."

"No, I have not."

Surprised, Elder Rich looked at Andrew and Rizpah Gibbons. "Has the girl not been taught?" he questioned.

"Rachel's been taught right well," Samuel stated, coming to the defense of his friends. "Fact is, she has a firm testimony of the truthfulness of the latter-day work."

"Is that true, Rachel? Are you a believer?"

Soberly the girl nodded. "I am."

"Tell me what you believe in. Would you do that for me?"

Rachel smiled, appreciating the man's sincere humility. "Of course. I believe in my Lord Jesus Christ, he whom my people call Shinob. I have felt his love, and I have heard his voice. I believe the words of the Book of Mormon, though I do not yet understand them all. And I believe that Brigham Young is *um-pug-iva Shinob*, a good and wise man who talks with God."

"Excellent!" Elder Rich declared. "I truly felt the Holy Spirit as you spoke those words. I hope that soon you will apply for baptism, for you are certainly worthy of it."

"I . . . I had not thought it good to ask for such a wondrous thing," Rachel declared shyly. "But such has been my desire for many seasons."

"Then you shall be baptized soon. Rachel, I assume that Sister Gibbons has told you why we are here."

"She has."

"Good. Then may I take a moment and explain all of this to you? As you are learning, right now most Mormons are white folks. But that should not be the case. God is the father of all the peoples on earth, and he wants all of them to come to him, partaking of his ordinances and preparing themselves for eternal life. One day the gospel will be preached to all people, no matter their nationality or color of skin, and then things will be made right for everybody. Unfortunately, that great work must be accomplished one step at a time.

"God the Father took the first step when he restored the gospel through the lad Joseph Smith. From there it spread rapidly across much of eastern America, and it has now made its way to the continent of Europe, where I must go from here. We are also spreading the gospel among your people, as well as among other tribes scattered across this great land.

"However, in this we are encountering much difficulty. Many of the natives of this land remain in their savage state, and it is a great trial for them to comprehend the words of God."

"What do you mean by 'savage state?' " Rachel abruptly asked.

"Why, the opposite of being in a civilized state," Elder Rich answered, surprised. "My dear Rachel, as Brigham Young says, civilization is simply the spirit of improvement, in learning and civil manners. The world may be said to have advanced in this so far as the arts and sciences are concerned; but, with these, they have mingled wicked ideas and practices, of which the savage Indian would be ashamed, and of which, fortunately, they are entirely ignorant."

"Savage is a bad thing, then?"

Elder Rich shifted uncomfortably. "Well, as opposed to being civilized, yes, it is bad, because it prevents progression."

"And you say only Indians are savage?"

"Oh, no!" Elder Rich smiled. "There are savages in every nation and civilization, including those that are most progressive. Why, I've seen Latter-day Saints do and say things that are terribly savage, far more destructive than the worst sort of non-civilization. And believe me, they're in much worse shape spiritually than any primitive Indian could be."

"So, what does it mean to be savage?" Rachel pressed while Samuel, Andrew, and Rizpah Gibbons suppressed smiles.

"I would say," Elder Rich responded carefully, "that it means being uninformed or unenlightened. For instance, most Indians are still savage or uncivilized, for they do not believe in making any improvements that will better their condition in the least. Their forefathers were once enlightened, and their knowledge was in advance of the knowledge of the present age. These natives, your people, belong to the house of Israel and are embraced in the promises and covenants made to Abraham, Isaac, and Jacob; but through their forefathers' transgressing the law of God, and breaking their covenants made with God, he hid his face from them, and they were left alone to follow the devices of their own evil hearts, until the whole race has sunk deep into barbarism."

"What is the word *barbarism?*" Rachel questioned immediately.

"*Barbarism* is another word for being savage."

For a moment Rachel paused, looking at the floor. Then, taking a deep breath, she lifted her gaze back to Elder Rich. "According to your words, I was a savage before Samuel Loper brought me to this people, for I knew nothing concerning them or their ways. Does this mean that my heart was evil?"

"I do not mean that personally," Elder Rich declared patiently. "In fact, I understand that your heart is pure and innocent. What I mean is that collectively the people who were your ancestors chose to disregard the light and knowledge God had given them. This does not mean your people are not good. It means only that they have lost the glory and knowledge they once had, and that they continue in a direction that will prevent them from regaining it.

"The Lord says this better than I do when he declares in the Book of Mormon: 'Because of their cursing which was upon them, they did become an idle people, full of mischief and subtlety, and did seek in the wilderness for beasts of prey.'

Neverthless, their ancient prophets have spoken good concerning them. It is prophesied by Nephi as follows:

169

'After the book (which is the Book of Mormon), of which I have spoken shall come forth, and be written unto the Gentiles, and sealed up again unto the Lord, there shall be many which shall believe the words which are written; and they shall carry them forth unto the remnant of our seed (the present American Indians). And then shall the remnant of our seed know concerning us, how that we came out from Jerusalem, and that they are descendants of the Jews. And the Gospel of Jesus Christ shall be declared among them; wherefore they shall be restored to the knowledge of their fathers, and also to the knowledge of Jesus Christ, which was had among their fathers. And then shall they rejoice; for they shall know that it is a blessing unto them from the hands of God; and their scales of darkness shall begin to fall from their eyes, and many generations shall not pass away among them, save they shall be a white and delightsome people.' "

"My skin is to become white?" Rachel asked in amazement.

Elder Rich chuckled. "That probably means clean or pure of heart rather than white skinned. I don't think the Lord cares about skin color. Rather, he is most concerned about heart color."

"I believe that." Rachel smiled. "And now I understand *savage*. It is any person who does not understand or know of Jesus Christ."

"That's how I define it, Rachel. If a person does not know Christ, has not partaken of his atonement by repenting of and obtaining a forgiveness of sins, and has no knowledge of or belief in Christ's saving ordinances, then that person is in a savage or barbarous condition.

"Further, as Christ declared, those who have risen above that condition by obtaining such knowledge and enlightenment are under the strict obligation of sharing their light with those who don't have it.

"That, Rachel, is our challenge, to help yours and all people climb from their primitive or savage state to a state of divine enlightenment, and that is why I have asked you to dress and come before me tonight."

"It is?" Rachel's voice echoed her surprise.

"That's right. It has come to the attention of Brigham Young that a tribe of Indians, the Moquis, believe a great many of the same things God has made known to us. Wishing to study their beliefs further, as well as to acquaint them more fully with the principles of the gospel as we understand them, Brother Young has directed that I organize an extensive mission to the Moquis. He specifically asked that I call you to be a part of that mission."

Her continued astonishment evident, Rachel could only stare. "But . . . but . . . ," she stammered, "I . . . I thought . . . "

Elder Rich smiled. "I know. You thought you had been asked down to be married to Brother Loper. And so you were. But that is the reason. President Young has asked that Brother Loper marry you as a plural wife, and that the two of you then serve together for one year among the Moquis. Thus they will not only learn something of our ways, but they will see that the fulness of the gospel can be lived by Indians as well as whites, and that it can civilize them as marvelously as it has you."

Hardly hearing the man, Rachel tried to control the anguished sense of helplessness that swept over her. It was not to be a marriage after all! At least not such a marriage as she had dreamed of. Instead it was a union of convenience, a practical joining of two people so they could fill an assignment. After that, what? After that, nothing! The mission would be over, and so would her marriage. Yes, and so, too, would her dream, the thin wisp of hope that had sustained her through so many long years of loneliness.

171

"Rachel, Brother Loper has accepted the call from President Young to spend a year among the Moquis. Will you?"

Quickly, desperately, Rachel glanced at the face of Samuel Loper. But whatever she had hoped to see was not there. Instead he stood looking at the floor, and from the way he was fidgiting, Rachel could tell he was truly miserable. Yet he had agreed to be obedient to the prophet. And so, therefore, must she.

"I will," she responded, her voice hardly above a whisper. And there was nothing she could do to keep her misery from the others in the room, Samuel Loper included.

PART FOUR

W hew!" Looking up at the glaring, brassy sky, Amanda Richins Loper wiped the sweat from her brow with the back of her hand. "I think this is the hottest day I've ever seen!" Then, with another sigh, she began once again stirring the contents of the soap barrel.

Rachel, carefully ladling first boiling fat and then boiling lye leached from wood ash into the mixture Amanda was stirring, had to agree. "It is very hot, especially for this late in the season. But this fire does not help, either."

"Umph," Amanda agreed as she stuck a long wisp of hair back behind her ear. "I'm glad you chose to work over the fire. This is all so new to me."

"It won't take much longer," Rachel stated as she ladled another quart of lye into the mix. "Once the lye and fat are all stirred in, then we will fill the barrel with more boiling water and stir it until it turns creamy. After that we simply let it stand for two or three months until it has turned to soap."

"How on earth did you learn all this?"

"Mother Gibbons taught me."

Amanda was astounded. "You mean this isn't how the Indians do it?"

"Goodness, no," Rachel laughed. "My people make their soap from the yucca plant, and it does not take such great effort as this. For myself it is a good soap, but Mother Gibbons prefers the lye soap because it is stronger, and so do many of the others here in the fort. It was in my mind that you would prefer this soap also."

Amanda nodded. "You're probably right. I suppose the molasses we made yesterday wasn't an Indian recipe, either?"

Rachel giggled. "No, that was also Mother Gibbons' recipe. Five bushels of parsnips boiled down make two gallons of molasses. You will enjoy it in the coming season of cold."

"I'm sure you're right. What's the Paiute word for fire?"

"*Kuna.*"

"Interesting. Have you spoken English all your life?"

"Oh, no. Only four years. It was then that Samuel bought me from my father with his rifle, and I came to live among the whites."

"I still can't imagine that!" Amanda was scornful. "What a barbaric custom!"

"Perhaps now that I am his wife, it should be called a dowry."

Amanda glanced at Rachel, and abruptly she laughed. "You're right. I'll bet a great deal of what we do seems barbaric to the Paiutes."

"I do not know the meaning of the word *barbaric.*"

"Oh. Well, maybe I should say *strange*. What customs seem strange to you, Rachel? I mean, seemed strange when you first came here?"

"Well," Rachel laughed, suddenly feeling embarrassed, "I will tell you the thing that Enos says."

"Enos?"

"Yes, the Ute warrior who will go to the Moquis with Jacob as interpreter. He says the thing that is strange about white people is that they have no roots. He says they are always trying to plant themselves, and yet in the end they will blow away in the wind because they are all born with wheels."

Amanda giggled but then sobered as she thought about it. "I hate to say so," she said slowly, "but he may have a point. We certainly do our share of gallivanting about. What about the whites do you personally find strange?"

"Well," Rachel replied, feeling embarrassed again, "it took many months before I accepted Mother Gibbons' feeling for modesty. I could see no sense in covering my body in hot weather, and I am certain I shocked many people before I saw the wisdom of it."

"You . . . you went naked?"

"I wore very little, at least when it was hot. It was also difficult for me to learn to work inside a cabin, for among my people the wickiup is small and is used only for sleeping. It was more than a year before I stopped feeling closed in, like I had crawled into a hole and could not get out."

"Are there other things?"

"Oh, yes. Many other things. It took a great deal of time for me to get used to seeing men working in the fields or helping with what you call housework. Among my people that is unseemly, for men and women each have their tasks, and there is much honor in that. Neither is it polite to gossip. When the Paiute see a thing happening to another that is bad, we stop it if we can. If we cannot, then we turn our backs and pretend that we have not seen it. That way we can never speak of it to others."

"How interesting!"

"I believe it is a good way. Another good way is that no one among our people has ownership of anything."

"But you . . . you had things."

"Oh, yes. But if I had something and another needed it, they were free to take it. And there was always politeness involved, so things did not simply turn up missing."

"Did you like that way?" Amanda asked.

"Well, I did not know that a thing could be stolen, or that one could be a thief, until I came to live with the whites. And except for one person, I had never seen a man or woman being cruel or unkind to another. That is not our way."

"You mean there was never a disagreement among the Paiutes?"

Rachel laughed. "There were many disagreements. But among my people, it was more important to be polite than it was to be right. Thus, disagreements were kept silent, and by talking back and forth, always in a quiet and friendly manner, people brought things to a settlement. If it could be seen that no settlement would be reached, one or another of those involved simply went away to live elsewhere for a time. There was no fighting among us, except in fun or occasionally in the choosing of a wife. And even that was not a bitter thing."

Rachel explained the custom of squaw-pulling. Then the talk turned to the slavery of Paiute children as it was being practiced by the Utes, the Navajos, and the Spanish. Finally, Rachel related again how it was that Samuel Loper had come to bring her to live among the whites. Soon the soap was completed, and the two exhausted young women sank onto the door-bench for a much-needed rest.

"*Pa-a tun-kam-ai,*" Rachel said as she drank deeply from the covered water barrel that stood in the shade of the porch overhang. "The water tastes good."

"It surely does," Amanda agreed as she took her turn. "And it feels good to sit down, too!"

"*Imik a-pu-ani,*" Rachel said softly as she turned and looked at the young woman who had become as her sister.

"You are a good person, Amanda. I am happy that Samuel Loper found you."

"Why, thank you," Amanda responded graciously. "So am I."

Rachel smiled and then looked away to where two boys were driving a small herd of cattle into the fort's corral, getting them ready for the next day. "It is in my heart to wish that you were going to the Moqui instead of me."

Amanda sighed. "I wish I was going, too. But *with* you, not *instead* of you. A year seems such a long time."

"A year of loneliness is a very long time indeed."

There was much meaning in Rachel's statement, and for a moment Amanda turned to look at her. "You mustn't feel that way," she finally declared. "Samuel cares very much for you, as well he should."

Rachel did not reply, and in the stillness a butterfly danced past, pausing only for a moment on the edge of the water barrel before lifting up and away over the wall of the fort.

"*A-siv-oits ung tuvits aus-in-tui,*" Rachel stated softly. "The butterfly has pretty wings."

"As do you," Amanda replied as she took Rachel's hand. "You are a lovely woman, Rachel, and Samuel feels it just as much as I do."

Rachel did not reply, but in her mind was the knowledge that it was not so. She was as a sister to Samuel Loper, nothing more. There was no man-woman feeling between them; no, and there never would be. She was only a Paiute girl whom he had married by way of commandment and whom he would put quietly aside as soon as this mission to the Moquis came to an end.

"I mean it, Rachel. Samuel and I are both thrilled that you are in our family!"

Rachel smiled, and her heart opened wide to this lovely woman who was only a little older than herself but who

179

was so willing to give. How sad that she could not give the one thing Rachel really wanted. But it was understandable that Samuel had eyes only for the lovely Amanda. She was tall and beautiful, she was happy and pleasant, and Samuel Loper should feel toward her as he did.

Still, perhaps it was enough that Rachel be near Samuel Loper, even though he did not have such feelings for her as she did for him. She told herself that often enough. Yet no matter how many times her brain said *mar-ung*, that thing, to her heart, somehow her heart could not find a way to hear it.

"Why is it that Brother Brigham is so interested in the Moqui people?" Amanda suddenly asked.

"The night he married us," Rachel answered, "Elder Rich told us that Brigham Young thinks perhaps the Moqui are descendants from the ancient Nephites, perhaps even the people of Ammon who covenanted to bury their weapons of war and never take them up again."

"Do the Moquis have that tradition?" Amanda asked.

"I have heard that they do. And if they have that tradition, then perhaps they will have many others that come from the Book of Mormon."

"How interesting!"

Rachel nodded. "Priscilla Hamblin told me they have a legend about being led to their mesas by three white prophets. Jacob is certain they are the three Nephite disciples who were allowed to tarry. Nor will the Moqui people leave their mesas until the three prophets return and give them permission. That's why Jacob hasn't been able to get any of them to move north, between our people and the Navajo."

"Have you ever been to their mesas?"

"No," Rachel replied with a shake of her head, "though even as a child I heard them discussed with wonder among my people. For this reason I am happy to be making this journey."

Amanda smiled. "And I'm happy for you. Have you heard who else is going?"

"Oh, yes. At least, most of them. Brother Rich told us their names the night he married us. Brother Marion Shelton and one other man are to spend this winter among them, studying their language and their beliefs about God. Besides Samuel, Jacob and his daughter Eliza, who is also Paiute, Thales Haskell, Taylor Crosby, John Young, and I think Benjamin Knell will be going. Of course Enos will go as interpreter. There are also others whose names I do not know. And my white father, Andrew Smith Gibbons, is to direct the affairs here at the fort during our absence."

Amanda sighed. "The fort will seem very empty with all of you gone."

Rachel did not reply.

"I . . . I just wish . . . " Abruptly Amanda turned and threw her arms around a startled Rachel, and for a moment she held her closely, weeping. "Al-already I miss both of . . . of you," she sobbed. "It will be so . . . so hard to have my baby all al-alone "

Rachel gasped. "You are to have a baby?"

Quickly Amanda pulled away, a smile showing through her tears. "Yes, but I have not dared tell Samuel. I don't want him to be worried about me . . . us, I mean."

"But you must tell him," Rachel stated firmly. "That way he and I can discuss it, and we can also exercise our faith together for you."

Now truly smiling, Amanda reached out and once again took Rachel into her arms. "You are so sweet," she whispered tenderly. "And of course you are right. I will tell him tonight —"

23

"Thales, did you get the jerky?"

Looking up from the mule he was packing, Thales Haskell waved at Jacob Hamblin. "Yep, and distributed so's it's not all on one animal. Same with the biscuits and flour."

Jacob nodded. "Good. Isaac, you got that boat of yours all ready?"

Isaac Riddle, already mounted, waved his hat. "She's ready, Jacob!"

"Fine. Amos, where're the beeves?"

Amos Thornton, standing beside his wife, pointed back toward the fort. "Enos has 'em yoked, Jacob. He'll be along directly."

Watching Brother Jacob give his directions amid the hustle and bustle of the scurrying missionaries was one of the most interesting things Rachel had ever seen. Oh, she had seen it all before but never from this perspective, as a participant rather than a bystander.

Now, as a hot wind gusted out of the south, scattering yellow cottonwood and sycamore leaves along with the dust raised by dozens of churning hooves and feet, Rachel found herself comparing these people with her own and feeling amazed at the difference.

When her people moved an encampment, they did so simply and quietly, without fanfare and without a great deal of preparation. When a move was to be made, they gathered together the things they needed, which were few, and left behind the things they did not need. After all, in another season they would be back, so wickiups were left standing, food was left stored in sealed pits, *manos* and *metates* were left in the forks of trees ready to use again, and so forth.

These white people, on the other hand, made much preparation and took so much with them that animals and wagons were needed to carry it all. Of course, to be gone a year was to be gone a long time, and because they could neither farm nor hunt while they were gone, many supplies would be needed. Rachel understood that, yet still she smiled at the noise and confusion that reigned around her.

Besides, though the scene appeared hectic, she had overheard Samuel telling Amanda that within a mile or so the order of travel would be established, the oxen and pack animals setting the pace, and the pattern would remain pretty much constant through the remainder of the journey.

"Very well," Jacob was saying in response to Amos Thornton. "Samuel, you and Rachel both ready?"

Samuel, standing next to his horse, nodded and then looked around for his young Paiute wife. But Rachel, wanting and yet not wanting to be near Samuel and Amanda, was standing discreetly behind the boat wagon so they might have a last few moments to themselves.

"You seen Rachel?" Samuel asked his tearful but composed young wife.

"Last I saw," the girl replied, wiping at her eyes, "she was talking to young George A. Smith."

Samuel grinned. "I should have knowed it. She loves watching that kid prance his hoss around."

"Rachel and everyone else. He's been playing his mouth organ all morning, tapping his little bell, and really putting on a show for the children. But I hate the song he keeps singing—"

"Now, Amanda."

"Well, I do. Have you listened to the words, about leaving his love behind and hanging his harp on a lonely tree? Oh, Samuel, I don't know if I can stand you being gone a whole year! What if something happens to you? How will I ever have the baby without you here?"

Samuel, still not used to the idea that he was going to be a father, shook his head. "I don't know much about that, Amanda. I truly don't. But there's lots of good women here that can help you better'n I can."

"But there's none of them can hold me and take away my lonelies better than you."

Samuel smiled and held his wife close. And Rachel, standing at the other side of the wagon, felt certain her own pains of loneliness were at least as great as those of the beautiful Amanda.

"The time'll go fast, Amanda," Samuel responded, his voice so low that Rachel was nearly unable to hear. "You'll see. Why, you'll be so busy you won't hardly notice—"

"Samuel, what . . . what if Jacob's right and something bad happens?"

For a moment Samuel stared off into the distance, unsure of what to say. Jacob had never had a premonition of trouble before, or if he had, he had never announced it publicly. But he had done so in meeting the night before, and Samuel knew better than to discount such words from an ordained apostle.

"Then I reckon it'll happen," he finally responded. "But this is my mission, Amanda. You wouldn't want me to turn away from it, would you?"

Slowly the young woman shook her head. "Samuel," she said then, her sudden tears falling unheeded, "be real careful, please. And take good care of Rachel. I love you both, and I . . . I couldn't stand l-losing either of . . . you."

Tenderly Samuel stroked his wife's back. "I'll do 'er, Amanda. And don't you spend the whole year fretting over such things, you hear. We'll both be fine."

"I . . . I hope so. Bye, Samuel honey."

"Adios," Samuel said huskily as he kissed his young wife.

Mounting then, Samuel reined over to where Jacob sat his horse, overseeing the final moments before departure.

It was October 1860, and so the hot, dry wind out of the south was very much out of season. Yet the thoughts of it not yet storming was the farthest thing from Rachel's mind. Silently she mounted her horse and drifted along after Samuel.

"How's Amanda?" Jacob was asking Rachel's husband as she drew rein.

"She'll be fine."

Jacob Hamblin nodded. "I know. But that don't make it any easier. Both my own Rachel and Priscilla struggle while I'm gone, but I think it's always harder on Priscilla. Is your Rachel ready to spend a year away from home?"

"She's always ready to do whatever is asked," Samuel replied simply, not even aware that Rachel was listening.

"She's an unusual girl," Jacob responded. "She could probably handle her assignment alone, but I didn't want her to have to. That's why I'm bringing Eliza along."

Rachel looked to where Jacob's adopted Indian daughter Eliza sat her horse. Like herself, Eliza had learned well the ways of the whites. But unlike her, Jacob's daughter did not seem quite as stable. Of course, that was probably just appearances, nothing more. And stable or not, she would provide good female companionship during the long months ahead.

"Sure wish I could get excited about this mission," Jacob suddenly said, speaking more to himself than to Samuel.

"You still have those feelings?"

"I do. But the worst of it is that I can't interpret them. All I know is that I feel differently than I've ever felt before when beginning a mission."

"Maybe you're just worrying over the Navajos."

"Could be. We've never run into them before, but two different Paiutes have told me that the Navajos are unhappy with us for crossing their lands to see the Moquis."

Samuel shook his head. "They're sure bitter enemies, the Navajos and the Moquis."

"That they are. Sort of makes me wish the Navajos hadn't linked us with them."

"But the Mormons have never troubled the Navajos," Samuel stated.

"I know," Jacob responded. "I just hope the Navajos remember that. To tell the truth, Samuel, I'm real nervous about taking young George A. Smith on such a dangerous journey as this might be."

Samuel glanced at the fifteen-year-old son of the apostle George A. Smith. The boy was seated jauntily astride the fancy black horse he called Vittick. Wild with everyone else, Vittick seemed to love young George A. as much as the youth loved the horse, and together they were something to watch. Galloping, turning, rearing on hind feet, high-stepping in perfect timing—Vittick was as much a thoroughbred as his young master.

"He'll stick it out," Samuel stated confidently.

"I'm certain he will," Jacob responded. "I . . . well, he's just a boy, and I feel a real burden of responsibility for him. I told his father that, too, but the boy had his heart so set on going—"

"He's not much of a boy any longer," Samuel stated easily.

"I know. At fifteen I was carrying a man's responsibilities, and I imagine it was the same with you. But now that I'm older, fifteen sure doesn't look as old as it used to.

"Well, it's about time to get moving. Excuse me, Samuel, and I'll call this assemblage to order."

Rachel watched as Jacob took off his hat and waved it in a large circle, a signal for order and quiet. Once that was accomplished, Jeheil McConnell was called to offer prayer, and then with wild whoops and subdued words of departure the party strung out and headed east along the Santa Clara. The Indian guide they called Enos led. Jacob came next, followed by Eliza Hamblin, George A. Smith, Jr., Amos Thornton, Samuel and Rachel, Jeheil McConnell, James Pierce, Isaac Riddle, Thales Haskell, and Jacob's brother Francis M. Hamblin. There were also several pack animals and the wagon carrying Isaac Riddle's boat, which was intended for use in crossing the Colorado River—if they could get it down the treacherous cliffs to the water. And once it was at the river, the wagon would be abandoned and the two oxen would be driven on as beeves, to be killed when the party needed more food.

It was a formidable looking group, Rachel thought as she surveyed the scene both before and behind her. All the men were heavily armed, and there was extra ammunition. They carried various trinkets and other gifts for the Indians, and enough clothing and so forth was packed onto the mules to last the entire party for a year.

Dropping slightly back, Samuel rode next to his wife. "Rachel," he asked, noting her tears, "you all right?"

Silently the woman made the sign that all was well. "I shall miss my sister Amanda," she stated then in Paiute, "and Mother and Father Gibbons and their family. I do not like leaving my family behind."

Samuel nodded with understanding. "Can't say as I blame you. Maybe we ought to join in singing with young George A. 'I'll hang my harp on a willow tree, and off to the wars again.' "

Samuel started singing, Rachel laughed at Samuel's funny way of doing it, and George A., hearing his song, turned back and grinned. And then he too began singing again. Soon all the company had joined in the song, all but Jacob Hamblin, who was still not able to shake the oppressive feeling that had so weighed him down the past few days.

And Rachel, watching Brother Hamblin ride along in silence, was suddenly filled with a terrible foreboding of her own.

24

Do you fear these people called the Diné?" Rachel asked Eliza as they rode side by side toward the confluence of the Santa Clara and the Rio Virgin.

"I know little of them," Eliza responded in Paiute. "It is said they make bad medicine for our people. I fear bad medicine."

Rachel made the sign that she felt the same. "My father is of the Diné," she said then, revealing to Eliza for the first time her own parentage.

"Can this be true?"

"It is so. He gave me to Samuel Loper many years ago, for he did not wish me to be a slave to the Diné or to be killed by them. We had been told that such is the way the Diné treat Paiute women and children."

Eliza shuddered, her imagination building rapid images of the horrors she might be forced to endure should they encounter the fierce Navajo. Rachel was dealing with the same fears, heightened by the knowledge she had of her own brother's hatred for her, manifested so openly when last she had seen him. And now she was being led into the very land where he had gone to dwell—

Crossing the roiling Rio Virgin just north of its confluence with the Santa Clara, the missionaries turned upriver and followed the stream in a northeasterly direction. With waves and shouts they passed scattered settlers who had been sent by Brigham Young to establish a cotton mission in what was starting to be called Utah's Dixie. And after a long and tiring first day, they finally made camp for the night beneath Hurricane Mesa near the small settlement of Toquerville.

"I'm telling you, Samuel," Thales Haskell said as he cleaned his plate of the food Rachel had helped prepare, "we've been missing out on a good bet. Rachel's cooking beats yours all hollow."

Isaac Riddle laughed. "I say amen to that sentiment."

Samuel nodded contentedly but kept silent.

"You and Eliza do very well, Sister Loper," Jacob agreed as he looked up from a letter he was penning to Elder George A. Smith about the progress of the party and about his young son. "Both of you will be a great blessing to us as well as to the Moquis."

Blushing, Rachel busied herself helping Jeheil McConnell, who had drawn cleanup duty for the first camp. Though Rachel had not drawn either cooking or cleanup duty, helping in those areas allowed her to feel useful, and she was more than willing to do it. Now, at the end of the first day's travel, the mood around the fire was festive, and young George A. Smith especially could not contain his enthusiasm.

"That was sure easier than I'd expected," he exclaimed. "I thought somebody said we'd have all kinds of problems with that wagon and boat."

Isaac Riddle laughed. "Listen, youngster, we were on good road today, and it'll be the same most of tomorrow.

After that we'll see how loud you crow. Maybe I ought to let *you* drive that fool wagon."

"If you do," Amos Thornton added, "I'll ride that horse of his for him."

"Hey," George A. responded, not realizing he was being teased, "nobody rides Vittick but me!"

"Easy, George," Samuel said as he put his hand on the boy's arm. "They're hurrahing you, is all. Everybody knows Vittick's a one-man horse."

Embarrassed, George grew silent, and Thales suddenly looked up. "All I ask," he said, his eyes filled with laughter and his hands beginning to gesture wildly, "is that *I* don't have to ride that fool wagon this trip. I recollect last time out I near busted my gut pushing our cart up those consarned sandhills. Then coming down the last one, she hit a bump and capsized bottom plumb up with Brother Isaac and me hanging for dear life to the stern."

There was general laughter, and Thales quickly warmed to his story.

"Well, we got her righted and all the fooferaw gathered and loaded, and after about thirty more steps she capsized again, and that time I went sailing end over teakettle and came near to perishing in a bed of pear cactus."

Everyone, including young George A., was laughing now, and Thales continued. "By then my faith in that cart was weakening, but we got her upright again and down the hill—and there she sank plumb to her hubs in deep sand. Well, she was rolling too heavy for me to endure that sort of happiness much longer, so I abandoned the project and set out with Brother Young to find water. By midnight all we'd found was more sand, so we camped dry, feeling mighty gloomy about our prospects. I don't rightly know what time the brethren dragged that cart in, but I do know I was glad I wasn't with 'em."

191

"You did look low-spirited when I arrived the next day," Jacob stated with a grin.

"Aw, that cart was a bad egg, Jacob, and you knowed it. I just hope this'n does better. Say, you remember that mule of Brother Crosby's called 'Devil'?"

"To my way of thinking, he was well-named," Samuel stated with a grin.

"I'd hope to shout he was! Crosby swore by 'im, but that critter was famous for jumping stiff-legged, turning his pack, and getting all tangled in the rigging. Somebody shoulda shot that sorry cuss."

"You mean Crosby or the mule?"

"I lent Crosby my spurs," Thales concluded after everyone had stopped chuckling, "and after becoming sufficiently acquainted with 'em, that mule finally give up and was gentle."

"And that's when *my* horse threw that sack of beans," Jacob stated with a wry smile. "Brethren, I do hope this trip turns out better than that."

There was silence around the fire, and then Jacob looked at where Rachel was sitting a little behind Samuel.

"Sister Loper, if my memory serves me right, you come from over in the country where we're headed. Isn't that so?"

"It is so," Rachel replied formally.

"And your father was Tanigoots?"

"That is so. His Navajo name is Dah-Nish-Uant."

"Dah-Nish-Uant," Francis Hamblin stated, speaking for the first time. "Don't recollect ever hearing of him."

"You've heard of him," Samuel stated with a soft laugh, "but owing to the peculiar way us whites like to massacre the Indian tongues, he's now called something else altogether."

"So, who is he?"

Leaning back, Samuel toed a burning stick further into

the fire. "Well, when I brought Rachel back to the Santa Clara and made the announcement that Tanigoots was now called Dah-Nish-Uant, Sister Gibbons right away changed that to Dawson. That only stuck with her and Rachel, but other folks thought Dah-Nish-Uant sounded an awful lot like Danish-Yank, so that handle was passed around for a spell. Then some wise old bird got to thinking that an Indian couldn't possibly be named Danish-Yank on account of no self-respecting Indian could've possibly heard of the Danes, so he upped and changed Danish-Yank to Spanish-Yank. That got real popular, but after a spell even Spanish-Yank wasn't good enough, and it got twisted and evolved again into the moniker we now use, which is Spaneshanks."

"Are you meaning to say," Thales Haskell stated incredulously, "that Tanigoots and Dah-Nish-Uant and old Chief Spaneshanks that I keep hearing about are all one and the same hombre?"

"As ever was," Samuel stated quietly. "Spaneshanks is Rachel's pa, all right. He used to be mighty friendly, but after what the army's been doing to the Navajos, stealing their sheep and taking them to California and then driving the people like cattle to Fort Defiance, I just hope he still is."

"Well," Jacob Hamblin stated quietly, echoing the sentiments of all there assembled, "for myself, I hope we don't have to deal with the Navajos at all. If we do, Brother Samuel, then my sentiments echo yours exactly. Of them all, Chief Spaneshanks is probably the best man for us to encounter."

"Yes," Rachel thought to herself as she spread her sleeping robes next to those of her husband, another trembling of fear spreading through her body. "But what if it is Peokon you must deal with, instead?"

It was afternoon of their fifth day out from Santa Clara,
and Samuel and Thales Haskell were riding side by side
just yards ahead of Rachel, all three of them travelling
ahead of the rest of the missionaries. The party had made
its way north and east past Virgin and Virgin Fields and
had camped at the new settlement of Grafton. The next
day they had turned south and picked their way carefully
up Horse Valley Wash and onto the Vermilion Cliffs Plateau, thus effectively bypassing the almost impassable
Hurricane Cliffs. Off to their right they had then passed
Elephant Butte, while in the distance to the southwest rose
Sand Mountain. With its huge sand dunes and nearly total
absence of water, the missionaries had given the area a
wide berth, circling far to the northeast before turning back
southwest in the direction of the Moqui. After passing
beneath Cottonwood Point and camping at the Cane Beds,
which Rachel of course remembered, they were now riding
eastward beneath the looming, multihued bulk of the Vermilion Cliffs. The Ute Indian called Enos had ridden ahead
to Yellow Rock Water or Pipe Springs, where they planned

to camp for the night, and he was scouting the springs for safety.

"I don't like it, Thales. I don't like it even a little!"

"You meaning Jacob?"

Samuel nodded. "As ever. He's quieter'n a tree full of owls at noontime."

"I've noticed. And it ain't like him to spook so easy."

For a moment the three rode in silence. "I don't reckon he's spooked," Samuel finally stated. "I think the Spirit's weighing heavily upon him."

"Ugly business if it is! You think the Lord's telling him we're heading for a massacre or something?"

"Could be, I reckon."

Rachel thought of that and felt her very heart turn cold. Though she did not really fear death, she had developed a terrible fear of being captured by the Navajos. Of course she did not fear her father, but if she were taken by Peokon—

"Well," Thales said finally as he watched a long-eared jackrabbit pound away into the distance, "It'd make sense of Jacob's feelings, all right."

"For all we know," Samuel stated as he unconsciously glanced back to make sure Rachel was all right, "the entire Navajo nation might be waiting for us."

"Yeah, and all painted up and feathered for war."

Samuel squinted and looked off toward the distant blue of Buckskin Mountain and the Kaibab Plateau, and Rachel, watching him, tried her best to read his thoughts. But it did no good, for since their marriage the man had become like a blank wall to her. Of course she knew that was because he had not desired her, at least in the way a man desires a woman. But still it troubled her, for she felt like a burden to him, a burden he would be glad to rid himself of just as soon as possible.

195

"Does sort of give a body the flutterin' fantods just thinking about war parties," Samuel finally stated.

"Amen and amen."

Just then a cottontail rabbit scurried out of a juniper deadfall, and with a soft word to her husband, Rachel turned aside her horse and rode to the hole down which the rabbit had fled. Dismounting, she took her hardened digging stick and gently probed the hole. Within moments she was pulling the rabbit forth while Samuel and Thales watched from a little distance away.

"How's Rachel getting along?" Thales asked, speaking softly but not so low that Rachel, with her acutely trained hearing, couldn't overhear.

Samuel looked at his friend. "How do you mean?"

Reaching up, Thales lifted his hat and ran his fingers through his hair, studying out in his mind how he might approach what it was he felt compelled to say to his friend. "Well," he finally stated, "it ain't too hard to tell the girl's scared. So's Eliza, only more so."

"Scared? What of?"

"The Navajo, I reckon. You ever talk to Rachel about that?"

Samuel shook his head. "Not that I recollect."

"You ever talk to her about much of anything?"

Samuel chuckled. "Don't reckon I have a whole lot to say."

"Well," Thales said as he studied the far horizon, choosing his words carefully as he went along, "I ain't meaning to interfere twixt a man and his wife, old friend, but one thing I learned before my own wife passed away is that womenfolk—white or red—set store by talking. I see the emptiness in Rachel's eyes, and I figure—well, maybe it'd help if you talked to her a little more."

With a sigh Samuel reached down and patted his horse's neck. "Could be you're right, Thales. Trouble is, the silence of the land has sort of gotten into my bones, if you know what I mean. I forget that others need to talk."

"You aren't so different there," Thales said softly.

"Besides," Samuel continued, doing his best to be honest with himself as well as with his friend, "talking to a woman ain't so easy for me. Never has been. It was easier when Rachel was just a little kid. I can talk to kids, and the last three or four snows I could make pretty good chin music with Rachel. But now — well, I just don't know what to say. I reckon that's especially true now that she's my wife."

For a moment both men were silent; the only sounds were the creaking of saddles as one or the other of them shifted weight. A little way off Rachel was busy killing and then pelting the rabbit, and neither of the men had any idea that she had been listening to their every word. Yet she had, and it was in her, for a moment, to mount up and simply ride away to her own people, thus sparing Samuel Loper the pain and discomfort of being married to a person for whom he felt nothing.

But then, thinking again of the fact that her marriage to Samuel Loper had been brought to pass by the Lord through the prophet Brigham Young, Rachel gave a long sigh. She would stay with it, she knew, and do her best to care for the man during their mission. That he would one day send her away, she was certain. And she was just as certain it would be when the mission to the Moquis was over. As to what she would do after that . . . well, perhaps it didn't really matter —

Putting both the rabbit and pelt into her rucksack, Rachel mounted her horse, and without another word the two men turned their mounts and rode on. With another sigh Rachel kicked her horse in the ribs, and moments later the three were moving across the dusty plain exactly as before, except that she was a little farther back.

Rachel did not want to be listening to the men, she truly didn't. Such a thing flew in the face of all she had been taught, both as a Paiute and as a white girl. And yet her curiosity was so intense that she could hardly help herself. Besides, despite the fact that she knew how he felt about her, Rachel loved to hear the sound of her husband's voice, and she loved to learn the things that seemed to flow so easily from his mouth when she wasn't near. Thus she urged her mount closer, keeping her eyes down but her ears busy in their task of listening—

They had now passed Lone Butte and crossed Cedar Ridge, and ahead and to their left the ragged edge of the cliffs broke away and dropped off eastward toward the patch of green now being called Pipe Springs. The sun hung low in the sky behind them, casting long shadows of men and horses across the sage and rabbitbrush through which they had been riding.

"Maybe there's a wildness in me, Thales," Samuel suddenly stated. "I have a love for the wind whispering through the dry grass, or the smell of woodsmoke in some lonesome rocky draw. Where other folks see desolation and wilderness, I see beauty and peace and solitude. There's a reaching in me for far-off places, and I can't seem to get shut of it no matter how I try."

Thales nodded but remained silent.

"I always have the feeling there's a promised land waiting for me somewhere out there," Samuel continued, pointing and then swinging his arm in a wide circle. "Not so much a place as something good I can learn or maybe do. I reckon I was born to look for it."

"I reckon I was, too," Thales said softly. "But I don't think we'll ever find it."

"I hope not." Samuel grinned. "I was born for the trail, not the hearth. I stay more'n a week or two at home, trying to act domesticated the way Amanda wants me to be, and

I get testy as a teased snake. We was born to discover, you and I, for the others who will come after us."

Thales nodded. "You're right. They'll live in a richer, more peaceful land, without the dangers we face. But we'll have made the trails, Samuel, and we'll have seen the land as God made it before folks have fouled it up."

"And they will," Samuel agreed. "You can certain bet on that."

Swinging his arm wide, Thales pointed at the wide expanse of wilderness through which they rode. "Yes, sir, Samuel, you'n me will have gone where the Indian goes, or the antelope or the wild sheep, and where few will ever be able to follow once we're done."

"More's the pity," Samuel declared softly, "for they'll never even know what they missed. They'll never be where the wind and sun and rain are their only companions. And they'll never hear the true songs of the earth, sung just as Rachel sings them every day of her life.

"Pa tried to hold me after Ma died, Thales, but I was too much like the Lamanite, with a yen inside me for the wide open, high-up lonesome. Whether it was the Tuscaroras I played with as a child, or the Sioux or the Shoshones or the Utes or the Paiutes or the Moquis or even the Navajos, there has always been in me that kinship, that feeling of brotherhood with them and the wind, that chokes me up with silence and fills me with awe. It ain't that I don't have a lot to say. It's just that I ain't been blessed with words powerful enough to say it."

In wonder Thales looked at his companion. "If you ain't," he said as he scratched at the back of his head, "then I'd like to meet the man who does."

Grinning, Samuel reached again to pat the neck of his horse. "Don't know where all that verbal lather came from," he stated apologetically, "especially since I ain't even winded. Speaking of talking to women, though, there's one thing I keep wondering."

"And that is?"

"How come it's so blasted much easier to talk to a horse?"

Thales chuckled. "Easier, maybe, but withal a whole lot less comforting."

Rachel found herself smiling at this, and in the midst of her smile, another cottontail rabbit erupted from beneath the feet of the men's horses. Knowing that it would add immeasurably to the supper she would be helping to cook, Rachel made the sign to Samuel that she would catch the small animal and bring it with her.

Calming his skittish horse, Samuel signed that he and Thales would ride on. And so, turning to chase down the rabbit, Rachel missed the part of the conversation she had most needed to hear.

"Samuel," Thales questioned as soon as they were alone, "does Rachel know you think of her as a woman?"

Suddenly serious, Samuel stared ahead. "I . . . don't reckon."

"You aiming to tell her?"

Slowly Samuel shook his head. "Wouldn't be fitting," he stated quietly.

"Why not?"

"She only married me out of obedience, Thales, so's we could fill this mission together. Beyond that she ain't got no interest in me."

Thales chuckled. "You truly think that. Then besides filling you with silence, all this sun and wind and blowing sand has made you blinder'n a cave-bound bat. The first time I ever laid eyes on her, almost exactly four years ago now, I could see that Rachel had set her woman's cap on sideways for you."

"That was a little-girl thing," Samuel stated with a wry

grin. "I knew it at the time and told her so. Now that she's growed up, things have changed."

Thales shook his head disgustedly. "Not likely. So far as I can see, the only thing changed is that you're married now, and you haven't yet told her you're happy about it."

"Have you talked to Amanda about this?"

"No. Why?"

"Well, she said the same thing just the other night," Samuel stated quietly. "She truly loves Rachel and figures I'm not doing right by her."

"Then when you going to repent?"

Miserably Samuel stared ahead. "I . . . don't rightly know. None of you seen the look on her face the night Elder Rich married us. I did, and it sure wasn't joyful. I'm telling you, Thales, she did not want to marry me!"

"But you did want to marry her?"

Samuel smiled. "I did, though I hadn't much thought on it until Brother Rich put the proposition to me. But lawsy, Thales. She's a good woman, and I mean downright, pure good. And bright? She palavers in English better'n I do, and she's always about two jumps ahead of Amanda and me in knowing what needs to be done around the place and how to do it. And poetic? You should hear her waxing eloquent on the beauties of nature or the foolishness of mankind. And I don't hardly know if I ever met a body what lived closer to the Spirit of the Lord than she does. She ain't got a guilty bone in her body, and she always does just exactly as she believes."

"Yep!" Thales grinned. "You're smitten, all right."

"I . . . I know. I wish I dared tell her how I feel. But I'm so plumb scared she'll think I'm foolish that I daren't say a word."

"She'd never do that."

Samuel chuckled. "Don't you believe it. That little gal says exactly what's on her mind, no matter who it is she's talking to. Come the end of this mission, she'll most likely tell me thank you and good riddance and not bat an eye. Tell you the truth, though. That ain't what I want."

"Have you asked the Lord for help?"

"Interesting you should ask that," Samuel declared as he lifted his hat and wiped the sweat from his brow. "Actually, I have been studying on it and praying that the Lord would give me some way of showing her how I feel. So far, though, he ain't seen fit to send me an answer."

"He will, just as soon as the time is right." Thales turned and looked back at the following group of missionaries. "They're about thirty minutes behind us," he said as he turned back, grinning, "at least if Rachel waits for them. And I reckon she will, since young George A.'s riding out to where she's after that rabbit. Samuel, you reckon that gives us enough time for a dip in yonder puddle?"

Samuel nodded, grinning. "Would be nice to get rid of some of this real estate I've been collecting."

And with a couple of wild whoops, the two men spurred their mounts up the final gentle slope toward Pipe Springs.

I'm telling you, I saw her do it!" young George A. exclaimed enthusiastically. "Sister Loper took that stick, stuck it down in the hole where that rabbit was hiding, gave it a twist or two, and out came the rabbit all wrapped up on the end of her stick. It was the slickest thing I ever saw!"

"Oh, come on," Jeheil McConnell scoffed. "I declare, George, your yarns are getting taller'n mine."

It was nearing dark at Pipe Springs, and the missionary party were ranged around where Rachel had directed that the fire be built. The animals were in a rope corral down in the trees, the wagon and boat were parked where they would make a windbreak, and the camp was as snug as could be expected. Yet the fitfully blowing wind, still hot and dry, served notice that the party needed to be concerned about where they were going to find water in the days to come.

"It's not a yarn, Brother McConnell," George A. protested, not realizing he was being teased again. "I swear it isn't! Tell him, Sister Loper! That's how you did it, isn't it."

Hiding her smile, Rachel kept her head down as she worked over the fire, pretending she did not hear. Actually the boy was right, for a cottontail rabbit's fur is loose, and a stick pushed against it and quickly twisted will capture the animal and bring it forth from its burrow nearly every time.

"She ain't answering," Isaac Riddle pressed with a smile, "because she's an honest woman. George, you're stretching things too much, and you know how your Pa feels about that. Next you'll probably tell us she slit the rabbit's hide with her knife and pulled it off entire, all in less'n a minute."

"That's right! That's *just* what she did. I never saw the like—"

"George," Amos Thornton laughed, "you keep this up, you'll be worse'n ol' Gun-locke Bill Hamblin, Jacob's brother."

"That's right," Thales chuckled. "You heard his latest whizzer? He's calling this place Pipe Springs now, on account of his claiming to have shot the bottom out of Dudley Leavitt's meerschaum pipe bowl a year or so ago while he was camping here. Fifty yards, he said it was, and that was with his handgun."

There was general laughter, and George A.'s face showed his relief that the scoffing was no longer directed at him.

"That was a certain lie, too," Samuel declared, his face serious. "I was here that day with ol' Bill, and he wanted to shoot that pipe out of Dudley's mouth. Bet Dudley fifty bucks he could do it, too. Of course Dudley wouldn't rise to the bet, not with the prospects of getting shot in the face looming so near. So Bill upped the ante and stuck the pipe in the rocks and fired away. Boys, it was sixty yards if it was an inch, and he holed that pipe square."

"Seventy yards," Francis Hamblin said quietly, "and it was dark when he did it. He told me so hisself."

Now everyone laughed, George could suddenly see what was happening, and he joined in with the rest of them.

"The food is ready," Rachel said then, interrupting the trend toward bigger and better yarns, and amid the general scrambling after Jacob had offered prayer, young George A. stopped near her.

"Sister Loper, how come you never stood up for yourself?"

Rachel smiled. "They were funning you, George. And please call me Rachel."

"All . . . all right . . . Rachel. I know they were funning me. But they weren't funning you. What you did was amazing. Truly I have never seen the like."

"It was nothing," Rachel stated modestly. "Only one of the ways of my people for getting *tab-oots*, the cottontail, out of his hole and into our bellies."

"*Tab-oots*, huh? How'd you know it wouldn't run?"

Smiling, Rachel filled George A.'s plate. "Because he is a timid little fellow," she explained as she worked, "too afraid to flee for his life. That is why he is mockingly called *tab-oots*, which means sun-killer."

"Sun-killer," George A. said with a questioning smile. "I don't think I understand."

"It is a long story," Rachel replied as she took for herself a plate of food. "Perhaps in a coming day there will be time to tell you the tale—"

"What's wrong with right now, after you eat?" the youth declared, his excitement obvious. "Hey, everybody, Sister Loper has a story for us after dinner, an honest-to-goodness Indian story!"

"No, I . . . I don't . . . " Rachel stammered, suddenly alarmed. "I am not *narro-gwe-nap*, I am not a storyteller."

"I'd like to hear it, ma'am," Francis Hamblin declared.

"So would I," Thales said with a smile. "Anything'd be better'n the foolishness these fellers try and pass off as truth."

"But . . . But I . . . couldn't . . . "

"Is this something that is sacred to you?" Jacob Hamblin asked then, his concern for the girl obvious.

"Oh, no! It is just that I . . . well, I fear that perhaps my words won't make sense."

Samuel, watching his young wife, knew suddenly that her fear was due to the fact that so many would be listening. Stage fright, his mother had called it. More than that, Rachel still felt herself to be less of a person than the whites among whom she had lived for so long. Perhaps if she could get used to talking more often with more people—

"Little One," he encouraged in Paiute after she had eaten in silence, "go ahead. Since we're in your *agunt*, your country, I think it would be a good thing if these men were taught a little about your people."

Noting bleakly that Samuel truly thought of her as Paiute rather than simply *pee-weun*, his wife, Rachel gave a sigh and nodded her obedience.

"If it is wanted," she said quietly, speaking in English, "I will make a telling concerning *tab-oots*, the cottontail."

"I want to hear," George A. declared immediately.

"So do we all," Jacob Hamblin agreed. "And Sister Loper, as you tell us your story, help us understand what made it an important story to the Paiute."

Rachel nodded while her mind raced to think of a way to do all that Brother Jacob had asked. How she loved the man, and how she respected him for his continual desire to understand all peoples, Indian and white. He was filled with such love, such concern—

"It is said by *narro-gwe-nap,* one who is a legend-keeper of my people," Rachel began, "that a long time ago, longer than the trees or even *timpi,* the rocks, can remember, the animals and the people who lived on *tu-weap,* the earth, all spoke the same language. They were ruled over by Tobats, who was the greatest God, and by his younger brother Shinob, who was the second greatest God, and who created the earth and all living creatures. Both of these Gods lived at Tobats-kan. Tobats was always old and sometimes cranky, and Shinob was always young and happy. Often Shinob ran errands for Tobats, and often he suggested ways for changes to be made that brought greater happiness to those who dwelt on the earth.

"Much time passed, and many changes were made that were good. But among the animals and the people, nothing was changed. Not their natures — not anything. They were allowed to think and do as they wished, and in that manner they learned many lessons."

"Can you give us an example?" Samuel asked quietly.

Rachel nodded. "One example I remember concerns *timpi,* the rock. In earliest times he had no name, but he could travel end over end and go wherever he wished. On the day when Tobats and Shinob found him, they laughed at him, for he had no shape, and then they gave him his name. But *timpi* was angry that he had been mocked, and he began chasing after Shinob, trying to slay him. Around and around the earth the rock chased Shinob, destroying many things as he passed, and no one could stop him. Finally, when Shinob was worn out and ready to drop down in despair, *y-bru-sats,* the nighthawk, came and began beating at *timpi* with her wings, slapping and slowing him down. This had such an effect that finally *timpi* broke in half at the spot where the nighthawk had repeatedly beat him with her wings. He was stopped at last, but Shinob, who was angry at the bad thing the rock had done,

207

took from him and his kind their ability to travel. He said that rocks must lie forever in beds and travel only when they were carried. If in anger they pull away from the mountains where they live, then they must break in pieces as they fall so they can no longer do what they tried to do to the God Shinob."

"So even rocks are considered living things?" Isaac Riddle asked.

"Oh, yes! And they are sullen and bad-tempered things, too. My people believe they must be handled with care or they will bring harm to all who disturb them."

"Well," Amos Thornton laughed, "that explains the stubbed toe I got last night. I should've been more careful how I moved that rock from under my bed."

"Yeah," Jeheil McConnell agreed. "You near hit me with it when you threw it aside, you big lummox."

All the men were laughing now, and Rachel was filled with the empty, hollow feeling that their mirth was a mocking of the things her people held sacred and dear. As she held herself from fleeing into the darkness, however, she identified one more stone in the wall of repression she was certain had been built to contain her.

"Do the Paiutes truly believe that everything is a living creature?" Amos Thornton asked, pressing the issue.

"Yes, everything. And because of this, everything is either a brother or a sister to the Nung-wa, the People, and so must be treated with respect."

"How do you treat a rock with respect?" Isaac Riddle continued.

"By being polite to it," Rachel responded.

"You mean your people talk to the rocks?"

Rachel smiled a little sadly. "Of course we do. We talk to all the creatures who inhabit this world. For instance, when we come to a pine-nut place, we talk to the ground and the mountain and everything. We ask to feel good and strong. We ask for cool breezes so we can sleep well at night. The pine nuts belong to the mountain, so we ask the mountain for some of its pine nuts to take home and eat. The water is the mountain's juice. It comes out of the mountain, so we ask the mountain for some of its juice to make us feel good and happy. Almost always the mountain is glad to oblige, and we come away from it with much food for the season of cold."

"You said almost always," probed Amos Thornton. "What happens if the mountain doesn't oblige you?"

"If for some reason the mountain is offended," Rachel responded, "then when we come for pine nuts the next season, there will be very few, and we will go away hungry. That is why we are always careful to be polite to all creatures. We wish for their friendship, not their enmity, so that we, too, can live well and in peace."

"Interesting, very interesting. If you talk to mountains and so forth, do they ever talk back?"

"Sometimes. But only if a person is willing to listen. If one does not believe, or does not take time to listen, then of course the creature will know it and remain silent."

"Makes sense," Francis Hamblin stated with a chuckle. "I know if somebody wasn't paying attention to me, I'd shut up in a hurry."

"It hasn't worked yet," somebody growled, and a wave of laughter spread around the fire.

"Say," George A. declared, interrupting the merriment, "we still haven't heard the story about the rabbit. Come on, Sister Loper, we're waiting."

With a small sigh Rachel looked at George A., who was only slightly younger than she was, and for whom she felt real affection. "All right," she stated without enthusiasm, "this is the story of *tab-oots* and why he is so timid."

In a soft and simple way Rachel then told the story of

the little cottontail who had set out to kill *tavaputs*, the sun, because it was so hot that all the other creatures were miserable. But the sun was wise and each day changed the place where he came up. When the little rabbit finally did hit him with an arrow, fire came out and burned nearly all the world, scorching the back of the rabbit's neck and turning his *kwa-sivi*, his tail, white. It was his tail that was made white, Rachel concluded, because that was the end of the cowardly rabbit that was facing the fire.

"There," Rachel declared when she had finished. "That is the end of my telling."

"That's a great story," George A. declared enthusiastically. "Tell us another!"

After much prodding Rachel began again, telling the tale of how the coyote's family left him, because he was cruel, to hide in the sky, where they became *poot-see*, stars, while the coyote, angry with them for leaving him, still howls up at them all night long. That was followed by the account of how *pah-ince*, the beaver, who was an arrogant and haughty fellow, lost all the hair from his beautiful tail and thus became a humble person. And finally, Rachel told of how *quan-ants*, the eagle, carrying on his back *to-wab*, the rattlesnake, to the great council of all the animals, was forced by the snake's tightly coiled body to walk all the way. Of course his head walked back and forth as much as his body did, for *quan-ants* is a stately fellow, and each time the head went back, the forked tongue of *to-wab* clipped off a feather. Thus when they finally arrived at the council, *quan-ants'* head was bald, and it has remained so ever since. Yet, because he suffered as a result of acting selflessly, he is still a very revered fellow and is much honored among all the people.

"I'll bet you have plenty more stories," George A. declared when Rachel had grown silent.

"There are a great many tales such as these that are

held in respect among my people," Rachel agreed. "As many, in fact, as there are lessons to teach or lessons to be learned."

"And your tales teach them well," Jacob agreed. "Brethren, as you can see, Sister Rachel's people used simple parables that concerned things they saw and understood to explain the deeper things of life that perhaps few will ever understand. I find it a thing of wonder that they teach in precisely the same way Jesus taught. Hearing tales such as these Sister Loper has told us tonight only reaffirms my belief that we are all children of the same great God, that the gospel was understood in this land as well as in Palestine, and that we are all watched over by his Holy Spirit."

For a moment there was silence, and Rachel found herself wondering why all the men didn't have the same feelings for her that Jacob had. More, why was it that Samuel Loper didn't feel that way? Why—

"I believe, once we get to the Moquis, that we will discover even further proof that our beliefs come from the same divine source."

"Brother Jacob," Rachel asked boldly in the brief silence that followed, "can you explain something for me?"

"Of course, Rachel. What is it?"

"For a long time I have wanted to know why you call the people of the high mesas Moqui."

"Because that's their name," Jacob replied, sounding a little confused.

"No, it isn't," Rachel stated with a shake of her head. "*Moqui* is a name given them by my father's people, the Diné. It is a name of derision, which means 'coward' or 'sissy.' "

There was a buzz of surprise around the fire. "Are you serious?" Jacob finally asked.

Quickly Rachel nodded. "The name was given them because they wouldn't come down off their mesas to fight."

"You see?" Jacob stated to no one in particular, "even their enemies recognize that they are the people of peace, just as the people of Ammon were. Cowardly, is it? Well, the people of Ammon certainly weren't cowards! Isn't it ironic that, even today, it takes more courage to avoid a fight than it does to take part in one?

"Rachel," he said then, turning back to the girl, "do you know their true name?"

"Yes," Rachel replied. "They call themselves Hopi, though I do not know the meaning of the name."

"Very well, that will come later. Brethren, from now on we will use the name *Hopi* in our conversations. I believe they deserve only our greatest respect. Do you approve of that, Rachel?"

Pleased, Rachel nodded. "I approve. I have loved the Hopi since they first gave Samuel the name Pu-am-ey."

The men laughed. "Pu-am-ey," Jeheil McConnell repeated. "Eagle-Who-Walks-on-the-Ground."

"I never did cotton much to that handle," Samuel stated self-consciously.

"Well," Jacob declared, laughing delightedly at his young friend. "Nevertheless it is a good name, for it describes you perfectly."

Samuel Loper grinned crookedly. "I reckon." Then he sat silently, his eyes staring off into the darkness, and the silence stretched out around the fire. *Waxots*, the frogs, cried continually from the nearby swamp, and then off in the trees *mu-u-pits*, the owl, made a talking.

Rachel, catching her breath, waited a moment. When the owl's talking was repeated, she turned and gazed at her husband, wondering. Then she felt her heart swelling again with the love-feelings she had carried for so many years.

212

Perhaps the Hopi had named him Eagle-Who-Walks-on-the-Ground, but to her, despite the fact that they could never be close to each other, no man could ever soar higher. In all the ways that showed a man to be true, he was like the eagle in flight, high and higher than all the others. What a lucky Paiute woman she had been just to know him. And what an unlucky woman she had been to have been born Paiute—

It is called *pahkk-kae-koh u'way,* the walking rain."

Rachel and George A. sat their horses on a slickrock outcropping overlooking the vast sweep of the distant Colorado River gorge and the desert beyond. It was afternoon, the hot wind was coming from first one direction and then another, and the only clouds in the sky were lying low and dark on the distant edge of the horizon.

"No kidding?" George A. was watching a sheet of virga, the tendrils of rain that trailed beneath the clouds, as it swept across the distant slickrock wilderness. "Walking rain. What a perfect name!"

"Among my father's people, the Diné," Rachel continued, "there is the Male-Rain, which brings with it thunder and lightning, and the Female-Rain, which is the gentle shower. When the two rains meet, as you see happening far off there in the west, then from their union will spring the green things of next spring."

George A. breathed deeply. "Rachel, I love it out here! I even love this awful heat. There is such a feeling of freedom that I can't begin to describe it. I want to sing, but I don't know the words—"

"There is a chant among my father's people," Rachel declared, "a song that is also a ceremony:

> Far as man can see,
> Comes the rain,
> Comes the rain with me.
>
> From the Rain-Mount,
> Rain-Mount far away,
> Comes the rain,
> Comes the rain with me.

Rachel paused, and George A. looked at her with wonder in his eyes. "I have never heard anything like that. Is there more?"

"Oh, yes," Rachel responded with a nervous laugh. "The chant is of lightning and thunder, of flying *pa-sof-piccli*, swallows, and growing corn, and it is meant to express gratitude to the Creator for his goodness."

"Do the Paiute people have such a chant?"

Rachel shook her head. "Chanting is not a thing my people do, except when we hold a cry for the dead. Yet we always give thanks, and I remember many times standing beside *pe-ats*, my mother, as she sang with reverence of the walking rain. I do not know where she got the song, for it was not of her people. But these are the words:

> Ho, you long-leg walkers.
> Ho, *Pah-cun-ab*
> Cloud-man with the
> walking rain.
>
> I thank you for the *pah*.
> I thank you already for the
> healing of the
> cracked-earth mesa.
>
> Ho, now my corn grows tall

Ho, now with *pah* the water
my corn grows tall
and brushes the feet of the
walking rain.

"Those were the words of her song, and after them
she would lift her face in gratitude to Tobats and Shinob
that they had once again healed our land and given us
food to eat."

"That's beautiful."

For more moments George and Rachel watched the
distant rainstorm sweep the horizon, the silence between
them a pleasing and comfortable thing.

"Rachel," George asked, his eyes still on the distant
storm, "may I ask you a question?"

"Certainly."

"Why are you so unhappy?"

Surprised, Rachel glanced at George A., and then
quickly away. "Why . . . do you say that I am unhappy?"

George A. shrugged. "I just see it, that's all. It's in
your eyes, mostly. Do you feel the same terrible feelings
that Jacob feels?"

"I . . . do not know," Rachel responded, her eyes also
on the distance.

"Sister Gibbons told me you're a real spiritual person,
so I'll bet that's it."

"*Imik a-pu-ani,*" Rachel said as she put her hand on
George's arm. "You are a good person, George. I think a
great deal of you, and I would answer you if I could. But
I do not know this thing. Perhaps what Jacob feels is a
part of it, or perhaps it is all of it. And perhaps the sadness
you see is different from anything that Jacob feels."

"Is it that you miss your people, Rachel? Won't they
let you go back to them?"

"I miss my people," Rachel responded after a moment's thought. "And it is true—I cannot go back. Yet it is not for the reason you suppose. I cannot go back because I am no longer the one who left. I have made changes they would not understand."

"They wouldn't accept you?"

Rachel smiled. "Oh, yes, they would accept me. But I could not accept them, or at least how they do certain things, think certain things, feel about certain things. Nor could I accept myself attempting to once again be like them. Besides, I am the wife of Samuel Loper."

"Yeah, I know. How come he never touches you or smiles at you or anything like that?"

Taken aback by the youth's boldness, Rachel did not know how to respond. She thought of an answer, rejected it in favor of another, rejected that one also, and then was saved by the distant shouts of some of the men with their party.

"Uh-oh," George A. declared as he wheeled his beautiful horse off the slickrock. "Sounds like trouble, Rachel. I'd better go help!"

With a click of her tongue, Rachel urged her horse down off the outcropping and onto the twisting path taken a short time earlier by the missionaries, following immediately behind George A. Outwardly she appeared calm, but inside, where all her feelings lived, Rachel was growing more frightened by the hour. And now the perceptiveness of young George A. frightened her even further. What would happen if any of the other missionaries saw her fears? Would she be sent back? Would she be given to the Diné? Or would she simply be left behind? Rachel did not know, but neither did she know how to stop the coldness that, despite the heat, was growing within her heart.

"You all right, Isaac?"

The voice was Jacob's, and even before rounding the corner of rock, Rachel could sense his exhausted concern.

217

"It isn't me," Isaac Riddle replied, his voice filled with disgust. "It's this consarned boat. She isn't going to make it around this fool corner!"

Coming abruptly on Isaac and his boat, Rachel and young George could see his plight. The steep trail, which was actually a twisting, narrow ravine filled with willows, simply did not leave room for Isaac's boat to negotiate the turns. The boat was too long, the wagon wheels were set too wide, and no one in the party had time to widen the cut so the boat could advance.

"You think we could dismantle it?" Amos Thornton asked as he came up from below.

"I could, at that," Isaac replied. "But it'd take most of a week to put her back together so's she'd be seaworthy."

"We don't have a week," Jacob responded quietly.

"How about pulling it back to the top and lowering it over the rim?"

"That's an idea," Jacob responded, acknowledging Jeheil McConnell's suggestion. "Thales, could it be done?"

Thales Haskell shook his head. "Not around here, it couldn't. The rim's too broken, and the drop to the bottom's way too far. We just don't have that much rope."

"Any other suggestions?" Jacob asked.

"I suggest we leave it," Samuel stated quietly. "We've crossed the river without a boat before, and I reckon we can do it again."

"Anybody else?"

Isaac Riddle sighed. "I'm with Samuel, Jacob. I made the boat especially for this trip, but its been nothing but trouble since we started, and I see no practical way of getting it to the water. If we can move it back off the trail and cover it with brush, then I reckon there's always another day."

Jacob nodded. "So be it. Boys, let's get this boat off the trail."

Quickly the oxen were unhitched and unyoked. Thirty minutes later the boat was in a side canyon covered with brush, and the entire party was again pushing their way down the willow-choked watercourse.

The descent was incredibly steep, terribly treacherous, and the toll it took on the already tired party was heavy. Yet they pushed forward, anxious to get on with the mission that was beginning to seem fraught with difficulty.

It had been a long trail, a lonely trail, and both people and horses were feeling the strain. From Pipe Springs they had made their way east and then southeast, following up Jacob's Canyon onto the Kaibab Plateau and some springs Jacob had dug out a few years before that were now being called Jacob's Pools. There, in the thick forests of ponderosa pine and quaking aspen, two men of Rachel's people had come to the camp and in return for food had agreed to guide them further east.

Descending from the Kaibab Plateau where it overlooked the desolate House Rock Valley, the party had immediately ascended again through the Vermilion Cliffs to the Paria Plateau. Like the Kaibab, the Paria, which meant "elk" in Paiute, was a mountainous plateau of wide open expanses interspersed with thick forest. Because it was lower, it was more arid than the Kaibab, but water had been sufficient and the missionaries had made good time. Now, however, the precipitous slickrock slopes and willow-tangled depths of Paria Canyon yawned ahead of them in surreal beauty, and with darkness coming, Rachel knew they were in for a dangerous time.

"We've got to get to the river before dark," Jacob stated as they paused on a high shelf for a brief rest. "Too much chance of losing a man or an animal on this trail, and we can't afford either one."

"You planning on crossing tonight?"

"I don't know, Francis. If the river's low, maybe. If it

219

isn't, well, even low the Colorado is dangerous water. If it's high, there just isn't any way we dare try it."

"I could do it," George A. declared. "Vittick and I could swim it easy."

Jacob smiled, as did several of the others. "We'll see, George. Most likely you could. But when we get to the river, we'll see."

For a moment then the party stood in silence, staring off into the dizzying distance. The steep ravine came to the shelf where they rested, which would have become a mighty waterfall during a rainstorm. But there the ravine ended in a cliff, and there was no obvious way to descend the next three or four hundred feet.

"We've been down this trail once afore," Thales stated as he looked around, "but I'll be dogged if I can remember exactly where it goes from here."

"Getting old, huh?" Samuel teased. "Well, boys, that Utah Indian showed us the lay of it not more'n a year ago, and since I ain't so old and decrepit as Thales, given a minute or two I reckon I can scare up what he showed us."

"Old!" Thales scoffed at Samuel. "I ain't so old as to tell that you couldn't scare up your own two hands on a moonlit night. I'll find the trail!"

"Both of you go ahead," Jacob agreed with a slight smile. "Samuel, you go left, Thales, you right. The rest of us will wait right here."

"Jacob," Amos Thornton said then, "it seems to me we went off over there to the left, but for some reason I'm like you and Thales. I can't exactly remember this part of the trail."

"I reckon the runoff last spring is what's changed things," Samuel said, looking around. "Let's just hope the trail wasn't destroyed."

Clicking his horse forward, Samuel rode left along the

shelf thirty feet or so to where it ended abruptly in a massive overhang of sandstone. Thales had ridden right, and Rachel, whose horse had followed Samuel of its own accord, watched as her husband reached the abutment and swung his mount toward the edge of the shelf. There he paused for a moment as if thinking, and then he looked up, grinning.

"I reckon this is it, boys," he called to the bunched party. "Leastwise it's something! If it ain't what I hope it is, well, it's sure been nice knowing you fine gentlemen. You too, Thales." And seconds later a smiling Samuel clucked his horse off the edge, and both he and the animal vanished.

With a sharp gasp Rachel urged her horse forward and was relieved to see her husband's hat vanishing below her field of vision. The animal she was riding reached the edge of the shelf, and only then did she see the lip of a narrow trail, leading downward. Abruptly Rachel's breath was stilled.

At her feet was an abyss of darkness, and around her were great fissured cliffs and upthrusts, an unbelievable jumble of stone now bathed in deep shadows and fading light. Awed, Rachel sat transfixed.

"Well," Jacob said as he came up behind her, paying no attention whatsoever to the surreal beauty of the scene, "we might as well get after it."

"She's not going to get any better," Amos Thornton agreed. "Let's do 'er!" And with that, he urged his horse past Rachel and over the lip of the gorge.

Following after him, Rachel clung to the saddle horn as her horse plunged down the almost unseen path, switching back and forth across the face of the cliff into the cool darkness below. Once, during a momentary pause, she glanced back up to see a thin tower of rock protruding far above her, looking for all the world like a great warning finger such as Rizpah Gibbons used when scolding her children. With a shudder Rachel turned quickly away, and as she listened to the distant but terrible roar of the river below, she knew the rock had been a warning, letting her know she would soon be in a land of swift and horrible danger.

Worse, she would essentially be in that land alone, and she had no idea what was going to happen to her!

Boys," Thales Haskell said, the urgency in his tone garnering everyone's attention, "we've got company."

After making the perilous descent into the canyon of the Paria, the missionaries had followed it downstream to the confluence of the Paria and Colorado Rivers. Now they were gathered in the almost eternal twilight of the deep canyon of the Colorado, the two rivers running as one before them, and the thunder of the pounding water reverberating from the monolithic walls looming overhead. But the river appeared unusually high, and it was obvious that rains somewhere upstream had created an unanticipated flood in the roiling red-brown waters.

George A. had again volunteered himself and his horse, Vittick, to try to cross, and a somber Jacob had just declared that he did not have good feelings about such a venture when Thales made his announcement.

Turning as one, the entire party watched as a group of horsemen rode down the sandbar toward them. And Rachel, her heart in her throat, was certain they were the feared Navajo.

"Samuel, can you tell who they are?" Thales asked quietly.

"Looks like Utes and at least one Apache—no, two. They're painted and armed, but the way that Apache's holding his rifle over his head, they ain't acting any too hostile. Reckon we'd better make a little *um-pug-iva*, a little medicine talk with 'em?"

"That's how I read it," Thales agreed. "Jacob, they're Utes and Apaches—sort of an unusual combination. But they look friendly, so I reckon we'd best palaver."

Jacob nodded. "Very well. Enos, go see what they want."

With a grunt of acknowledgement the Ute interpreter raised his hand in the universal sign of peace and nudged his horse toward the approaching group.

Rachel, still filled with the fear that now seemed never to go away, watched as the Utes and Apaches splashed their horses through a shallow portion of the river to come to a halt, clustered loosely about Enos. For several moments the conversation between the Indians went back and forth, their voices loud enough that they could be heard even over the continual roar of the water.

"Utes called Nahguts and others Enos not know," Enos declared after he had ridden back to the missionaries. "Apaches called Do-klini and Tubac."

"What are they doing here?" Jacob asked.

"Do-Klini say him allthesame mad at Navajo, maybeso him kill Navajo soon in big fight. Him say thousand Navajo warriors with Manuelito and Barboncito fight big fight at place called Fort Defiance in moon called *Sa-wha-mats-oits*, white man moon called April. Navajo not win, now heap mad, allthesame kill Apache, kill Ute, kill Mormonee, kill everybody. That why Do-klini come fight Navajo." Enos pointed to the rushing water. "Now river mad, plenty mad. Too much water now. Navajo one side, Do-klini other side.

224

Maybeso wait one moon till water not so mad, then go fight Navajo."

"Is he trying to tell us that the water is too high for us to cross?"

Enos smiled widely, nodding his head as he did so.

"Have they been waiting long?" Jacob asked.

"Some days, maybe many." Enos looked back at the Indians. "Do-klini say river smell like *dah-eh-sah* now, say it smell like death. Indians no afraid of Navajo bullets and arrows, even if whizz like mad bees, but fear angry water. They say Mormonee no cross, come camp with them."

Now Jacob looked at the Indians, who had been moving slowly closer. "They want us to camp with them?"

Again Enos smiled widely. "They see Rachel, call her *estune*. In 'Pache that mean mature woman, beautiful woman. Maybeso Do-Klini take Rachel, make wife. Maybeso Tubac take 'Lizabeth."

As Rachel's blood ran chill, Jacob nodded soberly. "Enos," he responded, "tell them the women are our wives. Thank them for warning us about the river. Tell them that we will be camping in our own camp."

Then Jacob turned to Isaac Riddle. "Isaac, break out some supplies and trade goods, and let's make sure these fellows leave happy."

Isaac did as he was bidden, and while Enos explained Jacob's words to the Utes and Apaches, who were now less than a dozen feet away, Samuel rode forward with the supplies. Though he understood very little Apache, he did understand Ute, and he could tell from what the Utes were saying that the Apache called Do-klini was much enamored with his wife Rachel.

For several moments the conversation went back and forth between Enos and Do-klini, Samuel listening silently and Rachel watching intently from a distance. Abruptly then it ended, and after Samuel had handed each of the men the supplies and trade goods he had brought forward, they turned and without a backward glance rode upriver.

"What else did Do-klini say?" Jacob asked as Samuel and Enos watched the departing riders.

"Him want Rachel heap bad," Enos replied, turning around. "That all."

"You told him no, of course."

"I make joke. I say Rachel wife of Pu-am-ey. I say Pu-am-ey fierce warrior, more fierce than all others. I say Pu-am-ey and Jacob make bad medicine. I say Pu-am-ey love Rachel, maybeso kill many braves keep her. Heap big joke."

Surprised at the man's words, Rachel glanced quickly at her husband. He was not smiling, but neither was he arguing with the Ute interpreter. Therefore were the man's words accepted. Samuel Loper did not love her and would not fight—

"What did he say to that?" Thales, who was smiling, asked then.

"Do-klini say *enthlay-sit-daou*. He say Enos is wise and calm person to warn him. Do-klini say thank you." Enos smiled again, widely. "I tell Do-klini it not any considerable thing I do. I tell him cover tracks of warning in his memory."

Thales and several of the others chuckled, and Jacob nodded with satisfaction. "Good," he declared. "Samuel and Thales, we'll set up camp back beyond those willows. You take charge. I noticed a level bench there, and away from the water a little, maybe we can hear ourselves think. Isaac, you bring the stock in and stake it tonight. We lost a beef here a year ago, and I don't want to lose another. Amos, you're cook, and Francis, you're tender. I don't want you boys throwing it off on the women, either. They've cooked nearly every night, and I want them to rest."

"What can I do?" George A. asked.

"You rest, too," Jacob declared, "and keep an eye out for those Indians. If you see any sign of them returning, I want to know about it.

"Boys," he concluded, "I don't know what to tell you to expect. Maybe the water will be lower in the morning, and maybe it won't. I suppose we'll just have to wait and see."

Then, as the party went to work, Jacob sighed heavily and turned his back to them. Slowly he walked downstream along the sandbar, his head bowed in thought, his spirits even heavier than before. And Rachel, watching him, knew there was trouble in her future, trouble she could do nothing to avoid.

It was a strange feeling, sitting with nothing to do, and soon her mind became so agitated with worry and fear that she arose and walked to the willows. With a knife she cut several willows of the same width, and these she quickly peeled and split. Then, while Eliza looked on, Rachel began coiling and plaiting them into the beginnings of a basket.

"Why do you do this thing?" Eliza finally asked.

"Mother Gibbons says that idle hands are the devil's tools," Rachel answered without looking up.

"Yes, and Priscilla Hamblin says that an idle mind is the devil's workshop," Eliza agreed. "Do you believe these white sayings?"

"I know I do not like my thoughts."

"If your hands are busy, do your thoughts go away?" Eliza was now speaking in Paiute.

Rachel shook her head. "Perhaps a little, but not enough."

"My thoughts do not go away even when I sleep," Eliza stated. "And I also have bad thoughts."

"Are they because of your father Jacob's thoughts?"

227

Rachel questioned without looking up. "Because he is troubled, is it so of you?"

"This I do not know. I know only that my heart is heavy with fear, and more and more I see that I am not a white girl like I had hoped to be."

Now Rachel looked up. "I did not think I would ever be a white girl," she said as tears came suddenly to her eyes. "But I did hope that one day I would be a person of worth to a husband."

"But . . . but you have a husband."

"That is so." Dropping her eyes, Rachel returned to her work on the basket, which was already taking shape.

"Rachel Iitats," Eliza pressed, slipping unconsciously into English, "I do not understand—"

"Neither do I," Rachel replied as she continued working on her basket. "Neither do I."

There's not much I dislike more than a dry camp." The speaker was Jeheil McConnell, and he was merely echoing the feelings of the other missionaries.

"Yeah," Amos Thornton agreed as he poked a small stick into the fire, "and two dry camps in a row can make a man mighty miserable."

"Or a horse. These animals of ours need water, and they need it bad."

"No worse'n I need to get shut of this rock in my mouth! Whoever said it helped a man from getting thirsty must've been touched in the head."

"Now, Amos, don't you go speaking disparagingly of that there pebble you're sucking on. After all, like the Paiutes say, it might be your little brother—"

Listening to the wry chuckles that followed, Rachel kept her hands as busy as possible. She did not want to listen! She would not take offense, not when so much depended on how she might respond. And so, swallowing her pain and anger, she made her hands work even harder.

She had finished her cooking basket and was coating

it with pitch she had gathered as they had passed through a small pinion forest. She was also doing her best to keep her eyes as well as her mind from wandering across the fire. For there, she knew, sat four old Navajos who had come up to them about two o'clock that afternoon, and who had been looking at her and discussing her ever since. The men showed no animosity toward her, yet they were Navajos, and her heart felt such fear toward the Navajos as a people that she was almost beside herself with terror.

The missionaries were camped in a small swale formed by shifting sand dunes, and their fire had been positioned as closely as possible to the base of *wah-ahp*, a lone cedar tree, which not only dispersed the smoke but diffused the light. Thus they remained hidden from more than a few yards away. Except for the fact that there was no water and little grass for the animals, it was a good camp, a safe camp, and Rachel knew that Samuel and Thales had chosen well.

"Is Jacob feeling any better about things?" Thales asked Francis Hamblin.

"Not so's you'd notice. He's off in the trees right now, he says standing guard. But he's praying, I reckon. Tell you the truth, boys, I haven't ever seen him like this. He's lower'n skunk smell in a well hole."

Thales stared into what was left of the tiny fire. "Well, I hope it isn't me he's getting those fluttering fantods about."

"He said it wasn't you, Thales, or any of the rest of us, either."

"A man can't help but wonder, the way he's acting."

"How would you act," Samuel asked, speaking for the first time since the evening meal, "happen you knew we were headed for disaster of some sort, and that the lot of us would see some serious hard times ahead?"

Thales smiled weakly. "I reckon I'd act about the same as he is, now you put it that way."

"That's how Jacob put it yesterday morning, just before we crossed the river."

"Well," George A. declared as he stood and stretched, "I meant what I said yesterday, too. No matter what comes, I will stick it to the last. That's what I came for."

Smiling at the youth who had become a close friend during the course of their journey, Rachel continued rubbing the pitch into the woven willow basket, sealing it so water could not possibly leak out. She knew it was silly for her to be going to such efforts when they had an ample supply of cooking kettles, but somehow she could not stop. Perhaps it did push back her fear. Perhaps it did help her control her thoughts—

"Maybe we should have followed these Navajos back to Spaneshanks," Isaac Riddle said, breaking the oppressive silence again. "After all, they seem friendly enough, and they said it was only fifteen miles to their camp."

"Some of our animals wouldn't have made it fifteen miles," Thales stated quietly.

"Not to mention we're on a mission," Jeheil added as he picked up a handful of sand and tossed it at the fire. "We start running from every fool threat somebody makes, we'll never get to the Hopis."

"Besides which, Isaac," Amos put in, "we had a discussion and all voted. You know the vote was to press ahead."

"I know," Isaac admitted dejectedly. "It's just that the thought of a bunch of Navajos waiting somewhere ahead to ambush and kill us doesn't do much for my digestion."

Samuel chuckled. "Or mine either. But we've always been protected so far, Isaac. Happen we really are attacked, which probably ain't too likely, well, I reckon we're just going to have to rely on the Lord again.

231

"Jeheil, is the livestock all hobbled and staked?"

"All except Vittick. George here just lets him roam about."

Samuel looked at young George A. "George, maybe you had ought to hobble that critter tonight. Navajos like horses, especially good ones, and I'd recommend you either hobble or stake that one of yours real close."

George A. smiled. "I'll stake him, Brother Samuel, and sleep on the rope."

"Good. Boys, since Jacob's not back, I'll volunteer to offer prayer. Then I reckon we'd ought to turn in."

As Samuel prayed, pleading for protection and wisdom, Rachel could not help but marvel. Her husband was a wonderful man, a very wonderful man. She loved everything about him, and she also admired everything about him. He was a man to make a woman proud to stand beside him. Only, he would not let her stand anywhere near him—

"You all right, Rachel?"

She and Samuel were lying in the darkness, the camp had settled down, and for some time Rachel had been trying to sleep. Yet sleep had not come, and now she rolled over and stared upward. "*U'way-ng wan-xkay-tu,*" she said by way of reply. "I think the rain is coming."

"It figures. It'll likely hit tomorrow, about the time we get to water."

"Most likely."

"So, you all right?"

Above her the stars glittered brightly in the cool desert air, and as Rachel looked at them, she suddenly felt terribly small and completely insignificant. There was so much of creation, so much for God to be worried about, and she was so small and unimportant—

"Rachel?"

Rachel knew she must answer her husband, of course.

232

But what could she say? If she spoke of her fear, he would mock her. And if she lied and told him all was well with her, then she would be better off not to answer at all. Still—

"The reason I was asking is because Eliza's so frightened. Jacob says she has some fool notion she's going to be taken by the Navajo and murdered or something. You know anything about that?"

"I know Eliza . . . fears . . . the Navajo."

"Do you?"

"I fear . . . something."

"But why?"

Rachel took a deep breath. "I do not know. Perhaps I fear Peokon, who has a terrible hatred for me."

Samuel chuckled. "Rachel, that was years ago. Besides, the chances of running into your brother are mighty slim."

"I know those men who sleep yonder come from the camp of my father."

Samuel leaned up on his elbow. "Who told you that? I thought you couldn't speak Navajo."

"My father taught me a few words, and I heard them speak his name."

Lying back down, Samuel stared upward. "Well, you're right about that. It seems old Dah-Nish-Uant, or Spaneshanks, sent them here to warn us. But that don't mean your brother's around. Ornery as he is, like as not somebody's already put an arrow or a bullet through him and put him out of all our misery."

Rachel considered that idea for an instant, wondering how she would feel if it were true, and then her husband continued, capturing her thoughts again.

"Rachel, there just ain't no call for you to be worrying. Like as not nothing's going to happen. And if it does, well, I'll take care of you. Amanda'd never forgive me if I didn't."

There was a chuckle in Samuel's voice, and Rachel

233

nearly wept it made her feel so bad. What was it about her, she wondered, that was so undesirable to this man? Why could he not see that he held her heart in his hands, and that it was a wondrous thing to hold? Why could he not see the depth of feeling she had for him, her love that had lived for so many long and lonely years?

Yes, he would try to care for her, but not because she meant anything to him. No, it was because she meant something to Amanda. But not him, not the man called Samuel Loper!

Bitterly Rachel rolled to her side, facing away from her husband, and when, moments later, she heard his heavy breathing, she stole from her bed and climbed to the brow of the nearest sand dune.

"Oh, Great Father," she pleaded as she huddled next to a small outcropping of rock, "give this foolish woman understanding. Thou hast given her all that she has asked, and yet she feels so lonely and miserable. How can such a thing be? Wilt thou please help her to understand?"

For long moments Rachel crouched next to the boulders, waiting. Above her a meteorite streaked across the night sky, and out in the desert a lone coyote yipped and cried his anger and distress that he had been left alone. Near her, Jacob suddenly materialized out of the darkness, making his way silently back to the camp, and Rachel almost called out to him. Yet she did not, for the man was already burdened enough, and quickly he was past and she was alone again with the night. Of course, Enos was still somewhere on guard, but he had grown so frightened when he had learned of the Navajo plot to attack and kill them all—

Shuddering at the thought, Rachel closed her eyes tightly against it, waiting for the answer she was sure God would send her, the understanding of her own misery she had pleaded for. Yet nothing came, and after a time she knew that nothing would. She was alone, truly alone, and there was no one she could turn to, not even the Great Father in the sky—

The deseret night was suddenly alive with movement, and Rachel's head came up with a jerk. Her eyes were wide and staring from her position on the brow of the dune, and her ears were tuned to the smallest sounds imaginable. Nothing moved, yet there was a stirring in the night around her, a whisper of sound across the dunes that was not of wind or coyote passing.

Perhaps it was her imagination. Rachel did not know. Yet she was certain she had heard a horse's hoof click ever so faintly against stone. Then a saddle creaked, or maybe a bridle chain jingled. She was sure of it. Somewhere wiry brush scraped on wool blanket, someone sighed, and a restless horse tried to nicker and was cut off. They were small sounds but different sounds, and suddenly she knew that the missionary company was not alone.

With a gasp of fear, Rachel turned from the rocky outcropping and slid down the dune. Then, as quickly as possible, she buried herself in the bedding next to her sleeping husband, getting as close to him as she could without waking him.

Samuel had told her that he thought her brother might be dead. But no, the evil Peokon was alive, and Rachel knew it. She could feel it in her heart. More, he was out there in the night, somewhere close—

Rachel," Samuel called, his voice low in the morning stillness, "hold up. Your pack's loose, and happen we don't
do some tightening you'll soon be losing it."

Obediently Rachel drew rein and dismounted. Then,
while Samuel tightened her cinch strap as well as the pack
behind her saddle, she stretched her back and glanced
around.

It was November 1, 1860, and they had been riding
since early morning. Hopeful of reaching water by noon,
Rachel knew they must be close. Of course she had no
real idea of where the water was, but the animals had
quickened their paces, and that was always an indication.

Clouds were building overhead, dark and ominous,
and in the gusty wind the temperature was starting to
drop. Rain would be good, Rachel thought, though it was
too bad it had not come sooner. The animals were truly
suffering, and the pebbles she and the others were holding
in their mouths did little to slake their own thirst.

For some time they had traveled through sand dunes,
a slow and laborious trek, but now they had emerged into

more open country, and the going had improved. As she looked across the vast and apparently empty desert, Rachel stretched again and wondered at the surreal beauty of the land. Except on certain low, cedar-studded hills, trees appeared almost nonexistent, and even the grass clumps were scarce. Instead it was a land of sand and rock, scarred by wind and tempered by heat and cold. Here and there the ground was broken by deep ravines or arroyos, and the only relief for the eyes was from low mesas that lifted slightly against the skyline.

Working their way south down Cornfield Valley and between Cedar Ridge and the Echo Cliffs, the missionaries had climbed what would be called Hamblin Wash southeastward to where it headed into Hamblin Ridge. Crossing that they had come upon the multicolored Moencopi Wash, which they had followed eastward to the Blue Wash. This wash skirted the vast bulk of Black Mesa, which yet lay before them, and would lead finally to the sky-brushing pueblos of the people that called themselves Hopi.

Now Rachel breathed deeply of the sharp desert air, wondering that she had felt such fear the night before. All was so peaceful now, and the country appeared so open that there could not possibly be danger.

"You all right, Samuel?" Jacob's voice sounded his concern.

"As ever. Rachel's pack was loose, and I'm just tightening these cinch straps while we're stopped."

"Well, don't get behind, folks. It's too quiet around here, and I don't have a good feeling—"

"*Kiiiiyeeeee!*"

The completely unexpected Navajo war cries were both shrill and unnerving, and as Rachel and Samuel spun toward the heart-stopping noise, Rachel's horse bolted. Vainly she reached for the reins, missed, and then stood frozen, staring as a large band of Navajo warriors burst from a nearby ravine and swept in a thunder of pounding hooves toward the dismounted couple.

For Rachel, time seemed to slow down, giving her the ability to see everything in excruciating detail. Samuel was trying to mount his horse, which, frightened and skittish, with eyes rolled back so only the whites were visible, was sidestepping away from him. Her own horse was buck-jumping down the line of missionaries, and both Amos Thornton and Jeheil McConnell were attempting to capture the animal. Jacob was shouting something as he and Isaac Riddle tried to calm the pack animals, though she could hear nothing of his words. Enos was sitting stock-still, his face sick with fear, and young George A. was simply sitting astride Vittick, staring in open-mouthed amazement, still too startled to react.

The Navajos, and there were at least thirty of them, were bearing directly at her. Dressed much as the Apaches at the river had been, their faces were painted, and each of them had a single eagle feather in his hair. For weapons they carried bows, arrows, war clubs, and a spear or two. There were also a few guns, though these were strangely silent, and Rachel found herself wondering why. Yet the very fierceness of their charge caused her breathing to stop and her heart to feel as though it would burst from her chest. Never had she been so frightened, so absolutely unable to move or cry out.

Onward the warriors of the Diné came, whooping and screaming and brandishing their weapons in threatening, frightening gestures. It was uncanny how the morning, so calm and still only seconds before, had been so quickly transformed into a time of terror by the cacophony of sound. Yet it had, and Rachel's mind labored to comprehend exactly what was happening.

Suddenly her attention was captured by one of the warriors, a leader who rode a fine, dark-gray pony with long legs and flaring nostrils. Bearing down upon her, the rider, whose mouth was closed in silence and whose dark eyes burned with hatred, pulled slightly ahead of the others. Then his weapons were switched to his left hand, he was leaning out and reaching with his right, and abruptly Rachel knew he meant to carry her away.

She wanted to scream but couldn't, she wanted to run but found her legs unable to move, and she could not remember when she had taken her last breath. In numb horror she stared as the silent, painted warrior came at her, and even in the fractions of seconds during which this was happening, she was still aware that Jacob was shouting instructions and that her husband was still trying to get his foot into the stirrup of his skittish, shifting horse.

And then in a cloud of dust, the warrior brought his pony to a rump-sliding halt before her. Instantly his free arm was around Rachel, around her neck and under her arm, and as she was being pulled from the ground she found herself staring into the hardened face of Peokon, her anger-filled older brother.

Instantly galvanized into a frenzy of activity, Rachel began fighting and kicking, doing her best to resist. Yet Peokon's arm was like an iron band, and despite her efforts she could feel herself being drawn across the withers of the gray pony.

Peokon was kneeing the animal to steady it, and he and Rachel were concentrating on each other, glaring at each other. Yet though Rachel recognized him, there was no sign of recognition in the man's eyes, no indication that he knew the identity of the woman he was intent on capturing. There was only the grim, silent hatred and fierce determination that he would not be thwarted in the thing he wanted.

Rachel could see this, and with despair she knew there was nothing she could do to stop it, nothing at all. She had been captured by the feared Peokon, and soon she would be killed, or worse —

And then suddenly her husband was there beside her. Somehow Samuel had mounted his horse and pulled it alongside the gray pony of her brother. But more, Rachel could see his face, and though for some reason she could not hear what he was shouting, she knew his fiercely shouted words were filled with a great and terrible anger.

But why —

And then, with a move so swift and sudden that Rachel could not believe it and even Peokon could not react, Samuel Loper lifted his quirt. With a cry and a vicious slash, he brought it forward and down, the double-thonged leather end opening wide the cheek of the startled Navajo warrior. Blood spurted forth, and as the man gasped in surprise and reached his hand from Rachel to his face, the frightened woman threw herself from the gray war pony to sprawl unceremoniously on the hard ground.

As Samuel's horse pranced around her, seeming to protect her, Rachel watched as her husband raised his quirt again. Peokon, his eyes burning with hatred, hurriedly backed away, and then Samuel leaned down and lifted Rachel quickly to a seat behind him.

"Hold on," he ordered brusquely, and with a jab of his spurs he sent his mount digging forward, back toward the missionaries. And Rachel, still somehow comprehending even the tiniest details of what was happening, saw the four old Navajos from her father's camp jabbering excitedly as they pointed their fingers at her and Samuel. She saw the awe and wonder in the face of young George A. Smith. She saw Jacob and the others bringing the pack animals to order. She saw her own horse being led toward her by Jeheil McConnell. She saw the enemy warriors milling uncertainly and then abruptly retreating into the wash from which they had emerged. And she saw finally that her arms were wrapped around her man.

Yes, they were wrapped tightly and most comfortably around the body of her husband —

Samuel, you and Rachel all right?"

"We're fine, Jacob," Samuel responded. Rachel was already off Samuel's horse and back onto her own skittish mount.

"Thank goodness." The relief in Jacob's voice was obvious, and Rachel knew he had been as concerned for her as he had been for her husband.

"Glory be!" George A. declared excitedly as he rode up, "that Navajo was trying to capture you, Rachel!"

"I . . . I know."

"But ol' Brother Samuel let him know what was what, all right. Did you see that, Rachel? Faster'n greased lightning he quirted that man in the face." George's animation echoed his enthusiasm. "I'd have dropped you, too, happen I'd been cut like that. Boy, oh boy, I'll bet that ol' Indian doesn't try that trick again!"

Still excited, George A. rode off, and Rachel sat still, trying to ease the fire that still burned in her lungs. She didn't think Peokon had recognized her, but she knew he would be back, and she knew the cut from Samuel's quirt would only fire his determination.

"Samuel," Jacob said, "you watch over Eliza and Rachel. Thales, didn't you tell me you had found a table-land somewhere around here with good graze and water and a narrow passage to it that could be easily defended?"

"I did, Jacob, last spring after my winter with the Hopi. It's off that way not more'n two miles."

"Very well. You're in charge of leading us to it. If we're attacked we can do better there than we can here in the open. Now everybody get going! Enos, in case they want to talk, you're taking up the rear with me."

As the frightened interpreter reined in beside Jacob, Thales signaled the remainder of the missionaries to fall in behind him. Her heart still beating wildly, Rachel did as she was instructed, following her husband. And as they rode away, bunched tightly together, Rachel looked back to see the Navajos gathering quickly and following after them. Only there were more even than before, seventy, maybe even a hundred warriors, and it didn't take an interpreter to understand that they were bent on mischief. Nor did it take an interpreter to understand that the long-legged gray pony ridden by her brother was moving out in front of the others.

They made a strange caravan, the missionaries and the Navajos. In the vast gulf of the threatening afternoon, all the animals were walking. Rachel and her group formed one tightly knit bunch, then came a sort of no-man's-land of fifty to seventy-five yards, and then came the larger group of Navajos, which was being continually augmented by riders drifting in from almost all directions. Nor did the Navajos seem in a hurry to catch up. They simply followed, silently, menacingly.

In front of her, Rachel could hear Eliza weeping fearfully, and she knew how the younger Paiute girl felt. Despite the fact that Samuel had saved her from the grasp of the evil Peokon, she knew that nothing had changed, nothing had ended. All of them were in terrible, fearful danger, she and Eliza most of all. It was now obvious that the Navajos wanted her, and the next time they attacked, Samuel Loper might not be so fortunate or so willing to risk himself.

Her heart hammering with a fear that would not go away, Rachel turned once again to look back. The war party was now impossibly large, and she knew abruptly that the missionaries were in the Navajos' power. They could not escape, and they were so outnumbered that even the thought of fighting seemed silly.

Suddenly one of the Navajos spurred his horse into a gallop, and instantly Jacob and Enos drew rein.

"Nobody else stop," Samuel shouted from directly behind Rachel. "Just keep moving, slow and easy. Thales, how much farther?"

"A half mile at the most," Thales called from the front of the group. "You got any ideas?"

"Not hardly. Yourself?"

"None worth more'n a pinch of snuff in a high wind. You keeping your eye on Jacob and Enos?"

"As ever." Samuel turned again and looked back, where the single Navajo who had galloped ahead was riding beside Jacob and the interpreter, shouting and gesturing with his weapons.

"Rachel," Samuel stated, his voice calm but firm, "if I have to stop, you take care of Eliza, you hear?"

Nodding her understanding, Rachel nonetheless felt herself grow cold with terror. How could she possibly care for Eliza when her own mind was so numb with fear? How could she—

Overhead the clouds continued to grow ever more dark and ominous. From the rocks ahead of them a raven called out, twice, and then lifted on sleek black wings to sail over their heads. With a shudder Rachel watched the spirit bird, a bird that brought omens of bad things to come. She was being warned of those things, she knew, for they would be done to her. They would be done to her and Eliza! Only for some reason she could not understand the words of the raven.

In the distance there was a brief flash of lightning, but it was so far away that Rachel could hear no thunder. Still, the storm was threatening, and if it hit they would be caught out in the open.

"Jacob's coming!"

Glancing back, Rachel saw that the Navajo had returned to his war party, and that Jacob and Enos were trotting forward. Yet they were taking their time and seemed in no particular hurry to catch up.

Suddenly Rachel realized that the missionary party was climbing. They were in the rocks, and the trail had narrowed to where not more than two horses could ride abreast. Jacob and Enos still followed behind, though they were drawing closer. The Navajos seemed to have slowed and from a distance appeared to be arguing with each other.

"All right, brethren," Thales finally shouted from somewhere up in front, "such as it is, we're here. Jeheil, you, Francis, and Samuel are the best shots, so get up into the rocks with your rifles. Isaac, you and Amos and I will hold these animals together and keep our eye on these four old fellows from Spaneshanks' camp. I reckon now we'll learn how much they really are our friends. Rachel, you and Eliza will have to help with the stock. You up to that?"

"I . . . think so."

"Good. I don't know what's coming, but if we all stick together—"

"Brother Haskell, what can I do?"

Surprised, Thales turned to young George A. Smith. "Mercy, boy, I most forgot about you. Why don't you and Vittick wait there where the trail comes out of the rocks. If you see trouble, or if Samuel signals to you, raise some dust and come tell me about it. You got that?"

George A. grinned. "You bet! Vittick and I will do it just right."

Wheeling, George A. was just starting to ride away

when Jacob and Enos emerged from the narrow pass and rode toward the group. Jacob's face was grim, and Rachel could not tell what Enos was thinking.

While Samuel scrambled into the rocks to keep watch, Jacob gathered the remainder of the party together.

"Boys," he said finally, "it doesn't look very good."

"They after scalps?" Amos asked.

"Well, from what Enos can tell, there are a couple of issues. First and foremost is that they don't want us doing any more trading with the Hopi. If we trade with the Navajos' enemies, then we become enemies to the Navajo ourselves."

"So, do we go on?"

For a moment Jacob dropped his head. "No," he stated finally, looking back up, "I don't think we do, at least not just yet. They've pretty well got us boxed, boys. We might make it, but our Lamanite brethren don't seem peacefully disposed, and I truly fear that we'd lose men, good men, in a fight we couldn't win no matter how it came out.

"No, I think the answer is to stop right here and trade our goods with the Navajos. Let's make friends with them and let the Lord soften their hearts a little. Then we'll see what presents itself."

"You said there were two issues," Francis stated then. "What's the second one."

Bleakly Jacob looked at his brother, and Rachel could sense that he was loathe to say what was coming. And suddenly, as surely as she was sitting there astride her horse, Rachel knew the second issue. She knew that she and Eliza were the subjects of the council between Jacob and the Navajo spokesman, and she knew that they were to be sacrificed for the good of the party. And Jacob's

words, spoken quietly into the still air, were absolute ver-
ification.

"They want the women," he stated quietly and with
deep finality. "If we give them up, maybe they'll let some
of the rest of us go."

Instantly Eliza was wailing in terror, and though Rachel remained silent, her tears were falling, and her heart seemed turned to stone.

In the distance but closer now, lightning flashed and thunder was rumbling. For an instant they were struck by a quick flurry of raindrops, but then it passed, racing over the small tabletop of the mesa and away. No one was really wet, but the smell of freshly wet earth was in the air, and Rachel wondered how such a clean, fresh scent could exist in the midst of such fearful circumstances. In flashes of lightning, she could see boldly illuminated the fringe of rocks where her husband lay hidden, and suddenly she wished he was beside her, hearing this, somehow stopping it from happening. Yet he was not, nor would he stop it if he were there. Abruptly she knew that, and the very thought turned her cold. Worse, with the exception of Jacob, these other men, who felt no ties at all to her and Eliza, would also turn them over—

"What'd you tell 'em?" Thales asked.

"I told them Rachel and Eliza were our wives," Jacob

said. "I know that's only partly true, but just as Abraham told Pharaoh that his wife was his sister, I felt justified in doing the same about Eliza."

"How did they take that?"

Jacob shook his head. "They said they'd let the husbands live, which means Samuel and me, but that the rest of you would have to die. Of course that's nonsense, but—"

"Company," George A. shouted as he rode wildly up to the group. "Samuel says there's two of 'em."

"Let them come in," Jacob said as he turned back. "Thales, let's get this camp set up. If we're going to do some trading, let's make it look official."

In short order the camp was established, fires were lit, meals were set to cook, and under heavy guard the stock was led to the spring to water. Meanwhile under Jacob's direction, the remaining men placed themselves strategically about the camp, their weapons evident, and Rachel and Eliza were made busy with the camp chores.

"Maybeso Navajo say him want trade," Enos said after the two warriors had ridden in and conversed with him at the edge of camp.

"Tell them they are welcome in the camp of their friends," Jacob replied quietly. "Tell them we are here representing the Great Spirit, who has declared that all men are brothers. In peace we welcome our brothers the Navajos."

Enos translated this to the best of his ability. Then the two Navajos nodded and, with slight smiles that looked evil to Rachel, took their places beside Jacob near the fire. Slowly then, and with dignity, Jacob took from the packs some of the trade items, which he presented to the two as gifts. They had come bearing blankets and silver items, but as darkness deepened it became apparent that they were not so much interested in trade as they were in re-

ceiving outright gifts. Yet in perfect calmness Jacob dealt
with them, with trembling limbs Rachel and Eliza fed them,
and finally, still smiling their thin smiles, the two mounted
and rode off the mesa and into the darkness.

"Navajo him heap mad," Enos volunteered as soon as
the men had gone. "Maybeso trade, allthesame fight, take
women, kill Mormons. Navajo him heap mad."

"What they so mad about?" George A. asked.

"Enos not know. Maybeso Jacob pray, him know."

"I have prayed, Enos," Jacob responded quietly, "and
I don't know much of anything."

"Navajo say him no kill Mormons if Mormons give
ammunition to Navajo. Maybeso trade plenty tomorrow.
Trade ammunition, trade women, no kill Mormons."

Not noticing the terror on the faces of Rachel and Eliza,
Jacob shook his head. "Boys, it seems to me our mission
needs to be brought to a conclusion right here. I think all
hope of reaching the Hopi is past. All in favor of trading
everything we have with the Navajos and then going
home, say aye."

There was a chorus of ayes.

"Any feel inclined to try and break through to the
Hopi?"

There was silence around the campfire.

"Very well, I feel justified in my decision to turn back
tomorrow after we have done some trading. I'd leave now,
tonight, but I feel we need to establish some sort of friendly
basis with these people. Otherwise we'll be fighting them
every time any of us ever tries to cross their land again."

"Not to mention we'd have to fight them all tonight."

Jacob nodded. "That's right. I truly feel our best chance
is by treating them as friends, trading with them."

"Do you think they'll really trade?"

"I do," Jacob replied. "They've given their word that
if we trade with them, we won't be harmed."

253

"Their word?" Amos questioned. "How can we trust people who are after our scalps?"

"What choice do we have?"

Quietly the men talked this over, and then from the group came another question.

"What about the women?"

Jacob looked up at the man who had spoken. "What do you mean?"

"Well, it's obvious the Navajos want them. And since the women are Indians like them, maybe we should consider giving them up."

Her heart pounding once again, Rachel stared in horror at the man who had spoken. There it was, the thing she had feared and even known from the very first. She and Eliza were only conveniences, worthless creatures who would be bartered or abandoned when their continued presence was no longer of value. They could expect no more! They could—

"It's a good thing Brother Samuel's up in the rocks instead of here listening to you," Thales Haskell stated, looking nowhere but into the fire. "He's not so peaceful as Jacob here, and I don't think he'd take kindly to such remarks about his wife."

"Say, I was only trying to—"

Jacob gave a deep sigh, and the man grew silent. "Suppose," Jacob said, calling the man by name, "some white feller from St. Louis came through the Santa Clara country and demanded your wife or daughter. Suppose he even threatened to kill you if you didn't hand them over, and he had half a hundred men to back him, all mad as hornets and armed to the teeth. Would you give them up?"

"Well, no, I wouldn't. But this seems a little different—"

"When you figure out *how* it's different, you be sure

and come tell me. I'd be beholding to know. Until then, I'll hear no more of this."

There was silence around the fire, and Rachel stood as though she had been struck dumb. Oh, she appreciated Jacob's comment, but she had always known how he felt toward her. On the other hand, the remark made by Thales Haskell had truly set her heart to beating. Would Samuel truly defend her as Thales had said? Even against his own people, would he—

"Jeheil," Jacob was continuing, "you get up in the rocks with Samuel and take first watch. I'll take second with Amos. Thales, you and Francis take last watch. Isaac, you and George A. watch over the women, and don't both of you sleep at once. So far as I know, there's only one trail into this place, but with maybe a hundred warriors out there, any number of them might take a fool notion to sneak in on us. Any questions?"

"I have one."

"What is it, George?"

"Do you think we'll have a fight?"

"I don't know, George, but I hope not. I certainly don't want a fight."

"Why not? These are bad people. I was thinking of how the Israelites had to go in at the Lord's command and wipe out the wicked inhabitants of the promised land. Maybe a few of these Navajos, like that fellow Brother Loper quirted, need the same treatment."

Jacob smiled. "Well, once a few years ago I figured another Indian I knew, a fellow by the name of Old Big Foot, needed killing. I set out to do it and got my chance. But when my gun misfired several times, and when Old Big Foot couldn't hit me at close range with half a dozen of his arrows, I concluded that the Lord did not want me shedding the blood of the Lamanites, or them mine. Instead I determined that I was to be a messenger of peace to them. Since then it has been made manifest to me by the Holy Ghost that if I would not thirst for the blood of the Indians, I would never fall by their hands. So far, you can see that I have not."

"Wow," George A. breathed, "that's wonderful. So you don't fear the Indians?"

"Oh, I fear what they can do, all right. We all do, George. We fear that, and we respect them. But I also love them, and so I have no fear for my own life. Do you understand the difference?"

Soberly George A. nodded. "I think so. I was going to tell you I wasn't afraid to fight if it came to it. But now let me say that I won't be afraid to love these Lamanite brethren like you do. And I'll try, Jacob. I surely will."

Jacob smiled. "I'm certain you will, George." Then he turned to Rachel and Eliza. "Sisters," he said gently, "put your hearts at ease. We'll take care of you, and so long as there's a breath of life left in my body, you'll be protected."

The words had the ring of truth to them, and Rachel knew that Jacob meant every word he said. But none of the others said a thing. And hours later, as Rachel tossed restlessly inside the tent she and Eliza were sharing, she was still unable to feel peace.

Was it possible that her husband truly cared for her? Was it possible that she was indeed a person of worth to him? In a marvelous and forthright manner he had risked his life to save her from her evil brother. She could not forget that, could not get it from her mind. And though she didn't understand enough of their words to make sense of them, even the old Navajos had obviously approved of what Samuel had done. Yet he had said nothing about it since, and he had made no further effort to touch her or hold her or console her in the midst of her great fear. She didn't understand that, for among the whites such affection was common. That he had shown none could only mean she had been right all along. She was not worthy of Samuel Loper's love. At least that was how she had been thinking. But now, she thought as she yawned sleepily, Thales Haskell had set her mind to racing again—

Dawn was in the sky when Rachel awakened, but the horizon was dark with thunderheads and crisscrossed with vivid, nearly continual lightening. A dampness in the air warned of the coming storm, and Rachel shivered in the early-morning cold.

"Rachel, are you awake?"

"I am, Eliza. Are you *spur-ay*? Are you cold?"

"No, but I . . . am frightened."

"Don't be frightened. It is only the storm. See? *U'way-ng wan-xkay-tu*, the rain is coming."

Momentarily blinded by a sudden flash of lightning that struck somewhere near, Rachel and Eliza lay still, awaiting the crash of thunder. It came, and with it, the rain.

It came with a roar and a rush. Lightning crashed and the smell of brimstone was in her nostrils and thunder rolled and reverberated against the rocks that rimmed the mesa. "*Ur pa-at-wan-an un-vai*," she whispered as Eliza cowered against her. "That was a long thunder."

Eliza responded only by weeping, and so as Rachel held her and tried to comfort her, the rain swept across the sparse meadow in driving sheets. And then, through the downpour, Rachel noticed her husband. He was seated before the smoldering and sputtering fire beside Jacob, water cascading from his hat, and the two were staring silently before them, both apparently lost in their thoughts.

Rachel crouched beneath the shelter of the canvas tent, Eliza trembling next to her, and waited. The rain, having expended its first violence, gradually diminished until it was only a trickle. However, thunder rumbled menacingly in the distance, and the sky was low and gray, the clouds swollen with rain that could let loose again at any moment.

And it was then that the Navajos, or most of them, anyway, came silently to the trading fire.

Navajo want ammunition. Say him want heap more."

"No," Jacob replied quietly, "no ammunition. We'll trade anything else we have spread out, but no ammunition."

Enos translated, and there was a murmuring of discontent about the trading fire. The clouds had lifted somewhat, and the trading had been going on for most of the morning. Twenty or more Navajos sat around the fire, with that many more standing behind them, watching. Rachel and Eliza were in the tent, keeping out of sight as much as possible, and Thales and Jeheil had taken the horses down to water. George, Isaac, and Amos were seated at the fire beside Jacob, and truthfully it seemed to all concerned as if things had gone remarkably well.

Overhead a vulture circled against the lowering sky, a solitary speck in the wide expanse of eternity. Rachel watched it, thinking of what it must be seeing, thinking it was only awaiting the death of something below—

"George," Jeheil McConnell said quietly, coming up behind the young man. "Your horse took off."

"What?"

"We were driving them back from water, and Vittick took a side trail. Thales and I tried to stop him, but you know Vittick won't listen to anyone else but you."

George A. grinned and rose to his feet. "Yeah, he's a ring-tailed wonder, all right. But don't worry. I'll go get him."

"Don't go alone," Jacob said, glancing up.

George A.'s smile grew wider. "I've got faith, Brother Jacob, just like you. But I'll see if I can find someone—"

"Jacob, Navajo him have many blanket," Enos stated, distracting Jacob. "Him want trade Eliza allthesame blanket, maybeso silver and skyrock."

Soberly Jacob shook his head. "You tell him," he replied, his voice so quiet that all present had to strain to hear, "that Mormons don't trade wives. Mormons love their wives. You tell him that, Enos."

Enos did, and the trading continued until, abruptly, a message was passed among the Navajos. Silently, and without further trading, they all arose and quickly departed.

"What happened?" Jacob demanded. "Enos, what's going on?"

"Enos not know. Maybeso Jacob pray, him know."

Disgustedly Jacob rose to his feet. "All right, everyone, something's going on. We all here?"

"All but George," Isaac responded. "He went after Vittick."

"Alone?"

"As far as I know."

"Glory," Jacob said with a shake of his head. "Samuel, you and Jeheil go after him. Enos, you get over into the rocks and see if you can hear what's up. The rest of you stay put. I don't have a good feeling about any of this, and I can't be worrying about where everyone is."

But Rachel, almost as if she couldn't stop herself, was following after her husband and Jeheil as they went in search of young George A. Smith.

Over a small rise they went, and then down a winding trail through the rocks, passing the route to the spring and continuing toward the bottom of the mesa. It was very still, and the feeling in the air was one Rachel had never experienced. It was as if all nature was hushed and waiting, as if—

They suddenly came upon young George A. Smith lying in the trail before them, his blood darkening the sand. A slow, cool wind twisted through the rocks, and leaves stirred on the brush, but nothing else moved. With a gasp Rachel rushed past her husband and Jeheil to the side of the fallen boy, who did his best to smile as Rachel lifted his head into her arms.

"I . . . I was trying to trust 'em," he said as he grimaced in pain. "Tell Jacob. But that one ol' Samuel quirted, he's a mean devil—"

As Rachel pulled George's hair back from his eyes, Vittick walked a few feet away, then looked back nervously, not liking the smell of blood. Then the animal walked a little farther and began to crop grass.

George A. did not move. The wind stirred the thin fringes on the arms of his buckskin shirt and moved his neckerchief. Rachel did not know what to do. She had no medicines, no herbs—

"How you feeling, George?" Samuel asked, feeling as helpless as Rachel. Jeheil had already gone hurrying back for Jacob.

"Mighty bad," the youth replied, his eyes wide. "They had Vittick, Samuel. Two of 'em. They were leading my horse off, so I took the bit of one of the Indian ponies and stopped 'em. They gave Vittick right up, so I mounted and started back. Then one of 'em, not the one you quirted, but another one, asked if he could see my pistol. Well, I was trying to trust 'em—"

"Oh, George, that was a fool thing to do."

George A. grimaced again. "I . . . I know. Now. But I gave it to him, and he handed it to the other one, the fellow you quirted. Quick as a wink he stuck that old pistol into my belly and shot. At first I thought maybe he'd missed, because I didn't feel anything. But he kept shooting, and all at once I sort of fell out of my saddle. I didn't mean to. I just started to fall and couldn't stop myself."

"George, don't talk now."

"It doesn't hurt to talk, Rachel." George did his best to smile. "Not any more'n it hurts keeping still. But that's when they got me with this arrow—"

"There're four arrows, George."

"Four? Lawsy, I only felt one. I was lying on the ground, and the one I'd given my gun to? He dismounted and pulled my shirt up over my head. That's when that other feller with the cut face shot those arrows into my back. Four of 'em. Who'd have thought that?

"Rachel, it sure feels good having you hold me like this. Makes me sort of wish I'd found me a lady friend. Maybe—"

Abruptly George gasped with pain, and Rachel, her tears falling freely, did her best to sooth him. And then Jacob was there, and Samuel was telling him what had happened.

"He's hurt bad?" Jacob finally questioned.

"I . . . I'm hurt terrible," George A. whispered from Rachel's lap. "But maybe, Brother Jacob, if you could give me a blessing—"

Samuel nodded in affirmation of Jacob's request, his own tears silently expressing his depth of feeling. "Three bullets in his stomach and four arrows in his back, Jacob. Looks like one of the bullets hit his spine low down, and three of the arrows are in mighty deep. I don't reckon he has much of a chance."

"Just . . . leave me," George pleaded. "I'm done for anyway, so you folks get on out of here. Go on, save yourselves."

"George," Jacob responded, kneeling in the trail beside the youth, "how could I ever face your father if we did that? Now you grit your teeth, because Samuel and I are going to put you back in Vittick's saddle."

"I . . . I can't sit—"

"We'll have to drape you until we get back to camp. Now hold on, because this'll likely hurt a mite."

"Jacob," the boy pleaded, his voice barely more than a whisper, "can't you just carry me in a . . . a blanket?"

"Well, if we had four of us—"

"I can carry a corner," Rachel stated quietly.

"Then we'll do it," Jacob stated as he unrolled a blanket from behind his saddle.

And with as much tenderness as possible, Samuel and Jacob lifted the wounded boy onto the blanket. They each took a corner, Jeheil took the third, and Rachel took the final one, and walking as gently as possible, they began the long trek back to camp.

It was late afternoon when Rachel and the others finally brought George A. to the camp on the tableland. There, while she sent Eliza scurrying about looking for yarrow and other medicinal plants, Rachel began cleaning George A.'s fearful wounds. It was Jacob who had to remove the arrows, as Rachel didn't have the heart to inflict further pain on her young friend.

"See," he gasped when the last arrow was out, "I told you I'd . . . stick it to the end."

Jacob smiled. "You've done fine, George."

Rachel then dressed the wounds, after which George A. spoke again.

"Jacob, could . . . I have that blessing now?"

"Of course, son. Brethren, would you all like to assist me?"

Silently the men who were not on guard stepped forward to place their hands on George's head, and Jacob blessed the youth that he would rest easy and that his pain would be made tolerable.

"Enos," he said after George A. had thanked him, "you

go find those Navajos and ask them what they mean by shooting a man after they had agreed to trade with us and then let us go in peace."

With a nod Enos mounted his horse and rode toward the narrow pass over which Jeheil McConnell was now watching. While the others sat watching young George A., Jacob walked a little way off and bowed his head in prayer.

This was all new to Rachel, for though she had seen death, she had never seen it administered so violently. And she was certain that the young boy who had befriended her was dying. With the kinds and number of wounds he had received, there was no way it could end otherwise. And so she grieved, her tears falling freely as she wiped the boy's fever-ridden brow with a damp cloth.

Neither had she ever felt such sorrow as that which seemed to weigh so heavily over the camp of missionaries. It was oppressive, almost smothering, and under the weight of it no one spoke, no one even looked at one another. Even the four old Navajos were silent, their faces impassive. Instead, all in the party seemed alone with their thoughts, even though all but Jacob, Enos, and Jeheil were clustered together near the fire. As Samuel stared silently at the earth, Rachel wondered about him, thinking deeply of the tears she had seen in his eyes when they had come upon the wounded boy. She had never seen Samuel Loper weep, and the tears had startled her more than she could say. But now—

"Here comes Enos."

Lifting her head, Rachel watched as the small Ute rode up and dismounted.

"Well," Jacob asked, walking back to the fire, "what did the rascals have to say?"

Enos shook his head dourly. "Navajo him say, tell Jacob no bury boy. Navajo eat him, allthesame Navajo women and children eat boy too."

"What?" Jacob was incredulous.

"Navajo him heap mad. Him wait on trail to Moquis. Him kill all Mormons who try go to Moquis. Say Mormons kill three Navajos, maybeso Navajos kill three Mormons. One dead, Jacob give two more for Navajo to kill. Then give women to Navajo, and Mormons go home in peace."

For a moment Jacob paced back and forth, his agitation obvious. The late afternoon sun broke through the clouds, but it was the nearby rocks that were illuminated, not the camp. There all seemed in darkness, punctuated by the soft groanings of the wounded George A.

"Let me get this straight," Jacob finally said as the group gathered near. "The Navajos think we killed three of their people, and they want to kill and eat three of ours in return. So they want me to hand over George A.'s body and two other men, as well as both women, and then they will let us go in peace?"

Solemnly Enos nodded.

"Well, of all the fool ideas—"

"Jacob, what're we going to do?"

"I don't know," Jacob replied slowly, shaking his head. "I just don't know. I've never in my life prayed harder, and the heavens seem like brass over our heads, the earth like iron beneath our feet. We cannot get to the Hopi, who are almost in sight we are so close, and our animals are so jaded it will be certain death trying to escape back to Santa Clara. So to tell you the truth, Isaac, I plumb don't know."

Firmly the Ute interpreter folded his arms. "Enos say give up men. Give up women. Maybeso then go home in peace. Heap better four die than all die."

Slowly Jacob sank to the earth. "You know," he said as he pushed a small stick into the fire, "just when I think we're making headway and bringing a little civilization into their lives, an Indian will say something like that. And

266

as reprehensible as the idea is to us, to Enos it is eminently practical to give up four lives in order to save half a dozen more."

"Only two die," Enos hastened to explain. "Women make slaves, allthesame maybeso make heap good wives."

"It's the same thing, you Lamanite scalawag," Thales growled softly to himself.

"That's right," Jacob agreed. "It is."

"Then Enos say Jacob make trade?"

"No, I did not say that!" Jacob declared, his own frustration obvious. "You go tell those fellows that while there may be only a few of us, we are well armed, and we will fight as long as there is one of us left to fight."

"Jacob make bad mistake," Enos declared sadly. "Heap bad mistake. Two die allthesame go home. Many die no go home. No not one. Bad mistake. Very bad."

"Maybe so," Jacob sighed. "But I'll tell you this, Enos. I would not give one red cent to live after I had given up two men to be murdered. I would rather die like a man than live like a dog!"

Still shaking his head, Enos remounted and rode away. Then the group sat in silence, the sparks and smoke from the tiny fire lifting into the darkening sky.

Slowly the afternoon faded into night. Samuel built up the fire, but other than that no one moved, no one spoke. Out on the mesa a coyote lifted its lonely voice to the night, and nearby a solitary cricket was quickly joined by a chorus of his fellows. One of the horses stamped a hoof and was still, a mule brayed noisily, and the morose feeling of the group continued unabated.

Occasionally young George A. groaned fitfully as he drifted in and out of consciousness. Seated near him, Rachel did her best to minister to his wounds. Yet they were horrid, and even the herbs she placed over them did little to help. Still she tried, keeping the boy's brow cool, and time drifted slowly along.

Returning some time later, Enos dismounted. And then, pointedly, he turned his back to the group and sat down, his arms folded in finality.

"Maybe Enos is right," Amos Thornton said quietly, his voice breaking the silence that had grown between them.

"Would you be one of the two men?" Samuel asked as he whittled thoughtfully on a small stick.

"If we drew lots, and the lot fell to me, I'd take it like a man."

"So would I," Jeheil McConnell acknowledged. "It sticks in my craw, though, giving up the women to God only knows what sort of fate. I don't think I could do that."

"What's the difference between them and us?" The question was asked angrily, even bitterly. "Besides, they're Indians, and they can adapt to Indian life, even slavery if it should come to that, a whole lot easier than all of us can adapt to dying."

Rachel listened in horror as the conversation bounced back and forth. She had been right! All along she had been right. She had never been white, and despite the fine words and generous giving of Rizpah Gibbons and the others at the fort, she could now see that the whites had never considered her as one of them. No matter her language skills and everything else she had forced herself to learn about being white, and no matter her marriage to the white missionary Samuel Loper, she was still an Indian, a dirty little Paiute squaw. And now that she and Eliza were no longer needed, whether to impress others or to make the whites feel better about themselves because they were being so benevolent in rearing them, they would be pushed aside like so much useless baggage.

It was so unfair! So wrong and so unfair—

"You bring Eliza here to die!" Eliza suddenly shouted at Jacob as tears coursed down her cheeks. "Eliza no fool! I think you Eliza's father. All the time I think that! But no, you enemy, make bad medicine for Eliza."

"Eliza, that just isn't so."

Now Rachel was weeping as deeply as Eliza. Jacob, not knowing what else to do or say, stood and paced around the fire, looking at the wounded young man each time he passed him by.

"Maybe we ought to bring it to a vote," someone said.

Jacob, in his pacing, did not even look at the man who had spoken.

"That sounds right to me," another agreed. "Besides, if we give up the women, maybe that'll satisfy the Navajos and they'll let us all go."

"Hmmm. That could very well be," a third man responded. "Very well, all in favor of having Enos turn the two Indian women over to the Navajos—"

"Boys?" The voice of Samuel Loper, not loud or forceful, nevertheless brought the verbal proceedings to an abrupt halt.

"As I see it," he continued, laying aside his whittled stick but not moving to fold his knife, "you've only got one little problem with your wondrous plan."

"And that is?"

"Me."

Rachel stared in shocked amazement. Was it possible that Samuel Loper was defending her again? He had done so against the Navajos, but against his own people? That could not be. Not when he cared nothing for her. Yet as Enos translated what was happening for the four old Navajos, they were suddenly talking and pointing their fingers at her and Samuel again—

And then to her further amazement, Rachel's husband was standing, his long arms lifting his lithe body off the ground until he was upright and facing the other missionaries.

"What . . . what's that supposed to mean?" he was asked.

Samuel smiled thinly. "It means I'm about to do something I should have done a long time ago." He turned and moved to where Rachel was standing next to George A. And then, wonder of all wonders, he was putting his arms around her and drawing her close so that she had no choice but to gaze up into his clear, blue-gray eyes.

"You're my wife, Little One," the man declared softly as he looked at no one but her, "given me in marriage by an apostle of the Lord Jesus Christ. Now, I don't hardly know how you feel about that. Probably you married me just to be obedient. But it meant a lot more than that to me. It surely did! Likely you won't have me after this mission is over. But if you will, then I'll be a happy man!"

Leaning forward, Samuel rested his forehead gently against the forehead of the dumbfounded Rachel. He kissed her lightly, tenderly, and she responded, and then she knew, finally, that the promise given her so many long seasons before by the whisper of Shinob, who was also her beloved Jesus, had been fulfilled.

CHAPTER

37

Abruptly Samuel released his wife and turned back to the others of the party. "Boys," he declared, his voice still soft and quiet, but now carrying a ring of power in it that Rachel had never heard, "I've already quirted one man defending my wife, and I reckon I'm up to taking on any of the rest of you that want to give her up to the Navajos, one at a time or altogether. You decide, for it just don't make no never mind with me."

"You'll have to whip me, too," Thales Haskell added as he stepped forward to stand beside his friends. "And believe me, I'm ready!"

"And I'll stand beside him," Jacob declared. "Eliza's my daughter, and she always will be. And I intend to see that she's treated as such."

There was a brief pause, broken only by a man's cough.

"Aw," a voice finally growled, "we were only throwing around ideas."

"Not very bright ones."

"We admit that, Jacob. But these are desperate times, and men sometimes think and say desperate things—"

271

"Well then, think and say no more," Jacob ordered. "We'll find a way out of this, and it won't be by sacrificing each other."

"You could leave me," the wounded George A. declared from his blanket, startling them all with his lucidity. "I'm a goner anyway, so it won't make much difference if you leave me behind. Then I sure won't be slowing you down."

"I won't do it, George," Jacob declared as he knelt beside the son of his good friend. "If we go, you'll be coming with us."

"But Jacob, I hurt something terrible, and I'd only slow you down—"

"We'll be fine. And George, you've got to bear up and take it. We can't leave you behind!" Standing, Jacob turned back to the others. "Listen, everyone. We'll be leaving here shortly, but we've got to make it look like we're still here and staying. So pack up, but do it leisurely, and don't take the camp equipment or the kettles. In fact, I even want breakfast cooking in the kettles when we ride out."

"Jacob, we try to run, they'll kill us sure."

"No, they won't," Jacob replied quietly as he faced his men. "Fact is, brethren, I promise you in the name of the Lord God of Israel that not another one of us will be injured on this mission. You write it down, for surely as I live, you will see it come to pass. Now let's get packed what we can take with us. Enos, see if our four old Navajo friends here will still guide us to Spaneshanks' camp."

Quickly turning back toward the group, Enos asked the question. "Navajo say we go now," the interpreter stated after a brief exchange.

"Good. Any questions?"

"What . . . about me?" George A. gasped. "How am I going to travel?"

"You ride Vittick," Jacob responded tenderly, "and

Jeheil will sit behind you, holding you in place. It's about the only way we can do it."

Quietly the youth stared upward. "Well," he finally breathed, "I said I'd stick it to the end, and I will. Load me on Vittick when you're ready, and I'll do my best not to complain."

"Thank you, son," Jacob declared soberly. "Now, are there any more questions?"

There were none, so one after another the men drifted into the darkness to saddle and pack their animals. Samuel built up the fire, adding fuel and clearing debris from around it so the flames could not spread, and then they were ready to go.

"Samuel Loper," Rachel asked then, speaking softly in Paiute, "do you know the meaning of the *um-pug-iva*, the talk the old Diné make when they point to us?"

"Don't you?" Samuel asked in surprise.

"Their words are too fast, and I cannot understand."

"I don't understand them either, Little One." Samuel smiled and took Rachel's hand in his own. "But Enos told me that they say, 'He is worthy of his woman. See how he fights for her.' "

Rachel's eyes grew wide. "Are those truly their words?"

"*Sohn-kohv-ee-ahn*. Do you worry that they are not?"

"I do not worry at all, *nuni koo-mahn*, my husband, for now you are with me."

And so, smiling peacefully to herself, Rachel went away with the others into the darkness of the night.

CHAPTER
38

They traveled along the side of the mesa by a trail no one but the old Navajos could see. But the old men found the way, and they went into the hills back of the mesa. The air was cool and there was no wind, nor were there stars or any light at all but a vague hint of a moon obscured by the clouds. It was so dark that Rachel could not see more than a few feet ahead of her. Sandhills rose around them and, in the distance, the sheer walls of a mesa, and there were scattered towers of rock like fingers upheld in warning. Yet now Rachel smiled when she saw them, for she knew the warning was for her, cautioning her to never doubt again —

It was a wondrous time for escaping, too dark for shadows, too black for the Navajos to see them going. Silently they moved, with only a whispering as the hooves of their horses moved through the shifting sand. They wove among the rocks and trees, their moving bodies like shuttles weaving back and forth through the woolen warp of a giant Navajo loom. The four old Navajos led the way, and the missionaries followed on faith, trusting to them and to their horses, which were searching out the way with each hooffall along the ground.

A horse nickered softly, a hoof clicked on a stone, young George A. groaned softly with his pain, someone shifted in his saddle and coughed. These were the only sounds. And Rachel, her heart breaking over the rapidly approaching death of George A., wondered that somehow she could still be happy. Yet she was, incredibly and peacefully happy, for she was still savoring the wondrous words she had heard her husband speak such a short time before. She was still cherishing the way he had finally held her to him, and she was still contemplating with joy the talk of the old Navajos, not that she was finally worthy of Samuel Loper, but that Samuel Loper was now worthy of her.

"Oh, Great Father," she breathed silently through tears of joy, "this woman gives thanks, for now her heart, the soul of her soul, feels joy in her man. Truly he is as the eagle, my Father, soaring high and higher, far and farther, just as a man should do. For that this woman gives thanks.

"But now it is in her mind to ask one other little thing, which to you is no great thing at all, but which to her is a great thing. O Great Jesus, whom she has come to know, you who brought Samuel Loper so surely into her life—will you please promise this foolish woman that she might soar always with him, soaring forever with the eagle of her heart?"

There was silence on the mountain where they rode, a stillness as if the earth was waiting. And then suddenly noo'i, the wind, came sighing through the rock formations and softly whispering past the silent riders. Then from nearby came the plaintive cry of pan-ah-wich, the night bird. Immediately he was answered by the call of his mate, far off but coming quickly closer, and with joy in her heart, Rachel Iitats Dawson Loper smiled into the night.

"Thank you, O beloved Jesus," she whispered as she lifted her face tearfully upward. "Now I know that I shall soar beside my husband, the great Pu-am-ey, in peace."

Author's Note

While the preceding story is fictional, it was inspired by the lives and experiences of Ira Hatch and Sarah Maraboots Dyson Hatch. Ira Hatch was born 5 August 1835 in Farmersville, Cattaragus County, New York. In 1840 his family moved to Hancock County, Illinois, took part in the general exodus of the Mormons to the west in 1846, and arrived in the valley of the Great Salt Lake in September 1849.

In 1853 young Ira was sent south with Dimmick B. Huntington to establish peace among the Indians of the Sevier River area. Not much was accomplished on this mission. In the October 1853 general conference, Ira was called on another Indian mission, to the Southwest Utah Territory. He departed for this mission early in the spring of 1854, at eighteen years of age, little understanding that he would spend the rest of his life on this mission.

In the spring of 1855 he was sent by Jacob Hamblin on a mission to the Paiute Kaibab-its, where he met the Navajo called Tanigoots. Late that fall Tanigoots summoned him back to his encampment, where he asked the young missionary to take his daughter Maraboots and rear her as a white girl. Ira agreed, exchanging his rifle for the girl, and she was then taken to the home of Andrew and Rizpah Gibbons in the settlement of Harmony; the couple began raising her as one of their own children.

Though Maraboots was probably born in 1843, her exact birth date is unknown. She was the daughter of Tanigoots/Dah-Nish-Uant and Ungka Poetes. Her maternal grandfather was Chief Kanosh, and her paternal grandfather was a Navajo chieftain, though his identity is unknown. And she was born, most likely, in southern Utah or northern Arizona.

Upon her arrival in Harmony, at about the age of twelve, she was given the name of Sarah Maraboots Dyson, and so she was called for the balance of her life.

Ira married Amanda Pace on 10 September 1859 in the Endowment House in Salt Lake City. Amanda, just barely seventeen at the time, had been born 11 September 1842 in Nauvoo, Illinois. Just one month later, in the middle of October 1859, Elder Charles C. Rich of the Council of the Twelve Apostles came to the Santa Clara and informed Ira that President Brigham Young wanted him to marry Sarah Maraboots Dyson so the two of them could fill a mission to the Hopi Indians. Ira's reply was, "I am willing if Sarah is."

When Sarah was awakened later that night and the situation was explained to her, she also agreed, providing that the ceremony be postponed until morning. When that proved inconvenient for Elder Rich, Sarah obliged him by dressing and standing beside the young missionary who had "purchased" her four years before, thus becoming his plural wife.

A year later, in the fall of 1860, their marriage still not consummated, Ira and Sarah began their long-awaited and arduous mission to the Hopi, the results of which are portrayed as accurately as possible, though fictionally, in the preceding story.

Amanda Pace Hatch died the following spring, in April of 1861, following complications in the birth of her first child, and Sarah became Ira's only living wife. Seven years later, on 11 October 1868, the two of them were sealed together for time and eternity in the Endowment House in Salt Lake City.

Finally it should be noted that young George A. Smith did die in the saddle during the missionary party's escape from the Navajo. His final words, after a last plea to be allowed to rest, were "Oh, well, go on then, but I wish I could die in peace." Shortly thereafter he passed away and was buried in a shallow hollow near the trail.

Several of the party recorded their feelings at this time. All stated that George A. was a favorite to everyone, and that the thoughts of watching his life's blood dripping out through the day, with his having no chance to rest in peace, and then thinking of leaving his body to be devoured by wolves and vultures and possibly mutilated by angry Indians was more than most of them could bear. It was a trial for all of them, but for Jacob, who bore the responsibility of leadership, and for Sarah, who had so cherished his hand of friendship, it was the worst. In fact, several months later Jacob returned to the site to gather the remains and return them to the boy's father. And Sarah never stopped speaking of the youth throughout the remainder of her life.

But now we are talking about human qualities, and that is where we ought to conclude, considering the joys and sorrows of Sarah and Ira Hatch. They were wonderful people, dedicated to their religion and to each other. For his entire life, which ended in September 1909, Ira served the Indians, whom he called his "red brethren." Sarah, who died in 1873 of complications following the birth of her fifth child, was a tiny, joyful woman who, despite the harshness of her frontier life, found happiness in everything about her. A song was always on her lips, and as Ira had hoped, she was able to take all that was good from her Paiute background, which was a great deal, and wed it to the gospel's truth she joyfully discovered among her adopted people. During her short life of about thirty years, as she and Ira established new homes in several different communities in Utah and Nevada, she not only gave birth to a family but also served in community positions and in the Relief Society. Truly did she and Ira learn that their two worlds, which they seemed to have so successfully joined together, were in reality one world, a world of love and brotherhood, where all creatures are given life by their Creator, and where all are equal to each other.